Puffin Books

Shane and Other Stories

Jack Schaefer was born in Cleveland, Ohio, in
November 1907. He was educated at Oberlin College,
Ohio and Columbia University, New York. He has
worked as an assistant director of education, an
Editor and a publisher. In 1975 he received the
Western Literature Association Distinguished
Achievement award.

Jack Schaefer says he has never consciously written
solely for children – or solely for adults – but for
readers, regardless of age.

Jack Schaefer

Shane
and Other Stories

PUFFIN BOOKS

PUFFIN BOOKS

Published by the Penguin Group
Penguin Books Ltd, 27 Wrights Lane, London W8 5TZ, England
Penguin Books USA Inc., 375 Hudson Street, New York, New York 10014, USA
Penguin Books Australia Ltd, Ringwood, Victoria, Australia
Penguin Books Canada Ltd, 10 Alcorn Avenue, Toronto, Ontario, Canada M4V 3B2
Penguin Books (NZ) Ltd, 182–190 Wairau Road, Auckland 10, New Zealand

Penguin Books Ltd, Registered Offices: Harmondsworth, Middlesex, England

First published by André Deutsch 1963
Published in Peacock Books 1964
Reprinted in Puffin Books 1980
Reprinted in Penguin Books 1989
Reissued in Puffin Books 1994
10 9 8 7 6 5

Printed in England by Clays Ltd, St Ives plc
Set in Linotype Pilgrim

Contents

Shane

I

He rode into our valley in the summer of '89. I was a kid then, barely topping the backboard of father's old chuck-wagon. I was on the upper rail of our small corral, soaking in the late afternoon sun, when I saw him far down the road where it swung into the valley from the open plain beyond.

In that clear Wyoming air I could see him plainly, though he was still several miles away. There seemed nothing remarkable about him, just another stray horseman riding up the road towards the cluster of frame buildings that was our town. Then I saw a pair of cowhands, loping past him, stop and stare after him with a curious intentness.

He came steadily on, straight through the town without slackening pace, until he reached the fork a half-mile below our place. One branch turned left across the river ford and on to Luke Fletcher's big spread. The other bore ahead along the right bank where we homesteaders had pegged our claims in a row up the valley. He hesitated briefly, studying the choice, and moved again steadily on our side.

As he came near, what impressed me first was his clothes. He wore dark trousers of some serge material tucked into tall boots and held at the waist by a wide belt, both of a soft black leather tooled in intricate design. A coat of the same dark material as the trousers was neatly folded and strapped to his saddle-roll. His shirt was finespun linen, rich brown in colour. The handkerchief knotted loosely around his throat was black silk. His hat was not the familiar stetson, not the familiar grey or muddy tan. It was a plain black, soft in texture, unlike any hat I had ever seen, with a creased crown and a wide curling brim swept down in front to shield the face.

All trace of newness was long since gone from these things. The dust of distance was beaten into them. They were worn and stained and several neat patches showed on the shirt. Yet a kind of magnificence remained and with it a hint of men and manners alien to my limited boy's experience.

Then I forgot the clothes in the impact of the man himself. He was not much above medium height, almost slight in build. He would have looked frail alongside father's square, solid bulk. But even I could read the endurance in the lines of that dark figure and the quiet power in its effortless, unthinking adjustment to every movement of the tired horse.

He was clean-shaven and his face was lean and hard and burned from high forehead to firm, tapering chin. His eyes seemed hooded in the shadow of the hat's brim. He came closer, and I could see that this was because the brows were drawn in a frown of fixed and habitual alertness. Beneath them the eyes were endlessly searching from side to side and forward, checking off every item in view, missing nothing. As I noticed this, a sudden chill, I could not have told why, struck through me in the warm and open sun.

He rode easily, relaxed in the saddle, leaning his weight lazily into the stirrups. Yet even in this easiness was a suggestion of tension. It was the easiness of a coiled spring, of a trap set.

He drew rein not twenty feet from me. His glance hit me, dismissed me, flicked over our place. This was not much, if you were thinking in terms of size and scope. But what there was was good. You could trust father for that. The corral, big enough for about thirty head if you crowded them in, was railed right to true sunk posts. The pasture behind, taking in nearly half of our claim, was fenced tight. The barn was small, but it was solid, and we were raising a loft at one end for the alfalfa growing green in the north forty. We had a fair-sized field in potatoes that year and father was trying a new corn he had sent all the way to Washington for and they were showing properly in weedless rows.

Behind the house, mother's kitchen garden was a brave sight.

The house itself was three rooms – two really, the big kitchen where we spent most of our time indoors and the bedroom beside it. My little lean-to room was added back of the kitchen. Father was planning, when he could get around to it, to build mother the parlour she wanted.

We had wooden floors and a nice porch across the front. The house was painted too, white with green trim, rare thing in all that region, to remind her, mother said when she made father do it, of her native New England. Even rarer, the roof was shingled. I knew what that meant. I had helped father split those shingles. Few places so spruce and well worked could be found so deep in the Territory in those days.

The stranger took it all in, sitting there easily in the saddle. I saw his eyes slow on the flowers mother had planted by the porch steps, then come to rest on our shiny new pump and the trough beside it. They shifted back to me, and again, without knowing why, I felt that sudden chill. But his voice was gentle and he spoke like a man schooled to patience.

'I'd appreciate a chance at the pump for myself and the horse.'

I was trying to frame a reply and choking on it, when I realized that he was not speaking to me but past me. Father had come up behind me and was leaning against the gate to the corral.

'Use all the water you want, stranger.'

Father and I watched him dismount in a single flowing tilt of his body and lead the horse over to the trough. He pumped it almost full and let the horse sink its nose in the cool water before he picked up the dipper for himself.

He took off his hat and slapped the dust out of it and hung it on a corner of the trough. With his hands he brushed the dust from his clothes. With a piece of rag pulled from his saddle-roll he carefully wiped his boots. He untied the handkerchief from around his neck and rolled his sleeves and dipped his arms in the trough, rubbing thoroughly and splashing water over his face. He shook his hands dry and used the handkerchief to remove the last drops from his face. Taking a comb from his shirt pocket, he smoothed back his long dark hair. All his movements were deft and sure, and with a quick precision he flipped down his sleeves, re-knotted the handkerchief, and picked up his hat.

Then, holding it in his hand, he spun about and strode directly towards the house. He bent low and snapped the stem of one of mother's petunias and tucked this into the hatband. In another moment the hat was on his head, brim swept down in swift, unconscious gesture, and he was swinging gracefully into the saddle and starting towards the road.

I was fascinated. None of the men I knew were proud like that about their appearance. In that short time the kind of magnificence I had noticed had emerged into plainer view. It was in the very air of him. Everything about him showed the effects of long use and hard use, but showed too the strength of quality and competence. There was no chill on me now. Already I was imagining myself in hat and belt and boots like those.

He stopped the horse and looked down at us. He was refreshed and I would have sworn the tiny wrinkles around his eyes were what with him would be a smile. His eyes were not restless when he looked at you like this. They were still and steady and you knew the man's whole attention was concentrated on you even in the casual glance.

'Thank you,' he said in his gentle voice and was turning into the road, back to us, before father spoke in his slow, deliberate way.

'Don't be in such a hurry, stranger.'

I had to hold tight to the rail or I would have fallen backwards into the corral. At the first sound of father's voice, the man and the horse, like a single being, had wheeled to face us, the man's eyes boring at father, bright and deep in the shadow of the hat's brim. I was shivering, struck through once more. Something intangible and cold and terrifying was there in the air between us.

I stared in wonder as father and the stranger looked at each other a long moment, measuring each other in an unspoken fraternity of adult knowledge beyond my reach. Then the warm sunlight was flooding over us, for father was smiling and he was speaking with the drawling emphasis that meant he had made up his mind.

'I said don't be in such a hurry, stranger. Food will be on the table soon and you can bed down here tonight.'

The stranger nodded quietly as if he too had made up his mind. 'That's mighty thoughtful of you,' he said, and swung down and came towards us, leading his horse. Father slipped into step beside him and we all headed for the barn.

'My name's Starrett,' said father. 'Joe Starrett. This here,' waving at me, 'is Robert MacPherson Starrett. Too much name for a boy. I make it Bob.'

The stranger nodded again. 'Call me Shane,' he said. Then to me: 'Bob it is. You were watching me for quite a spell coming up the road.'

It was not a question. It was a simple statement. 'Yes...' I stammered. 'Yes. I was.'

'Right,' he said. 'I like that. A man who watches what's going on around him will make his mark.'

A man who watches.... For all his dark appearance and lean, hard look, this Shane knew what would please a boy. The glow of it held me as he took care of his horse, and I fussed around, hanging up his saddle, forking over some hay, getting in his way and my own in my eagerness. He let me slip the bridle off and the horse, bigger and more powerful than I had thought now that I was close beside it, put its head down patiently for me and stood quietly while I helped him curry away the caked dust. Only once did he stop me. That was when I reached for his saddle-roll to put it to one side. In the instant my fingers touched it, he was taking it from me and he put it on a shelf with a finality that indicated no interference.

When the three of us went up to the house, mother was waiting and four places were set at the table. 'I saw you through the window,' she said, and came to shake our visitor's hand. She was a slender, lively woman with a fair complexion even our weather never seemed to affect and a mass of light brown hair she wore piled high to bring her, she used to say, closer to father's size.

'Marian,' father said, 'I'd like you to meet Mr Shane.'

'Good evening, ma'am,' said our visitor. He took her hand and bowed over it. Mother stepped back and, to my surprise, dropped in a dainty curtsy. I had never seen her do that before. She was an unpredictable woman. Father and I would have painted the house three times over and in rainbow colours to please her.

'And a good evening to you, Mr Shane. If Joe hadn't called

you back, I would have done it myself. You'd never find a decent meal up the valley.'

She was proud of her cooking, was mother. That was one thing she learned back home, she would often say, that was of some use out in this raw land. As long as she could still prepare a proper dinner, she would tell father when things were not going right, she knew she was still civilized and there was hope of getting ahead. Then she would tighten her lips and whisk together her special most delicious biscuits and father would watch her bustling about and eat them to the last little crumb and stand up and wipe his eyes and stretch his big frame and stomp out to his always unfinished work like daring anything to stop him now.

We sat down to supper and a good one. Mother's eyes sparkled as our visitor kept pace with father and me. Then we all leaned back and while I listened the talk ran on almost like old friends around a familiar table. But I could sense that it was following a pattern. Father was trying, with mother helping and both of them avoiding direct questions, to get hold of facts about this Shane and he was dodging at every turn. He was aware of their purpose and not in the least annoyed by it. He was mild and courteous and spoke readily enough. But always he put them off with words that gave no real information.

He must have been riding many days, for he was full of news from towns along his back trail as far as Cheyenne and even Dodge City and others beyond I had never heard of before. But he had no news about himself. His past was fenced as tightly as our pasture. All they could learn was that he was riding through, taking each day as it came, with nothing particular in mind except maybe seeing a part of the country he had not been in before.

Afterwards mother washed the dishes and I dried and the two men sat on the porch, their voices carrying through the open door. Our visitor was guiding the conversation now and in no time at all he had father talking about his own plans. That was no trick. Father was ever one to argue his ideas whenever he could find a listener. This time he was going strong.

'Yes, Shane, the boys I used to ride with don't see it yet. They will some day. The open range can't last forever. The fence lines are closing in. Running cattle in big lots is good business only for the top ranchers and it's really a poor business at that. Poor in terms of the resources going into it. Too much space for too little results. It's certain to be crowded out.'

'Well, now,' said Shane, 'that's mighty interesting. I've been hearing the same quite a lot lately and from men with pretty clear heads. Maybe there's something to it.'

'By Godfrey, there's plenty to it. Listen to me, Shane. The thing to do is pick your spot, get your land, your own land. Put in enough crops to carry you and make your money play with a small herd, not all horns and bone, but bred for meat and fenced in and fed right. I haven't been at it long, but already I've raised stock that averages three hundred pounds more than that long-legged stuff Fletcher runs on the other side of the river and it's better beef, and that's only a beginning.

'Sure, his outfit sprawls over most of this valley and it looks big. But he's got range rights on a lot more acres than he has cows and he won't even have those acres as more homesteaders move in. His way is wasteful. Too much land for what he gets out of it. He can't see that. He thinks we small fellows are nothing but damned nuisances.'

'You are,' said Shane mildly. 'From his point of view, you are.'

'Yes, I guess you're right. I'll have to admit that. Those of us here now would make it tough for him if he wanted to use the range behind us on this side of the river as he used to. Altogether we cut some pretty good slices out of it. Worse still, we block off part of the river, shut the range off from the water. He's been grumbling about that off and on ever since we've been here. He's worried that more of us will keep coming and settle on the other side too, and then he will be in a fix.'

The dishes were done and I was edging to the door. Mother nailed me as she usually did and shunted me off to bed. After she had left me in my little back room and went to join the men on the porch, I tried to catch more of the words. The voices were too low. Then I must have dozed, for with a start I realized that father and mother were again in the kitchen. By now, I gathered, our visitor was out in the barn in the bunk father had built there for the hired man who had been with us for a few weeks in the spring.

'Wasn't it peculiar,' I heard mother say, 'how he wouldn't talk about himself?'

'Peculiar?' said father. 'Well, yes. In a way.'

'Everything about him is peculiar.' Mother sounded as if she was stirred up and interested. 'I never saw a man quite like him before.'

'You wouldn't have. Not where you come from. He's a special brand we sometimes get out here in the grass country. I've come across a few. A bad one's poison. A good one's straight grain clear through.'

'How can you be so sure about him? Why, he wouldn't even tell where he was raised.'

'Born back east a ways would be my guess. And pretty far south. Tennessee maybe. But he's been around plenty.'

'I like him.' Mother's voice was serious. 'He's so nice and polite and sort of gentle. Not like most men I've met out here. But there's something about him. Something underneath the gentleness. . . . Something . . .' Her voice trailed away.

'Mysterious?' suggested father.

'Yes, of course. Mysterious. But more than that. Dangerous.'

'He's dangerous all right.' Father said it in a musing way. Then he chuckled. 'But not to us, my dear.' And then he said what seemed to me a curious thing. 'In fact, I don't think you ever had a safer man in your house.'

2

In the morning I slept late and stumbled into the kitchen to find father and our visitor working their way through piles of mother's flapjacks. She smiled at me from over by the stove. Father slapped my rump by way of greeting. Our visitor nodded at me gravely over his heaped-up plate.

'Good morning, Bob. You'd better dig in fast or I'll do away with your share too. There's magic in your mother's cooking. Eat enough of these flannel cakes and you'll grow a bigger man than your father.'

'Flannel cakes! Did you hear that, Joe?' Mother came whisking over to tousle father's hair. 'You must be right. Tennessee or some such place. I never heard them called that out here.'

Our visitor looked up at her. 'A good guess, ma'am. Mighty close to the mark. But you had a husband to help you. My folks came out of Mississippi and settled in Arkansas. Me, though – I was fiddle-footed and left home at fifteen. Haven't had anything worth being called a real flannel cake since.' He put his hands on the table edge and leaned back and the little wrinkles at the corners of his eyes were plainer and deeper. 'That is, ma'am, till now.'

Mother gave what in a girl I would have called a giggle. 'If I'm any judge of men,' she said, 'that means more.' And she whisked back to the stove.

That was how it was often in our house, kind of jolly and warm with good feeling. It needed to be this morning because there was a cool greyness in the air and before I had even begun to slow on my second plate of flapjacks the wind was rushing down the valley with the rain of one of our sudden summer storms following fast.

Our visitor had finished his breakfast. He had eaten so many flapjacks that I had begun to wonder whether he really would cut into my share. Now he turned to look out of the window and his lips tightened. But he pushed back from the table and started to rise. Mother's voice held him to his chair.

'You'll not be travelling in any such weather. Wait a bit and it'll clear. These rains don't last long. I've another pot of coffee on the stove.'

Father was getting his pipe going. He kept his eyes carefully on the smoke drifting upward. 'Marian's right. Only she doesn't go far enough. These rains are short. But they sure mess up the road. It's new. Hasn't settled much yet. Mighty soggy when wet. Won't be fit for travelling till it drains. You better stay over till tomorrow.'

Our visitor stared down at his empty plate as if it was the most important object in the whole room. You could see he liked the idea. Yet he seemed somehow worried about it.

'Yes,' said father. 'That's the sensible dodge. That horse of yours was pretty much beat last night. If I was a horse doctor now, I'd order a day's rest right off. Damned if I don't think the same prescription would do me good too. You stick here the day and I'll follow it. I'd like to take you around, show you what I'm doing with the place.'

15

He looked pleadingly at mother. She was surprised and with good reason. Father was usually so set on working every possible minute to catch up on his plans that she would have a tussle making him ease some once a week out of respect for the Sabbath. In bad weather like this he usually would fidget and stomp about the house as if he thought it was a personal insult to him, a trick to keep him from being out and doing things. And here he was talking of a whole day's rest. She was puzzled. But she played right up.

'You'd be doing us a favour, Mr Shane. We don't get many visitors from outside the valley. It'd be real nice to have you stay. And besides –' She crinkled her nose at him the way she did when she would be teasing father into some new scheme of hers. 'And besides – I've been waiting for an excuse to try a deep-dish apple pie I've heard tell of. It would just be wasted on these other two. They eat everything in sight and don't rightly know good from poor.'

He was looking up, straight at her. She shook a finger at him. 'And another thing. I'm fair bubbling with questions about what the women are wearing back in civilization. You know, hats and such. You're the kind of man would notice them. You're not getting away till you've told me.'

Shane sat back in his chair. A faint quizzical expression softened the lean ridges of his face. 'Ma'am, I'm not positive I appreciate how you've pegged me. No one else ever wrote me down an expert on ladies' millinery.' He reached out and pushed his cup across the table towards her. 'You said something about more coffee. But I draw the line on more flannel cakes. I'm plumb full. I'm starting in to conserve space for that pie.'

'You'd better!' Father was mighty pleased about something. 'When Marian puts her mind to cooking, she makes a man forget he's got any limits to his appetite. Only don't you go giving her fancy notions of new hats so she'll be sending off to the mail-order house and throwing my money away on silly frippery. She's got a hat.'

Mother did not even notice that. She knew father was just talking. She knew that whenever she wanted anything real much and said so, father would bust himself trying to get it for her. She whisked over to the table with the coffee pot, poured a fresh round, then set it down within easy reach and sat down herself.

I thought that business about hats was only a joke she made up to help father persuade our visitor to stay. But she began almost at once, pestering him to describe the ladies he had seen in Cheyenne and other towns where the new styles might be. He sat there, easy and friendly, telling her how they were wearing wide floppy-brimmed bonnets with lots of flowers in front on top and slits in the brims for scarves to come through and be tied in bows under their chins.

Talk like that seemed foolish to me to be coming from a grown man. Yet this Shane was not bothered at all. And father listened as if he thought it was all right, only not very interesting. He watched them most of the time in a good-natured quiet, trying every so often to break in with his own talk about crops and steers and giving up and trying again and giving up again with a smiling shake of his head a' those two. And the rain outside was a far distance away and r .eaningless because the friendly feeling in our kitchen was enough to warm all our world.

Then Shane was telling about the annual stock show at Dodge City and father was interested and excited, and it was mother who said: 'Look, the sun's shining.'

It was so clear and sweet you wanted to run out and breathe the brilliant freshness. Father must have felt that way because he jumped up and fairly shouted, 'Come on, Shane. I'll show you what this hopscotch climate does to my alfalfa. You can almost see the stuff growing.'

Shane was only a step behind him, but I beat them to the door. Mother followed and stood watching awhile on the porch as we three started out, picking our path around the puddles and the taller clumps of grass bright with the raindrops. We covered the whole place pretty thoroughly, father talking all the time, more enthusiastic about his plans than he had been for many weeks. He really hit his stride when we were behind the barn where we could have a good view of our little herd spreading out through the pasture. Then he stopped short. He had noticed that Shane was not paying much attention. He was quiet as could be for a moment when he saw that Shane was looking at the stump.

That was the one bad spot on our place. It stuck out like an old scarred sore in the cleared space back of the barn – a big old stump, all jagged across the top, the legacy of some great tree that must have died long before we came into the valley and finally been snapped by a heavy windstorm. It was big enough, I used to think, so that if it was smooth on top you could have served supper to a good-sized family on it.

But you could not have done that because you could not have got them close around it. The huge old roots humped out in every direction, some as big about as my waist, pushing out and twisting down into the ground like they would hold there to eternity and past.

Father had been working it off and on, gnawing at the roots with an axe, ever since he finished poling the corral. The going was slow, even for him. The wood was so hard that he could not sink the blade much more than a quarter-inch at a time. I guess it had been an old burr oak. Not many of those grew that far up in the Territory, but the ones that did grew big and hard. Ironwood we called it.

Father had tried burning brushpiles against it. That old stump just jeered at fire. The scorching seemed to make the wood harder than ever. So he was fighting his way around root by root. He never thought he had much time to spare on it. The rare occasions he was real mad about something he would stomp out there and chew into another root.

He went over to the stump now and kicked the nearest root, a smart kick, the way he did every time he passed it. 'Yes,' he said. 'That's the millstone round my neck. That's the one fool thing about this place I haven't licked yet. But I will. There's no wood ever grew can stand up to a man that's got the strength and the will to keep hammering at it.'

He stared at the stump like it might be a person sprouting in front of him. 'You know, Shane, I've been feuding with this thing so long I've worked up a spot of affection for it. It's tough. I can admire toughness. The right kind.'

He was running on again, full of words and sort of happy to be letting them out, when he noticed again that Shane was not paying much attention, was listening to some sound in the distance. Sure enough, a horse was coming up the road.

Father and I turned with him to look towards town. In a moment we saw it as it cleared the grove of trees and tall bushes about a quarter-mile away, a high-necked sorrel drawing a light buckboard wagon. The mud was splattering from its hooves, but not bad, and it was stepping free and easy. Shane glanced sideways at father.

'Not fit for travelling,' he said softly. 'Starrett, you're poor shakes as a liar.' Then his attention was on the wagon and he was tense and alert, studying the man upright on the swaying seat.

Father simply chuckled at Shane's remark. 'That's Jake Ledyard's outfit,' he said, taking the lead towards our lane. 'I thought maybe he'd get up this way this week. Hope he has that cultivator I've been wanting.' *L237,575*

Ledyard was a small, thin-featured man, a peddler or trader who came through every couple of months with things you could not get at the general store in town. He would pack in his stock on a mule-team freighter driven by an old, white-haired Negro who acted like he was afraid even to speak without permission. Ledyard would make deliveries in his buckboard, claiming a hard bargain always and picking up orders for articles to bring on the next trip. I did not like him, and not just because he said nice things about me he did not mean for father's benefit. He smiled too much and there was no real friendliness in it.

By the time we were beside the porch, he had swung the horse into our lane and was pulling it to a stop. He jumped down, calling greetings. Father went to meet him. Shane stayed by the porch, leaning against the end post.

'It's here,' said Ledyard. 'The beauty I told you about.' He yanked away the canvas covering from the body of the wagon and the sun was bright on a shiny new seven-pronged cultivator lying on its side on the floor boards. That's the best buy I've toted this haul.'

'Hm-m-m-m,' said father. 'You've hit it right. That's what I've been wanting. But when you start chattering about a best buy that always means big money. What's the tariff?'

'Well, now.' Ledyard was slow with his reply. 'It cost me more than I figured when we was talking last time. You might think it a bit steep. I don't. Not for a new beauty like that

there. You'll make up the difference in no time with the work you'll save with that. Handles so easy even the boy here will be using it before long.'

'Pin it down,' said father. 'I've asked you a question.'

Ledyard was quick now. 'Tell you what, I'll shave the price, take a loss to please a good customer. I'll let you have it for a hundred and ten.'

I was startled to hear Shane's voice cutting in, quiet and even and plain. 'Let you have it? I reckon he will. There was one like that in a store in Cheyenne. List price sixty dollars.'

Ledyard shifted part way around. For the first time he looked closely at our visitor. The surface smile left his face. His voice held an ugly undertone. 'Did anyone ask you to push in on this?'

'No,' said Shane, quietly and evenly as before. 'I reckon no one did.' He was still leaning against the post. He did not move and he did not say anything more. Ledyard turned to father, speaking rapidly.

'Forget what he says, Starrett. I've spotted him now. Heard of him half a dozen times along the road up here. No one knows him. No one can figure him. I think I can. Just a stray wandering through, probably chased out of some town and hunting cover. I'm surprised you'd let him hang around.'

'You might be surprised at a lot of things,' said father, beginning to bite off his words. 'Now give it to me straight on the price.'

'It's what I said. A hundred and ten. Hell, I'll be out money on the deal anyway, so I'll shave it to a hundred if that'll make you feel any better.' Ledyard hesitated, watching father. 'Maybe he did see something in Cheyenne. But he's mixed up. Must have been one of those little makes – flimsy and barely half the size. That might match his price.'

Father did not say anything. He was looking at Ledyard in a steady, unwavering way. He had not even glanced at Shane. You might have believed he had not even heard what Shane had said. But his lips were folding into a tight line like he was thinking what was not pleasant to think. Ledyard waited and father did not say anything and the climbing anger in Ledyard broke free.

'Starrett! Are you going to stand there and let that – that

tramp nobody knows about call me a liar? Are you going to take his word over mine? Look at him! Look at his clothes! He's just a cheap, tinhorn –'

Ledyard stopped, choking on whatever it was he had meant to say. He fell back a step with a sudden fear showing in his face. I knew why even as I turned my head to see Shane. That same chill I had felt the day before, intangible and terrifying, was in the air again. Shane was no longer leaning against the porch post. He was standing erect, his hands clenched at his sides, his eyes boring at Ledyard, his whole body alert and alive in the leaping instant.

You felt without knowing how that each teetering second could bring a burst of indescribable deadliness. Then the tension passed, fading in the empty silence. Shane's eyes lost their sharp focus on Ledyard and it seemed to me that reflected in them was some pain deep within him.

Father had pivoted so that he could see the two of them in the one sweep. He swung back to Ledyard alone.

'Yes, Ledyard, I'm taking his word. He's my guest. He's here at my invitation. But that's not the reason.' Father straightened a little and his head went up and he gazed into the distance beyond the river. 'I can figure men for myself. I'll take his word on anything he wants to say any day of God's whole year.'

Father's head came down and his voice was flat and final. 'Sixty is the price. Add ten for a fair profit, even though you probably got it wholesale. Another ten for hauling it here. That tallies to eighty. Take that or leave that. Whatever you do, snap to it and get off my land.'

Ledyard stared down at his hands, rubbing them together as if they were cold. 'Where's your money?' he said.

Father went into the house, into the bedroom where he kept our money in a little leather bag on the closet shelf. He came back with the crumpled bills. All this while Shane stood there, not moving, his face hard, his eyes following father with a strange wildness in them that I could not understand.

Ledyard helped father heave the cultivator to the ground, then jumped to the wagon seat and drove off like he was glad to get away from our place. Father and I turned from watching him into the road. We looked around for Shane and he was not in sight. Father shook his head in wonderment. 'Now where do you suppose –' he was saying, when we saw Shane coming out of the barn.

He was carrying an axe, the one father used for heavy kindling. He went directly around the corner of the building. We stared after him and we were still staring when we heard it, the clear ringing sound of steel biting into wood.

I never could have explained what that sound did to me. It struck through me as no single sound had ever done before. With it ran a warmth that erased at once and forever the feelings of sudden chill terror that our visitor had evoked in me. There were sharp hidden hardnesses in him. But these were not for us. He was dangerous as mother had said. But not to us as father too had said. And he was no longer a stranger. He was a man like father in whom a boy could believe in the simple knowing that what was beyond comprehension was still clean and solid and right.

I looked up at father to try to see what he was thinking, but he was starting towards the barn with strides so long that I had to run to stay close behind him. We went around the far corner and there was Shane squared away at the biggest uncut root of that big old stump. He was swinging the axe in steady rhythm. He was chewing into that root with bites almost as deep as father could drive.

Father halted, legs wide, hands on hips. 'Now lookahere,' he began, 'there's no call for you –'

Shane broke his rhythm just long enough to level a straight look at us. 'A man has to pay his debts,' he said, and was again swinging the axe. He was really slicing into that root.

He seemed so desperate in his determination that I had to speak. 'You don't owe us anything,' I said. 'Lots of times we have folks in for meals and –'

Father's hand was on my shoulder. 'No, Bob. He doesn't mean meals.' Father was smiling, but he was having to blink several times together and I would have sworn that his eyes were misty. He stood in silence now, not moving, watching Shane.

It was something worth seeing. When father worked on that old stump, that was worth seeing too. He could handle an axe mighty well and what impressed you was the strength and will of him making it behave and fight for him against the tough old wood. This was different. What impressed you as Shane found what he was up against and settled to it was the easy way the power in him poured smoothly into each stroke. The man and the axe seemed to be partners in the work. The blade would sink into the parallel grooves almost as if it knew itself what to do and the chips from between would come out in firm and thin little blocks.

Father watched him and I watched the two of them and time passed over us, and then the axe sliced through the last strip and the root was cut. I was sure that Shane would stop. But he stepped right around to the next root and squared away again and the blade sank in once more.

As it hit this second root, father winced like it had hit him. Then he stiffened and looked away from Shane and stared at the old stump. He began to fidget, throwing his weight from one foot to the other. In a short while more he was walking around inspecting the stump from different angles as if it was something he had never seen before. Finally he gave the nearest root a kick and hurried away. In a moment he was back with the other axe, the big double-bladed one that I could hardly heft from the ground.

He picked a root on the opposite side from Shane. He was not angry the way he usually was when he confronted one of those roots. There was a kind of serene and contented look on his face. He whirled that big axe as if it was only a kid's tool. The striking blade sank in maybe a whole half-inch. At the sound Shane straightened on his side. Their eyes met over the top of the stump and held and neither one of them said a word. Then they swung up their axes and both of them said plenty to that old stump.

3

It was exciting at first watching them. They were hitting a fast pace, making the chips dance. I thought maybe each one would cut through a root now and stop. But Shane finished his and looked over at father working steadily away and with a grim little smile pulling at his mouth he moved on to another root. A few moments later father smashed through his with a blow that sent the axe head into the ground beneath. He wrestled with the handle to yank the head loose and he too tackled another root without even waiting to wipe off the dirt. This began to look like a long session, so I started to wander away. Just as I headed around the corner of the barn, mother came past the corner.

She was the freshest, prettiest thing I had ever seen. She had taken her hat and stripped the old ribbon from it and fixed it as Shane had told her. Some of the flowers by the house were in a small bouquet in front. She had cut slits in the brim and the sash from her best dress came around the crown and through the slits and was tied in a perky bow under her chin. She was stepping along daintily, mighty proud of herself.

She went up close to the stump. Those two choppers were so busy and intent that even if they were aware she was there they did not really notice her.

'Well,' she said, 'aren't you going to look at me?'

They both stopped and they both stared at her.

'Have I got it right?' she asked Shane. 'Is this the way they do it?'

'Yes, ma'am,' he said. 'About like that. Only their brims are wider.' And he swung back to his root.

'Joe Starrett,' said mother, 'aren't you at least going to tell me whether you like me in this hat?'

'Lookahere, Marian,' said father, 'you know damned well that whether you have a hat on or whether you don't have a hat on, you're the nicest thing to me that ever happened on God's green earth. Now stop bothering us. Can't you see we're busy?' And he swung back to his root.

Mother's face was a deep pink. She pulled the bow out and the hat from her head. She held it swinging from her hand by the sash ends. Her hair was mussed and she was really mad.

'Humph,' she said. 'This is a funny kind of resting you're doing today.'

Father set the axe head on the ground and leaned on the handle. 'Maybe it seems funny to you, Marian. But this is the best resting I've had for about as long as I can remember.'

'Humph,' said mother again. 'You'll have to quit your resting for a while anyhow and do what I suppose you'll call work. Dinner's hot on the stove and waiting to be served.'

She flounced around and went straight back to the house. We all tagged her in and to an uncomfortable meal. Mother's always believed you should be decent and polite at mealtime, particularly with company. She was polite enough now. She was being special sweet, talking enough for the whole table of us without once saying a word about her hat lying where she had thrown it on the chair by the stove. The trouble was that she was too polite. She was trying too hard to be sweet.

As far as you could tell, though, the two men were not worried by her at all. They listened absently to her talk, chiming in when she asked them direct questions, but otherwise keeping quiet. Their minds were on that old stump and whatever it was that old stump had come to mean to them and they were in a hurry to get at it again.

After they had gone out and I had been helping mother with the dishes awhile, she began humming low under her breath and I knew she was not mad any more. She was too curious and puzzled to have room for anything else.

'What went on out there, Bob?' she asked me. 'What got into those two?'

I did not rightly know. All I could do was try to tell her about Ledyard and how our visitor had called him on the cultivator. I must have used the wrong words, because, when I told her about Ledyard talking mean and the way Shane acted, she got all flushed and excited.

'What do you say, Bob? You were afraid of him? He frightened you? Your father would never let him do that.'

'I wasn't frightened of him,' I said, struggling to make her see the difference. 'I was – well, I was just frightened. I was scared of whatever it was that might happen.'

She reached out and rumpled my hair. 'I think I understand,' she said softly. 'He's made me feel a little that way too.' She went to the window and stared towards the barn. The steady rhythm of double blows, so together they sounded almost as one, was faint yet clear in the kitchen. 'I hope Joe knows what he's doing,' she murmured to herself. Then she turned to me. 'Skip along out, Bob. I'll finish myself.'

It was no fun watching them now. They had eased down to a slow, dogged pace. Father sent me once for the hone, so they could sharpen the blades, and again for a spade so he could clear the dirt away from the lowest roots, and I realized he might keep me running as long as I was handy. I slipped off by myself to see how mother's garden was doing after the rain and maybe add to the population in the box of worms I was collecting for when I would go fishing with the boys in town.

I took my time about it. I played pretty far afield. But no matter where I went, always I could hear that chopping in the distance. You could not help beginning to feel tired just to hear it, to think how they were working and staying at it.

Along the middle of the afternoon, I wandered into the barn. There was mother by the rear stall, up on a box peering through the little window above it. She hopped down as soon as she heard me and put a finger to her lips.

'I declare,' she whispered. 'In some ways those two aren't even as old as you are, Bob. Just the same –' She frowned at me in such a funny, confiding manner that I felt all warm inside. 'Don't you dare tell them I said so. But there's something splendid in the battle they're giving that old monster.' She went past me and towards the house with such a brisk air that I followed to see what she was going to do.

She whisked about the kitchen and in almost no time at all she had a pan of biscuits in the oven. While they were baking she took her hat and carefully sewed the old ribbon into its old place. 'Humph,' she said, more to herself than to me. 'You'd think I'd learn. This isn't Dodge City. This isn't even a whistle stop. It's Joe Starrett's farm. It's where I'm proud to be.'

Out came the biscuits. She piled as many as she could on a plate, popping one of the leftovers into her mouth and giving me the rest. She picked up the plate and marched with it out behind the barn. She stepped over the cut roots and set the plate on a fairly smooth spot on top of the stump. She looked at the two men, first one and then the other. 'You're a pair of fools,' she said. 'But there's no law against me being a fool too.' Without looking at either of them again, she marched away, her head high, back towards the house.

The two of them stared after her till she was out of sight. They turned to stare at the biscuits. Father gave a deep sigh, so deep it seemed to come all the way from his heavy work shoes. There was nothing sad or sorrowful about it. There was just something in him too big to be held tight in comfort. He let his axe fall to the ground. He leaned forward and separated the biscuits into two piles beside the plate, counting them even. One was left on the plate. He set this by itself on the stump. He took up his axe and reached it out and let it drop gently on the lone biscuit exactly in the middle. He rested the axe against the stump and took the two halves of the biscuit and put one on each pile.

He did not say a word to Shane. He pitched into one pile and Shane did into the other, and the two of them faced each other over the last uncut roots, munching at those biscuits as if eating them was the most serious business they had ever done.

Father finished his pile and dabbled his fingers on the plate for the last crumbs. He straightened and stretched his arms high and wide. He seemed to stretch and stretch until he was a tremendous tower of strength reaching up into the late afternoon sun. He swooped suddenly to grab the plate and toss it to me. Still in the same movement he seized his axe and swung it in a great arc into the root he was working on. Quick as he was, Shane was right with him, and together they were talking again to that old stump.

I took the plate in to mother. She was peeling apples in the kitchen, humming gaily to herself. 'The wood-box, Bob,' she said, and went on humming. I carried in stove-lengths till the box would not hold any more. Then I slipped out before she might think of more chores.

I tried to keep myself busy down by the river skipping flat stones across the current all muddy still from the rain. I was able to for a while. But that steady chopping had a peculiar fascination. It was always pulling me towards the barn. I simply could not grasp how they could stick at it hour after hour. It made no sense to me, why they should work so when routing out that old stump was not really so important. I was wavering in front of the barn, when I noticed that the chopping was different. Only one axe was working.

I hurried around back. Shane was still swinging, cutting into

27

the last root. Father was using the spade, was digging under one side of the stump, bringing the dirt out between the cut roots. As I watched, he laid the spade aside and put his shoulder to the stump. He heaved against it. Sweat started to pour down his face. There was a little sucking sound and the stump moved ever so slightly.

That did it. Of a sudden I was so excited that I could hear my own blood pounding past my eardrums. I wanted to dash to that stump and push it and feel it move. Only I knew father would think I was in the way.

Shane finished the root and came to help him. Together they heaved against the stump. It angled up nearly a whole inch. You could begin to see an open space in the dirt where it was ripping loose. But as soon as they released the pressure, it fell back.

Again and again they heaved at it. Each time it would angle up a bit further. Each time it would fall back. They had it up once about a foot and a half, and that was the limit. They could not get past it.

They stopped, breathing hard, mighty streaked now from the sweat rivulets down their faces. Father peered underneath as best he could. 'Must be a taproot,' he said. That was the one time either of them had spoken to the other, as far as I knew, the whole afternoon through. Father did not say anything more. And Shane said nothing. He just picked up his axe and looked at father and waited.

Father began to shake his head. There was some unspoken thought between them that bothered him. He looked down at his own big hands and slowly the fingers curled until they were clenched into big fists. Then his head stopped shaking and he stood taller and he drew a deep breath. He turned and backed in between two cut root ends, pressing against the stump. He pushed his feet into the ground for firm footholds. He bent his knees and slid his shoulders down the stump and wrapped his big hands around the root ends. Slowly he began to straighten. Slowly that huge old stump began to rise. Up it came, inch by inch, until the side was all the way up to the limit they had reached before.

Shane stooped to peer under. He poked his axe into the opening and I heard it strike wood. But the only way he could get in position to swing the axe into the opening was to drop on his right knee and extend his left leg and thigh into the opening and lean his weight on them. Then he could bring the axe sweeping in at a low angle close to the ground.

He flashed one quick glance at father beside and behind him, eyes closed, muscles locked in that great sustained effort, and he dropped into position with the whole terrible weight of the stump poised above nearly half of his body, and sent the axe sweeping under in swift powerful strokes.

Suddenly father seemed to slip. Only he had not slipped. He had straightened even further. The stump had leaped up a few more inches. Shane jumped out and up and tossed his axe aside. He grabbed one of the root ends and helped father ease the stump down. They both were blowing like they had run a long way. But they would not stay more than a minute before they were heaving again at the stump. It came up more easily now and the dirt was tearing loose all around it.

I ran to the house fast as I could. I dashed into the kitchen and took hold of mother's hand. 'Hurry!' I yelled. 'You've got to come!' She did not seem to want to come at first and I pulled at her. 'You've got to see it! They're getting it out!' Then she was excited as I was and was running right with me.

They had the stump way up at a high angle. They were down in the hole, one on each side of it, pushing up and forward with hands flat on the under part reared before them higher than their heads. You would have thought the stump was ready to topple over clear of its ancient foundation. But there it stuck. They could not quite push it the final inches.

Mother watched them battling with it. 'Joe,' she called, 'why don't you use some sense? Hitch up the team. Horses will have it out in no time at all.'

Father braced himself to hold the stump still. He turned his head to look at her. 'Horses!' he shouted. All the pent silence of the two of them that long afternoon through was being shattered in the one wonderful shout. 'Horses! Great jumping Jehosaphat! No! We started this with manpower and, by Godfrey, we'll finish it with manpower!'

He turned his head to face the stump once more and dropped it lower between his humped shoulders. Shane, opposite him, stiffened, and together they pushed in a fresh assault. The stump quivered and swayed a little – and hung fixed at its crazy high angle.

Father grunted in exasperation. You could see the strength building up in his legs and broad shoulders and big corded arms. His side of the upturned stump rocked forward and Shane's side moved back and the whole stump trembled like it would twist down and into the hole on them at a grotesque new angle.

I wanted to shout a warning. But I could not speak, for Shane had thrown his head in a quick sideways gesture to fling his hair from falling over his face and I had caught a glimpse of his eyes. They were aflame with a concentrated cold fire. Not another separate discernible movement did he make. It was all of him, the whole man, pulsing in the one incredible surge of power. You could fairly feel the fierce energy suddenly burning in him, pouring through him in the single co-ordinated drive. His side of the stump rocked forward even with father's and the whole mass of the stump tore loose from the last hold and toppled away to sprawl in ungainly defeat beyond them.

Father climbed slowly out of the hole. He walked to the stump and placed a hand on the rounded bole and patted it like it was an old friend and he was perhaps a little sorry for it. Shane was with him, across from him, laying a hand gently on the old hard wood. They both looked up and their eyes met and held as they had so long ago in the morning hours.

The silence should have been complete. It was not because someone was shouting, a high-pitched, wordless shout. I realized that the voice was mine and I closed my mouth. The silence was clean and wholesome, and this was one of the things you could never forget whatever time might do to you in the furrowing of the years, an old stump on its side with root ends making a strange pattern against the glow of the sun sinking behind the far mountains and two men looking over it into each other's eyes.

I thought they should join hands so close on the bole of the stump. I thought they should at least say something to each other. They stood quiet and motionless. At last father turned and came towards mother. He was so tired that the weariness showed in his walk. But there was no weariness in his voice.

'Marian,' he said, 'I'm rested now. I don't believe any man since the world began was ever more rested.'

Shane too was coming towards us. He too spoke only to mother. 'Ma'am, I've learned something today. Being a farmer has more to it than I ever thought. Now I'm about ready for some of that pie.'

Mother had been watching them in a wide-eyed wonder. At his last words she let out a positive wail. 'Oh-h-h – you – you – men! You made me forget about it! It's probably all burned!' And she was running for the house so fast she was tripping over her skirt.

The pie was burned all right. We could smell it when we were in front of the house and the men were scrubbing themselves at the pump-trough. Mother had the door open to let the kitchen air out. The noises from inside sounded as if she might be throwing things around. Kettles were banging and dishes were clattering. When we went in, we saw why. She had the table set and was putting supper on it and she was grabbing the things from their places and putting them down on the table with solid thumps. She would not look at one of us.

We sat down and waited for her to join us. She put her back to us and stood by the low shelf near the stove staring at her big pie tin and the burned stuff in it. Finally father spoke kind of sharply. 'Lookahere, Marian. Aren't you ever going to sit down?'

She whirled and glared at him. I thought maybe she had been crying. But there were no tears on her face. It was dry and pinched-looking and there was no colour in it. Her voice was sharp like father's. 'I was planning to have a deep-dish apple pie. Well, I will. None of your silly man foolishness is going to stop me.'

She swept up the big tin and went out the door with it. We heard her on the steps, and a few seconds later the rattle of the cover of the garbage pail. We heard her on the steps again. She came in and went to the side bench where the dish-pan was and began to scrub the pie tin. The way she acted, we might not have been in the room.

Father's face was getting red. He picked up his fork to begin eating and let it drop with a little clatter. He squirmed on his chair and kept taking quick side looks at her. She finished scrubbing the tin and went to the apple barrel and filled her wooden bowl with fat round ones. She sat by the stove and started peeling them. Father fished in a pocket and pulled out his old jack-knife. He moved over to her, stepping softly. He reached out for an apple to help her.

She did not look up. But her voice caught him like she had flicked him with a whip. 'Joe Starrett, don't you dare touch a one of these apples.'

He was sheepish as he returned to his chair. Then he was downright mad. He grabbed his knife and fork and dug into the food on his plate, taking big bites and chewing vigorously. There was nothing for our visitor and me to do but follow his example. Maybe it was a good supper. I could not tell. The food was only something to put in your mouth. And when we finished, there was nothing to do but wait because mother was sitting by the stove, arms folded, staring at the wall, waiting herself for her pie to bake.

We three watched her in a quiet so tight that it hurt. We could not help it. We would try to look away and always our eyes would turn back to her. She did not appear to notice us. You might have said she had forgotten we were there.

She had not forgotten because as soon as she sensed that the pie was done, she lifted it out, cut four wide pieces, and put them on plates. The first two she set in front of the two men. The third one she set down for me. The last one she laid at her own place and she sat down in her own chair at the table. Her voice was still sharp.

'I'm sorry to keep you men waiting so long. Your pie is ready now.'

Father inspected his portion like he was afraid of it. He needed to make a real effort to take his fork and lift a piece. He chewed on it and swallowed and he flipped his eyes sideways at mother and back again quickly to look across the table at Shane. 'That's prime pie,' he said.

Shane raised a piece on his fork. He considered it closely. He put it in his mouth and chewed on it gravely. 'Yes,' he said. The quizzical expression on his face was so plain you could not possibly miss it. 'Yes. That's the best bit of stump I ever tasted.'

What could a silly remark like that mean? I had no time to

wonder, for father and mother were acting so queer. They both stared at Shane and their mouths were sagging open. Then father snapped his shut and he chuckled and chuckled till he was swaying in his chair.

'By Godfrey, Marian, he's right. You've done it, too.'

Mother stared from one to the other of them. Her pinched look faded and her cheeks were flushed and her eyes were soft and warm as they should be, and she was laughing so that the tears came. And all of us were pitching into that pie, and the one thing wrong in the whole world was that there was not enough of it.

4

The sun was already well up the sky when I awakened the next morning. I had been a long time getting to sleep because my mind was full of the day's excitement and shifting moods. I could not straighten out in my mind the way the grown folks had behaved, the way things that did not really matter so much had become so important to them.

I had lain in my bed thinking of our visitor out in the bunk in the barn. It scarce seemed possible that he was the same man I had first seen, stern and chilling in his dark solitude, riding up our road. Something in father, something not of words or of actions but of the essential substance of the human spirit, had reached out and spoken to him and he had replied to it and had unlocked a part of himself to us. He was far off and unapproachable at times even when he was right there with you. Yet somehow he was closer, too, than my uncle, mother's brother, had been when he visited us the summer before.

I had been thinking, too, of the effect he had on father and mother. They were more alive, more vibrant, like they wanted to show more what they were, when they were with him. I could appreciate that because I felt the same way myself. But it puzzled me that a man so deep and vital in his own being, so ready to respond to father, should be riding a lone trail out of a closed and guarded past.

I realized with a jolt how late it was. The door to my little room was closed. Mother must have closed it so I could sleep undisturbed. I was frantic that the others might have finished breakfast and that our visitor was gone and I had missed him. I pulled on my clothes, not even bothering with buttons, and ran to the door.

They were still at the table. Father was fussing with his pipe. Mother and Shane were working on a last round of coffee. All three of them were subdued and quiet. They stared at me as I burst out of my room.

'My heavens,' said mother. 'You came in here like something was after you. What's the matter?'

'I just thought,' I blurted out, nodding at our visitor, 'that maybe he had ridden off and forgotten me.'

Shane shook his head slightly, looking straight at me. 'I wouldn't forget you, Bob.' He pulled himself up a little in his chair. He turned to mother and his voice took on a bantering tone. 'And I wouldn't forget your cooking, ma'am. If you begin having a special lot of people passing by at mealtimes, that'll be because a grateful man has been boasting of your flannel cakes all along the road.'

'Now there's an idea,' stuck in father as if he was glad to find something safe to talk about. 'We'll turn this place into a boarding house. Marian'll fill folks full of her meals and I'll fill my pockets full of their money. That hits me as a mighty convenient arrangement.'

Mother sniffed at him. But she was pleased at their talk and she was smiling as they kept on playing with the idea while she stirred me up my breakfast. She came right back at them, threatening to take father at his word and make him spend all his time peeling potatoes and washing dishes. They were enjoying themselves even though I could feel a bit of constraint behind the easy joshing. It was remarkable, too, how natural it was to have this Shane sitting there and joining in almost like he was a member of the family. There was none of the awkwardness some visitors always brought with them. You did feel you ought to be on your good behaviour with him, a mite extra careful about your manners and your speech. But not stiffly so. Just quiet and friendly about it.

He stood up at last and I knew he was going to ride away

from us and I wanted desperately to stop him. Father did it for me.

'You are certainly a man for being in a hurry. Sit down, Shane. I've a question to ask you.'

Father was suddenly very serious. Shane, standing there, was as suddenly withdrawn into a distant alertness. But he dropped back into his chair.

Father looked directly at him. 'Are you running away from anything?'

Shane stared at the plate in front of him for a long moment. It seemed to me that a shade of sadness passed over him. Then he raised his eyes and looked directly at father.

'No. I'm not running away from anything. Not in the way you mean.'

'Good.' Father stooped forward and stabbed at the table with a forefinger for emphasis. 'Look, Shane, I'm not a rancher. Now you've seen my place, you know that. I'm a farmer. Something of a stockman, maybe. But really a farmer. That's what I decided to be when I quit punching cattle for another man's money. That's what I want to be and I'm proud of it. I've made a fair start. This outfit isn't as big as I hope to have it some day. But there's more work here already than one man can handle if it's to be done right. The young fellow I had ran out on me after he tangled with a couple of Fletcher's boys in town one day.' Father was talking fast and he paused to draw breath.

Shane had been watching him intently. He moved his head to look out the window over the valley to the mountains marching along the horizon. 'It's always the same,' he murmured. He was sort of talking to himself. 'The old ways die hard.' He looked at mother and then at me, and as his eyes came back to father he seemed to have decided something that had been troubling him. 'So Fletcher's crowding you,' he said gently.

Father snorted.

'I don't crowd easy. But I've got a job to do here and it's too big for one man, even for me. And none of the strays that drift up this way are worth a damn.'

'Yes?' Shane said. His eyes were crinkling again, and he was one of us again and waiting.

'Will you stick here awhile and help me get things in shape for the winter?'

Shane rose to his feet. He loomed up taller across the table than I had thought him. 'I never figured to be a farmer, Starrett. I would have laughed at the notion a few days ago. All the same, you've hired yourself a hand.' He and father were looking at each other in a way that showed they were saying things words could never cover. Shane snapped it by swinging towards mother. 'And I'll rate your cooking, ma'am, wages enough.'

Father slapped his hands on his knees. 'You'll get good wages and you'll earn 'em. First off, now why don't you drop into town and get some work clothes. Try Sam Grafton's store. Tell him to put it on my bill.'

Shane was already at the door. 'I'll buy my own,' he said, and was gone.

Father was so pleased he could not sit still. He jumped up and whirled mother around. 'Marian, the sun's shining mighty bright at last. We've got ourselves a man.'

'But, Joe, are you sure what you're doing? What kind of work can a man like that do? Oh, I know he stood right up to you with that stump. But that was something special. He's been used to good living and plenty of money. You can tell that. He said himself he doesn't know anything about farming.'

'Neither did I when I started here. What a man knows isn't important. It's what he is that counts. I'll bet you that one was a cowpuncher when he was younger and a top hand too. Anything he does will be done right. You watch. In a week he'll be making even me hump or he'll be bossing the place.'

'Perhaps.'

'No perhapsing about it. Did you notice how he took it when I told him about Fletcher's boys and young Morley? That's what fetched him. He knows I'm in a spot and he's not the man to leave me there. Nobody'll push him around or scare him away. He's my kind of a man.'

'Why, Joe Starrett. He isn't like you at all. He's smaller and he looks different and his clothes are different and he talks different. I know he's lived different.'

'Huh?' Father was surprised. 'I wasn't talking about things like that.'

Shane came back with a pair of dungaree pants, a flannel

shirt, stout work shoes, and a good, serviceable stetson. He disappeared into the barn and emerged a few moments later in his new clothes, leading his horse unsaddled. At the pasture gate he slipped off the halter, turned the horse in with a hearty slap, and tossed the halter to me.

'Take care of a horse, Bob, and it will take care of you. This one now has brought me better than a thousand miles in the last few weeks.' And he was striding away to join father, who was ditching the field out past the growing corn where the ground was rich but marshy and would not be worth much till it was properly drained. I watched him swinging through the rows of young corn, no longer a dark stranger but part of the place, a farmer like father and me.

Only he was not a farmer and never really could be. It was not three days before you saw that he could stay right beside father in any kind of work. Show him what needed to be done and he could do it, and like as not would figure out a better way of getting it done. He never shirked the meanest task. He was ever ready to take the hard end of any chore. Yet you always felt in some indefinable fashion that he was a man apart.

There were times when he would stop and look off at the mountains and then down at himself and any tool he happened to have in his hands as if in wry amusement at what he was doing. You had no impression that he thought himself too good for the work or did not like it. He was just different. He was shaped in some firm forging of past circumstance for other things.

For all his slim building he was plenty rugged. His slenderness could fool you at first. But when you saw him close in action, you saw that he was solid, compact, that there was no waste weight on his frame just as there was no waste effort in his smooth, flowing motion. What he lacked alongside father in size and strength, he made up in quickness of movement, in instinctive co-ordination of mind and muscle, and in that sudden fierce energy that had burned in him when the old stump tried to topple back on him. Mostly this last slept in him, not needed while he went easily through the day's routine. But when a call came, it could flame forward with a driving intensity that never failed to frighten me.

I would be frightened, as I had tried to explain to mother, not at Shane himself, but at the suggestion it always gave me of things in the human equation beyond my comprehension. At such times there would be a concentration in him, a single-ness of dedication to the instant need, that seemed to me at once wonderful and disturbing. And then he would be again the quiet, steady man who shared with father my boy's allegiance.

I was beginning to feel my oats about then, proud of myself for being able to lick Ollie Johnson at the next place down the road. Fighting, boy style, was much in my mind.

Once, when father and I were alone, I asked him: 'Could you beat Shane? In a fight, I mean.'

'Son, that's a tough question. If I had to, I might do it. But, by Godfrey, I'd hate to try it. Some men just plain have dynamite inside them, and he's one. I'll tell you, though. I've never met a man I'd rather have more on my side in any kind of trouble.'

I could understand that and it satisfied me. But there were things about Shane I could not understand. When he came in to the first meal after he agreed to stay on with us, he went to the chair that had always been father's and stood beside it wait-ing for the rest of us to take the other places. Mother was sur-prised and somewhat annoyed. She started to say something. Father quieted her with a warning glance. He walked to the chair across from Shane and sat down like this was the right and natural spot for him and afterwards he and Shane always used these same places.

I could not see any reason for the shift until the first time one of our homestead neighbours knocked on the door while we were eating and came straight on in as most of them usually did. Then I suddenly realized that Shane was sitting opposite the door where he could directly confront anyone coming through it. I could see that was the way he wanted it to be. But I could not understand why he wanted it that way.

In the evenings after supper when he was talking lazily with us, he would never sit by a window. Out on the porch he would always face the road. He liked to have a wall behind him and not just to lean against. No matter where he was, away from the table, before sitting down he would swing his chair into position, back to the nearest wall, not making any show, simply putting it there and bending into it in one easy motion. He did not even seem to be aware that this was unusual. It was part of his fixed alertness. He always wanted to know everything happening around him.

This alertness could be noted, too, in the watch he kept, without appearing to make any special effort, on every approach to our place. He knew first when anyone was moving along the road and he would stop whatever he was doing to study carefully any passing rider.

We often had company in the evenings, for the other homesteaders regarded father as their leader and would drop in to discuss their affairs with him. They were interesting men in their own fashions, a various assortment. But Shane was not anxious to meet people. He would share little in their talk. With us he spoke freely enough. We were, in some subtle way, his folks. Though we had taken him in, you had the feeling that he had adopted us. But with others he was reserved; courteous and soft-spoken, yet withdrawn beyond a line of his own making.

These things puzzled me and not me alone. The people in town and those who rode or drove in pretty regularly were all curious about him. It was a wonder how quickly everyone in the valley, and even on the ranches out in the open country, knew that he was working with father.

They were not sure they liked having him in their neighbourhood. Ledyard had told some tall tale about what happened at our place that made them stare sharply at Shane whenever they had a chance. But they must have had their own measure of Ledyard, for they did not take his story too straight. They just could not really make up their minds about Shane and it seemed to worry them.

More than once, when I was with Ollie Johnson on the way to our favourite fishing hole the other side of town, I heard men arguing about him in front of Mr Grafton's store. 'He's like one of these here slow-burning fuses,' I heard an old mule-skinner say one day. 'Quiet and no sputtering. So quiet you forget it's burning. Then it sets off one hell of a blow-off of trouble when it touches powder. That's him. And there's been trouble brewing in this valley for a long spell now. Maybe it'll be good when it comes. Maybe it'll be bad. You just can't tell.' And that puzzled me too.

What puzzled me most, though, was something it took me nearly two weeks to appreciate. And yet it was the most striking thing of all. Shane carried no gun.

In those days guns were as familiar all through the Territory as boots and saddles. They were not used much in the valley except for occasional hunting. But they were always in evidence. Most men did not feel fully dressed without one.

We homesteaders went in mostly for rifles and shot-guns when we had any shooting to do. A pistol slapping on the hip was a nuisance for a farmer. Still every man had his cartridge belt and holstered Colt to be worn when he was not working or loafing around the house. Father buckled his on whenever he rode off on any trip, even just into town, as much out of habit, I guess, as anything else.

But this Shane never carried a gun. And that was a peculiar thing because he had a gun.

I saw it once. I saw it when I was alone in the barn one day and I spotted his saddle-roll lying on his bunk. Usually he kept it carefully put away underneath. He must have forgotten it this time, for it was there in the open by the pillow. I reached to sort of feel it – and I felt the gun inside. No one was near, so I unfastened the straps and unrolled the blankets. There it was, the most beautiful-looking weapon I ever saw. Beautiful and deadly-looking.

The holster and filled cartridge belt were of the same soft black leather as the boots tucked under the bunk, tooled in the same intricate design. I knew enough to know that the gun was a single-action Colt, the same model as the Regular Army issue that was the favourite of all men in those days, and that old-timers used to say was the finest pistol ever made.

This was the same model. But this was no Army gun. It was black, almost blue-black, with the darkness not in any enamel but in the metal itself. The grip was clear on the outer curve, shaped to the fingers on the inner curve, and two ivory plates were set into it with exquisite skill, one on each side.

The smooth invitation of it tempted your grasp. I took hold and pulled the gun out of the holster. It came so easily that I could hardly believe it was there in my hand. Heavy like father's, it was somehow much easier to handle. You held it up to aiming level and it seemed to balance itself into your hand.

It was clean and polished and oiled. The empty cylinder, when I released the catch and flicked it, spun swiftly and noiselessly. I was surprised to see that the front sight was gone, the barrel smooth right down to the end, and that the hammer had been filed to a sharp point.

Why should a man do that to a gun? Why should a man with a gun like that refuse to wear it and show it off? And then, staring at that dark and deadly efficiency, I was again suddenly chilled, and I quickly put everything back exactly as before and hurried out into the sun.

The first chance I tried to tell father about it. 'Father,' I said, all excited, 'do you know what Shane has rolled up in his blankets?'

'Probably a gun.'

'But – but how did you know? Have you seen it?'

'No. That's what he would have.'

I was all mixed up. 'Well, why doesn't he ever carry it? Do you suppose maybe it's because he doesn't know how to use it very well?'

Father chuckled like I had made a joke. 'Son, I wouldn't be surprised if he could take that gun and shoot the buttons off your shirt with you awearing it and all you'd feel would be a breeze.'

'Gosh agorry! Why does he keep it hidden in the barn then?'

'I don't know. Not exactly.'

'Why don't you ask him?'

Father looked straight at me, very serious. 'That's one question I'll never ask him. And don't you ever say anything to him about it. There are some things you don't ask a man. Not if you respect him. He's entitled to stake his claim to what he considers private to himself alone. But you can take my word for it, Bob, that when a man like Shane doesn't want to tote a gun you can bet your shirt, buttons and all, he's got a mighty good reason.'

That was that. I was still mixed up. But whenever father gave you his word on something, there was nothing more to be said. He never did that except when he knew he was right. I started to wander off.

'Bob.'

'Yes, father.'

'Listen to me, son. Don't get to liking Shane too much.'

'Why not? Is there anything wrong with him?'

'No-o-o-o. There's nothing wrong about Shane. Nothing you could put that way. There's more right about him than most any man you're ever likely to meet. But — ' Father was throwing around for what to say. 'But he's fiddle-footed. Remember. He said so himself. He'll be moving on one of these days and then you'll be all upset if you get to liking him too much.'

That was not what father really meant. But that was what he wanted me to think. So I did not ask any more questions.

5

Two weeks went rocking past, and soon it did not seem possible that there ever had been a time when Shane was not with us. He and father worked together more like partners than boss and hired man. The amount they could get through in a day was a marvel. The ditching father had reckoned would take him most of the summer was done in less than a month. The loft was finished and the first cutting of alfalfa stowed away.

We would have enough fodder to carry a few more young steers through the winter for fattening next summer, so father rode out of the valley and all the way to the ranch where he worked once and came back herding a half-dozen more. He was gone two days. He came back to find that Shane, while he was gone, had knocked out the end of the corral and posted a new section making it half again as big.

'Now we can really get going next year,' Shane said as father sat on his horse staring at the corral like he could not quite believe what he saw. 'We ought to get enough hay off that new field to help us carry forty head.'

'Oho!' said father. 'So we can get going. And we ought to get enough hay.' He was pleased as could be because he was scowling at Shane the way he did at me when he was tickled silly over something I had done and did not want to let on that he was. He jumped off his horse and hurried up to the house where mother was standing on the porch.

'Marian,' he demanded right off, waving at the corral, 'whose idea was that?'

'Well-l-l,' she said, 'Shane suggested it.' Then she added slyly, 'But I told him to go ahead.'

'That's right.' Shane had come up beside him. 'She rode me like she had spurs to get it done by today. Kind of a present. It's your wedding anniversary.'

'Well, I'll be damned,' said father. 'So it is.' He stared foolishly at one and then the other of them. With Shane there watching, he hopped on the porch and gave mother a kiss. I was embarrassed for him and I turned away – and hopped about a foot myself.

'Hey! Those steers are running away!'

The grown folks had forgotten about them. All six were wandering up the road, straggling and separating. Shane, that soft spoken man, let out a whoop you might have heard halfway to town and ran to father's horse, putting his hands on the saddle and vaulting into it. He fairly lifted the horse into a gallop in one leap and that old cowpony of father's lit out after those steers like this was fun. By the time father reached the corral gate, Shane had the runaways in a compact bunch and padding back at a trot. He dropped them through the gateway neat as pie.

He was tall and straight in the saddle the few seconds it took father to close the gate. He and the horse were blowing a bit and both of them were perky and proud.

'It's been ten years,' he said, 'since I did anything like that.'

Father grinned at him. 'Shane, if I didn't know better, I'd say you were a faker. There's still a lot of kid in you.'

The first real smile I had seen yet flashed across Shane's face. 'Maybe. Maybe there is at that.'

I think that was the happiest summer of my life.

The only shadow over our valley, the recurrent trouble between Fletcher and us homesteaders, seemed to have faded away. Fletcher himself was gone most of those months. He had gone to Fort Bennett in Dakota and even on East to Washington, so we heard, trying to get a contract to supply beef to the Indian agent at Standing Rock, the big Sioux reservation over beyond the Black Hills. Except for his foreman, Morgan, and several surly older men, his hands were young, easy-going cow-boys who made a lot of noise in town once in a while but rarely did any harm and even then only in high spirits. We liked them – when Fletcher was not there driving them into harassing us in constant shrewd ways. Now, with him away, they kept to the other side of the river and did not bother us. Sometimes, riding in sight on the other bank, they might even wave to us in their rollicking fashion.

Until Shane came, they had been my heroes. Father, of course, was special all to himself. There could never be anyone quite to match him. I wanted to be like him, just as he was. But first I wanted, as he had done, to ride the range, to have my own string of ponies and take part in an all-brand round-up and in a big cattle drive and dash into strange towns with just such a rollicking crew and with a season's pay jingling in my pockets.

Now I was not so sure. I wanted more and more to be like Shane, like the man I imagined he was in the past fenced off so securely. I had to imagine most of it. He would never speak of it, not in any way at all. Even his name remained mysterious. Just Shane. Nothing else. We never knew whether that was his first name or last name or, indeed, any name that came from his family. 'Call me Shane,' he said, and that was all he ever said. But I conjured up all manner of adventures for him, not tied to any particular time or place, seeing him as a slim and dark and dashing figure coolly passing through perils that would overcome a lesser man.

I would listen in what was closely akin to worship while my two men, father and Shane, argued long and amiably about the cattle business. They would wrangle over methods of feed-ing and bringing steers up to top weight. But they were agreed that controlled breeding was better than open range running and that improvement of stock was needed even if that meant spending big money on imported bulls. And they would specu-late about the chances of a railroad spur ever reaching the valley, so you could ship direct without thinning good meat off your cattle driving them to market.

It was plain that Shane was beginning to enjoy living with us and working the place. Little by little the tension in him was fading out. He was still alert and watchful, instinct with that unfailing awareness of everything about him. I came to realize that this was inherent in him, not learned or acquired, simply a part of his natural being. But the sharp edge of conscious alertness, almost of expectancy of some unknown trouble always waiting, was wearing away.

Yet why was he sometimes so strange and stricken in his own secret bitterness? Like the time I was playing with a gun Mr Grafton gave me, an old frontier model Colt with a cracked barrel someone had turned in at the store.

I had rigged a holster out of a torn chunk of oilcloth and a belt of rope. I was stalking around near the barn, whirling every few steps to pick off a skulking Indian, when I saw Shane watching me from the barn door. I stopped short, thinking of that beautiful gun under his bunk and afraid he would make fun of me and my sorry old broken pistol. Instead he looked gravely at me.

'How many you knocked over so far, Bob?'

Could I ever repay the man? My gun was a shining new weapon, my hand steady as a rock as I drew a bead on another one.

'That makes seven.'

'Indians or timber wolves?'

'Indians. Big ones.'

'Better leave a few for the other scouts,' he said gently. 'It wouldn't do to make them jealous. And look here, Bob. You're not doing that quite right.'

He sat down on an upturned crate and beckoned me over. 'Your holster's too low. Don't let it drag full arm's length. Have it just below the hip, so the grip is about halfway between your wrist and elbow when the arm's hanging limp. You can take the gun then as your hand's coming up and there's still room to clear the holster without having to lift the gun too high.'

'Gosh agorry! Is that the way the real gunfighters do?'

A queer light flickered in his eyes and was gone. 'No. Not all of them. Most have their own tricks. One likes a shoulder holster; another packs his gun in his pants belt. Some carry two guns, but that's a show-off stunt and a waste of weight. One's enough, if you know how to use it. I've even seen a man have a tight holster with an open end and fastened on a little swivel to the belt. He didn't have to pull the gun then. Just swung up the barrel and blazed away from the hip. That's mighty fast for close work and a big target. But it's not certain past ten or fifteen paces and no good at all for putting your shot right where you want it. The way I'm telling you is as good as any and better than most. And another thing – '

He reached and took the gun. Suddenly, as for the first time, I was aware of his hands. They were broad and strong, but not heavy and fleshy like father's. The fingers were long and square on the ends. It was funny how, touching the gun, the hands seemed to have an intelligence all their own, a sure movement that needed no guidance of thought.

His right hand closed around the grip and you knew at once it was doing what it had been created for. He hefted the old gun, letting it lie loosely in the hand. Then the fingers tightened and the thumb toyed with the hammer, testing the play of it.

While I gaped at him, he tossed it swiftly in the air and caught it in his left hand and in the instant of catching, it nestled snugly into his hand too. He tossed it again, high this time, and spinning end over end, and as it came down, his right hand flicked forward and took it. The forefinger slipped through the trigger guard and the gun spun, coming up into firing position in the one unbroken motion. With him that old pistol seemed alive, not an inanimate and rusting metal object, but an extension of the man himself.

'If it's speed you're after, Bob, don't split the move into parts. Don't pull, cock, aim, and fire. Slip back the hammer as you bring the gun up and squeeze the trigger the second it's up level.'

'How do you aim it, then? How do you get a sight on it?'

'No need to. Learn to hold it so the barrel's right in line with the fingers if they were out straight. You won't have to waste time bringing it high to take a sight. Just point it, low and quick and easy, like pointing a finger.'

Like pointing a finger. As the words came, he was doing it. The old gun was bearing on some target over by the corral and the hammer was clicking at the empty cylinder. Then the hand around the gun whitened and the fingers slowly opened and the gun fell to the ground. The hand sank to his side, stiff and awkward. He raised his head and the mouth was a bitter gash in his face. His eyes were fastened on the mountains climbing in the distance.

'Shane! Shane! What's the matter?'

He did not hear me. He was back somewhere along the dark trail of the past.

He took a deep breath, and I could see the effort run through him as he dragged himself into the present and a realization of a boy staring at him. He beckoned to me to pick up the gun. When I did he leaned forward and spoke earnestly.

'Listen, Bob. A gun is just a tool. No better and no worse than any other tool, a shovel – or an axe or a saddle or a stove or anything. Think of it always that way. A gun is as good – and as bad – as the man who carries it. Remember that.'

He stood up and strode off into the fields and I knew he wanted to be alone. I remembered what he said all right, tucked away unforgettably in my mind. But in those days I remembered more the way he handled the gun and the advice he gave me about using it. I would practise with it and think of the time when I could have one that would really shoot.

And then the summer was over. School began again and the days were growing shorter and the first cutting edge of cold was creeping down from the mountains.

6

More than the summer was over. The season of friendship in our valley was fading with the sun's warmth. Fletcher was back and he had his contract. He was talking in town that he would need the whole range again. The homesteaders would have to go.

He was a reasonable man, he was saying in his smooth way, and he would pay a fair price for any improvements they had put in. But we knew what Luke Fletcher would call a fair price. And we had no intention of leaving. The land was ours by right of settlement, guaranteed by the government. Only we knew, too, how far away the government was from our valley way up there in the Territory.

The nearest marshal was a good hundred miles away. We did not even have a sheriff in our town. There never had been any reason for one. When folks had any lawing to do, they would head for Sheridan, nearly a full day's ride away. Our town was small, not even organized as a town. It was growing, but it was still not much more than a roadside settlement.

The first people there were three or four miners who had come prospecting after the blow-up of the Big Horn Mining Association about twenty years before, and had found gold traces leading to a moderate vein in the jutting rocks that partially closed off the valley where it edged into the plain. You could not have called it a strike, for others that followed were soon disappointed. Those first few, however, had done fairly well and had brought in their families and a number of helpers.

Then a stage and freighting line had picked the site for a relay post. That meant a place where you could get drinks as well as horses, and before long the cowboys from the ranches out on the plain and Fletcher's spread in the valley were drifting in of an evening. With us homesteaders coming now, one or two almost every season, the town was taking shape. Already there were several stores, a harness and blacksmith shop, and nearly a dozen houses. Just the year before, the men had put together a one-room schoolhouse.

Sam Grafton's place was the biggest. He had a general store with several rooms for living quarters back of it in one half of his rambling building, a saloon with a long bar and tables for cards and the like in the other half. Upstairs he had some rooms he rented to stray drummers or anyone else stranded overnight. He acted as our postmaster, an elderly man, a close bargainer but honest in all his dealings. Sometimes he served as a sort of magistrate in minor disputes. His wife was dead. His daughter Jane kept house for him and was our school-teacher when school was in session.

Even if we had had a sheriff, he would have been Fletcher's man. Fletcher was the power in the valley in those days. We homesteaders had been around only a few years and the other people still thought of us as there by his sufferance. He had been running cattle through the whole valley at the time the miners arrived, having bought or bulldozed out the few small ranchers there ahead of him. A series of bad years working up to the dry summer and terrible winter of '86 had cut his herds about the time the first of the homesteaders moved in and he had not objected too much. But now there were seven of us in all and the number rising each year.

It was a certain thing, father used to say, that the town would grow and swing our way. Mr Grafton knew that too, I guess, but he was a careful man who never let thoughts about the future interfere with present business. The others were the kind to veer with the prevailing wind. Fletcher was the big man in the valley, so they looked up to him and tolerated us. Led to it, they probably would have helped him run us out. With him out of the way, they would just as willingly accept us. And Fletcher was back, with a contract in his pocket, wanting his full range again.

There was a hurried counsel in our house soon as the news was around. Our neighbour towards town, Lew Johnson, who heard it in Grafton's store, spread the word and arrived first. He was followed by Henry Shipstead, who had the place next to him, the closest to town. These two had been the original home-steaders, staking out their hundred and eighties two years before the drought and riding out Fletcher's annoyance until the cut in his herds gave him other worries. They were solid, dependable men, old-line farmers who had come West from Iowa.

You could not say quite as much for the rest, straggling in at intervals. James Lewis and Ed Howells were two middle-aged cowhands who had grown dissatisfied and tagged father into the valley, coming pretty much on his example. Lacking his energy and drive, they had not done too well and could be easily discouraged.

Frank Torrey from farther up the valley was a nervous, fidgety man with a querulous wife and a string of dirty kids growing longer every year. He was always talking about pulling up stakes and heading for California. But he had a stubborn streak in him, and he was always saying, too, that he'd be damned if he'd make tracks just because some big-hatted rancher wanted him to.

Ernie Wright, who had the last stand up the valley butting

out into the range still used by Fletcher, was probably the weakest of the lot. Not in any physical way. He was a husky, likeable man, so dark-complected that there were rumours he was part Indian. He was always singing and telling tall stories. But he would be off hunting when he should be working and he had a quick temper that would trap him into doing fool things without taking thought.

He was as serious as the rest of them that night. Mr Grafton had said that this time Fletcher meant business. His contract called for all the beef he could drive in the next five years and he was determined to push the chance to the limit.

'But what can he do?' asked Frank Torrey. 'The land's ours as long as we live on it and we get title in three years. Some of you fellows have already proved up.'

'He won't really make trouble,' chimed in James Lewis. 'Fletcher's never been the shooting kind. He's a good talker, but talk can't hurt us.' Several of the others nodded. Johnson and Shipstead did not seem to be so sure. Father had not said anything yet and they all looked at him.

'Jim's right,' he admitted. 'Fletcher hasn't ever let his boys get careless thataway. Not yet anyhow. That ain't saying he wouldn't, if there wasn't any other way. There's a hard streak in him. But he won't get real tough for a while. I don't figure he'll start moving cattle in now till spring. My guess is he'll try putting pressure on us this fall and winter, see if he can wear us down. He'll probably start right here. He doesn't like any of us. But he doesn't like me most.'

'That's true.' Ed Howells was expressing the unspoken verdict that father was their leader. 'How do you figure he'll go about it?'

'My guess on that,' father said – drawling now and smiling a grim little smile like he knew he was holding a good hole card in a tight game – 'my guess on that is that he'll begin by trying to convince Shane here that it isn't healthy to be working with me.'

'You mean the way he –' began Ernie Wright.

'Yes.' Father cut him short. 'I mean the way he did with young Morley.'

I was peeping around the door of my little room. I saw Shane sitting off to one side, listening quietly as he had been right along. He didn't seem the least bit surprised. He did not seem the least bit interested in finding out what had happened to young Morley. I knew what had. I had seen Morley come back from town, bruised and a beaten man, and gather his things and curse father for hiring him and ride away without once looking back.

Yet Shane sat there quietly as if what had happened to Morley had nothing to do with him. He simply did not care what it was. And then I understood why. It was because he was not Morley. He was Shane.

Father was right. In some strange fashion the feeling was abroad that Shane was a marked man. Attention was on him as a sort of symbol. By taking him on father had accepted in a way a challenge from the big ranch across the river. What had happened to Morley had been a warning and father had deliberately answered it. The long unpleasantness was sharpened now after the summer lull. The issue in our valley was plain and would in time have to be pushed to a showdown. If Shane could be driven out, there would be a break in the homestead ranks, a defeat going beyond the loss of a man into the realm of prestige and morale. It could be the crack in the dam that weakens the whole structure and finally lets through the flood.

The people in town were more curious than ever, not now so much about Shane's past as about what he might do if Fletcher tried any move against him. They would stop me and ask me questions when I was hurrying to and from school. I knew that father would not want me to say anything and I pretended that I did not know what they were talking about. But I used to watch Shane closely myself and wonder how all the slow-climbing tenseness in our valley could be so focused on one man and he seem to be so indifferent to it.

For of course he was aware of it. He never missed anything. Yet he went about his work as usual, smiling frequently now at me, bantering mother at mealtimes in his courteous manner, arguing amiably as before with father on plans for next year. The only thing that was different was that there appeared to be a lot of new activity across the river. It was surprising how often Fletcher's cowboys were finding jobs to do within view of our place.

Then one afternoon, when we were stowing away the second

and last cutting of hay, one fork of the big tongs we were using to haul it up to the loft broke loose. 'Have to get it welded in town,' father said in disgust and began to hitch up the team.

Shane stared over the river where a cowboy was riding lazily back and forth by a bunch of cattle. 'I'll take it in,' he said.

Father looked at Shane and he looked across the way and he grinned. 'All right. It's as good a time as any.' He slapped down the final buckle and started for the house. 'Just a minute and I'll be ready.'

'Take it easy, Joe.' Shane's voice was gentle, but it stopped father in his tracks. 'I said I'll take it in.'

Father whirled to face him. 'Damn it all, man. Do you think I'd let you go alone? Suppose they – ' He bit down on his own words. He wiped a hand slowly across his face and he said what I had never heard him say to any man. 'I'm sorry,' he said. 'I should have known better.' He stood there silently watching as Shane gathered up the reins and jumped to the wagon seat.

I was afraid father would stop me, so I waited till Shane was driving out of the lane. I ducked behind the barn, around the end of the corral, and hopped into the wagon going past. As I did, I saw the cowboy across the river spin his horse and ride rapidly off in the direction of the ranch-house.

Shane saw it, too, and it seemed to give him a grim amusement. He reached backwards and hauled me over the seat and sat me beside him.

'You Starretts like to mix into things.' For a moment I thought he might send me back. Instead he grinned at me. 'I'll buy you a jack-knife when we hit town.'

He did, a dandy big one with two blades and a corkscrew. After we left the tongs with the blacksmith and found the welding would take nearly an hour, I squatted on the steps on the long porch across the front of Grafton's building, busy whittling, while Shane stepped into the saloon side and ordered a drink. Will Atkey, Grafton's thin, sad-faced clerk and bartender, was behind the bar and several other men were loafing at one of the tables.

It was only a few moments before two cowboys came galloping down the road. They slowed to a walk about fifty yards off and with a show of nonchalance ambled the rest of the way to

Grafton's, dismounting and looping their reins over the rail in front. One of them I had seen often, a young fellow everyone called Chris, who had worked with Fletcher several years and was known for a gay manner and reckless courage. The other was new to me, a sallow, pinch-cheek man, not much older, who looked like he had crowded a lot of hard living into his years. He must have been one of the new hands Fletcher had been bringing into the valley since he got his contract.

They paid no attention to me. They stepped softly up on the porch and to the window of the saloon part of the building. As they peered through, Chris nodded and jerked his head towards the inside. The new man stiffened. He leaned closer for a better look. Abruptly he turned clear about and came right down past me and went over to his horse.

Chris was startled and hurried after him. They were both so intent they did not realize I was there. The new man was lifting the reins back over his horse's head when Chris caught his arm.

'What the hell?'

'I'm leaving.'

'Huh? I don't get it.'

'I'm leaving. Now. For good.'

'Hey, listen. Do you know that guy?'

'I didn't say that. There ain't nobody can claim I said that. I'm leaving, that's all. You can tell Fletcher. This is a hell of a country up here anyhow.'

Chris was getting mad. 'I might have known,' he said. 'Scared, eh. Yellow.'

Colour rushed into the new man's sallow face. But he climbed on his horse and swung out from the rail. 'You can call it that,' he said flatly and started down the road, out of town, out of the valley.

Chris was standing still by the rail, shaking his head in wonderment. 'Hell,' he said to himself, 'I'll brace him myself.' He stalked up on the porch, into the saloon.

I dashed into the store side, over to the opening between the two big rooms. I crouched on a box just inside the store where I could hear everything and see most of the other room. It was long and fairly wide. The bar curved out from the opening and ran all the way along the inner wall to the back wall, which closed off a room Grafton used as an office. There was a row of windows on the far side, too high for anyone to look in from outside. A small stairway behind them led up to a sort of balcony across the back with doors opening into several little rooms.

Shane was leaning easily with one arm on the bar, his drink in his other hand, when Chris came to perhaps six feet away and called for a whisky bottle and a glass. Chris pretended he did not notice Shane at first and bobbed his head in greeting to the men at the table. They were a pair of mule-skinners who made regular trips into the valley freighting in goods for Grafton and the other shops. I could have sworn that Shane, studying Chris in his effortless way, was somehow disappointed.

Chris waited until he had his whisky and had gulped a stiff shot. Then he deliberately looked Shane over like he had just spotted him.

'Hello, farmer,' he said. He said it as if he did not like farmers.

Shane regarded him with grave attention. 'Speaking to me?' he asked mildly and finished his drink.

'Hell, there ain't nobody else standing there. Here, have a drink of this.' Chris shoved his bottle along the bar. Shane poured himself a generous slug and raised it to his lips.

'I'll be damned,' flipped Chris. 'So you drink whisky.'

Shane tossed off the rest in his glass and set it down. 'I've had better,' he said, as friendly as could be. 'But this will do.'

Chris slapped his leather chaps with a loud smack. He turned to take in the other men. 'Did you hear that? This farmer drinks whisky! I didn't think these plough-pushing dirt-grubbers drank anything stronger than soda pop!'

'Some of us do,' said Shane, friendly as before. Then he was no longer friendly and his voice was like winter frost. 'You've had your fun and it's mighty young fun. Now run home and tell Fletcher to send a grown-up man next time.' He turned away and sang out to Will Atkey. 'Do you have any soda pop? I'd like a bottle.'

Will hesitated, looked kind of funny, and scuttled past me

into the store room. He came back right away with a bottle of the pop Grafton kept there for us school kids. Chris was standing quiet, not so much mad, I would have said, as puzzled. It was as though they were playing some queer game and he was not sure of the next move. He sucked on his lower lip for a while. Then he snapped his mouth and began to look elaborately around the room, sniffing loudly.

'Hey, Will!' he called. 'What's been happening in here? It smells. That ain't no clean cattleman smell. That's plain dirty barnyard.' He stared at Shane. 'You, farmer. What are you and Starrett raising out there? Pigs.'

Shane was just taking hold of the bottle Will had fetched him. His hand closed on it and the knuckles showed white. He moved slowly, almost unwillingly, to face Chris. Every line of his body was as taut as stretched whipcord, was alive and somehow rich with an immense eagerness. There was that fierce concentration in him, filling him, blazing in his eyes. In that moment there was nothing in the room for him but that mocking man only a few feet away.

The big room was so quiet the stillness fairly hurt. Chris stepped back involuntarily, one pace, two, then pulled up erect. And still nothing happened. The lean muscles along the sides of Shane's jaw were ridged like rock.

Then the breath, pent in him, broke the stillness with a soft sound as it left his lungs. He looked away from Chris, past him, over the tops of the swinging doors beyond, over the roof of the shed across the road, on into the distance where the mountains loomed in their own unending loneliness. Quietly he walked, the bottle forgotten in his hand, so close by Chris as almost to brush him yet apparently not even seeing him, through the doors and was gone.

I heard a sigh of relief near me. Mr Grafton had come up from somewhere behind me. He was watching Chris with a strange, ironic quirk at his mouth corners. Chris was trying not to look pleased with himself. But he swaggered as he went to the doors and peered over them.

'You saw it, Will,' he called over his shoulder. 'He walked out on me.' Chris pushed up his hat and rolled back on his heels and laughed. 'With a bottle of soda pop too!' He was still laughing as he went out and we heard him ride away.

'That boy's a fool,' Mr Grafton muttered.

Will Atkey came sidling over to Mr Grafton. 'I never pegged Shane for a play like that,' he said.

'He was afraid, Will.'

'Yeah. That's what was so funny. I would've guessed he could take Chris.'

Mr Grafton looked at Will as he did often, like he was a little sorry for him. 'No, Will. He wasn't afraid of Chris. He was afraid of himself.' Mr Grafton was thoughtful and perhaps sad too. 'There's trouble ahead, Will. The worst trouble we've ever had.'

He noticed me, realizing my presence. 'Better skip along, Bob, and find your friend. Do you think he got that bottle for himself?'

True enough Shane had it waiting for me at the blacksmith shop. Cherry pop, the kind I favoured most. But I could not enjoy it much. Shane was so silent and stern. He had slipped back into the dark mood that was on him when he first came riding up our road. I did not dare say anything. Only once did he speak to me, and I knew he did not expect me to understand or to answer.

'Why should a man be smashed because he has courage and does what he's told? Life's a dirty business, Bob. I could like that boy.' And he turned inward again to his own thought and stayed the same until we had loaded the tongs in the wagon and were well started home. Then the closer we came, the more cheerful he was. By the time we swung in towards the barn, he was the way I wanted him again, crinkling his eyes at me and gravely joshing me about the Indians I would scalp with my new knife.

Father popped out the barn door so quick you could tell he had been itching for us to return. He was busting with curiosity, but he would not come straight out with a question to Shane. He tackled me instead.

'See any of your cowboy heroes in town?'

Shane cut in ahead of me. 'One of Fletcher's crew chased us in to pay his respects.'

'No,' I said, proud of my information. 'There was two of them.'

'Two?' Shane said it. Father was the one who was not surprised. 'What did the other one do?'

'He went up on the porch and looked in the window where you were and came right back down and rode off.'

'Back to the ranch?'

'The other way. He said he was leaving for good.'

Father and Shane looked at each other. Father was smiling. 'One down and you didn't even know it. What did you do to the other?'

'Nothing. He passed a few remarks about farmers. I went back to the blacksmith shop.'

Father repeated it, spacing the words like there might be meanings between them. 'You – went – back – to – the – blacksmith – shop.'

I was worried that he must be thinking what Will Atkey did. Then I knew nothing like that had even entered his head. He switched to me. 'Who was it?'

'It was Chris.'

Father was smiling again. He had not been there but he had the whole thing clear. 'Fletcher was right to send two. Young ones like Chris need to hunt in pairs or they might get hurt.' He chuckled in a sort of wry amusement. 'Chris must have been considerable surprised when the other fellow skipped. And more when you walked out. It was too bad the other one didn't stick around.'

'Yes,' Shane said, 'it was.'

The way he said it sobered father. 'I hadn't thought of that. Chris is just cocky enough to take it wrong. That can make things plenty unpleasant.'

'Yes,' said Shane again, 'it can.'

7

It was just as father and Shane had said. The story Chris told was common knowledge all through the valley before the sun set the next day and the story grew in the telling. Fletcher had an advantage now and he was quick to push it. He and his foreman, Morgan, a broad slab of a man with flattened face and head small in proportion to great sloping shoulders, were ·shrewd at things like this and they kept their men primed to rowel us homesteaders at every chance.

They took to using the upper ford, up above Ernie Wright's stand, and riding down the road past our places every time they had an excuse for going to town. They would go by slowly, looking everything over with insolent interest and passing remarks for our benefit.

The same week, maybe three days later, a covey of them came riding by while father was putting a new hinge on the corral gate. They acted like they were too busy staring over our land to see him there close.

'Wonder where Starrett keeps the critters,' said one of them. 'I don't see a pig in sight.'

'But I can smell 'em!' shouted another one. With that they all began to laugh and whoop and holler and went tearing off, kicking up a lot of dust and leaving father with a tightness around his mouth that was not there before.

They were impartial with attentions like that. They would hand them out anywhere along the line an opportunity offered. But they liked best to catch father within earshot and burn him with their sarcasm.

It was crude. It was coarse. I thought it silly for grown men to act that way. But it was effective. Shane, as self-sufficient as the mountains, could ignore it. Father, while it galled him, could keep it from getting him. The other homesteaders, though, could not help being irritated and showing they felt insulted. It roughed their nerves and made them angry and restless. They did not know Shane as father and I did. They were not sure there might not be some truth in the big talk Chris was making.

Things became so bad they could not go into Grafton's store without someone singing out for soda pop. And wherever they went, the conversation nearby always snuck around somehow to pigs. You could sense the contempt up in town, in people who used to be neutral, not taking sides.

The effect showed, too, in the attitude our neighbours now had towards Shane. They were constrained when they called to see father and Shane was there. They resented that he was linked to them. And as a result their opinion of father was changing.

That was what finally drove Shane. He did not mind what they thought of him. Since his session with Chris he seemed to have won a kind of inner peace. He was as alert and watchful as ever, but there was a serenity in him that had erased entirely the old tension. I think he did not care what anyone anywhere thought of him. Except us, his folks. And he knew that with us he was one of us, unchangeable and always.

But he did care what they thought of father. He was standing silently on the porch the night Ernie Wright and Henry Shipstead were arguing with father in the kitchen.

'I can't stomach much more,' Ernie Wright was saying. 'You know the trouble I've had with those blasted cowboys cutting my fence. Today a couple of them rode over and helped me repair a piece. Helped me, damn them! Waited till we were through, then said Fletcher didn't want any of my pigs getting loose and mixing with his cattle. My pigs! There ain't a pig in this whole valley and they know it. I'm sick of the word.'

Father made it worse by chuckling. Grim, maybe, yet still a chuckle. 'Sounds like one of Morgan's ideas. He's smart. Mean, but –'

Henry Shipstead would not let him finish. 'This is nothing to laugh at, Joe. You least of all. Damn it, man, I'm beginning to doubt your judgement. None of us can keep our heads up around here any more. Just a while ago I was in Grafton's and Chris was there blowing high about your Shane must be thirsty because he's so scared he hasn't been in town lately for his soda pop.'

Both of them were hammering at father now. He was sitting back, saying nothing, his face clouding.

'You can't dodge it, Joe.' This was Wright. 'Your man's responsible. You can try explaining all night, but you can't change the facts. Chris braced him for a fight and he ducked out – and left us stuck with those stinking pigs.'

'You know as well as I do what Fletcher's doing,' growled Henry Shipstead. 'He's pushing us with this and he won't let up till one of us gets enough and makes a fool play and starts something so he can move in and finish it.'

'Fool play or not,' said Ernie Wright. 'I've had all I can take. The next time one of those –'

Father stopped him with a hand up for silence. 'Listen. What's that?'

It was a horse, picking up speed and tearing down our lane into the road. Father was at the door in a single jump, peering out.

The others were close behind him. 'Shane?'

Father nodded. He was muttering under his breath. As I watched from the doorway of my little room. I could see that his eyes were bright and dancing. He was calling Shane names, cursing him, softly, fluently. He came back to his chair and grinned at the other two. 'That's Shane,' he told them and the words meant more than they seemed to say. 'All we can do now is wait.'

They were a silent crew waiting. Mother got up from her sewing in the bedroom where she had been listening as she always did and came into the kitchen and made up a pot of coffee and they all sat there sipping at the hot stuff and waiting.

It could not have been much more than twenty minutes before we heard the horse again, coming swiftly and slewing around to make the lane without slowing. There were quick steps on the porch and Shane stood in the doorway. He was breathing strongly and his face was hard. His mouth was a thin line in the bleakness of his face and his eyes were deep and dark. He looked at Shipstead and Wright and he made no effort to hide the disgust in his voice.

'Your pigs are dead and buried.'

As his gaze shifted to father, his face softened. But the voice was still bitter. 'There's another one down. Chris won't be bothering anybody for quite a spell.' He turned and disappeared and we could hear him leading the horse into the barn.

In the quiet following, hoof beats like an echo sounded in the distance. They swelled louder and this second horse galloped into our lane and pulled to a stop. Ed Howells jumped to the porch and hurried in.

'Where's Shane?'

'Out in the barn,' father said.

'Did he tell you what happened?'

'Not much,' father said mildly. 'Something about burying pigs.'

Ed Howells slumped into a chair. He seemed a bit dazed. The words came out of him slowly at first as he tried to make the others grasp just how he felt. 'I never saw anything like it,' he said, and he told about it.

He had been in Grafton's store buying a few things, not caring about going into the saloon because Chris and Red Marlin, another of Fletcher's cowboys, had hands in the evening poker game, when he noticed how still the place was. He went over to sneak a look and there was Shane just moving to the bar, cool and easy as if the room was empty and he the only one in it. Neither Chris nor Red Marlin was saying a word, though you might have thought this was a good chance for them to cut loose with some of their raw sarcasm. One look at Shane was enough to tell why. He was cool and easy, right enough. But there was a curious kind of smooth flow to his movements that made you realize without being conscious of thinking about it that being quiet was a mighty sensible way to be at the moment.

'Two bottles of soda pop,' he called to Will Atkey. He leaned his back to the bar and looked the poker game over with what seemed a friendly interest while Will fetched the bottles from the store. Not another person even twitched a muscle. They were all watching him and wondering what the play was. He took the two bottles and walked to the table and set them down, reaching over to put one in front of Chris.

'The last time I was in here you bought me a drink. Now it's my turn.'

The words sort of lingered in the stillness. He got the impression, Ed Howells said, that Shane meant just what the words said. He wanted to buy Chris a drink. He wanted Chris to take that bottle and grin at him and drink with him.

You could have heard a bug crawl, I guess, while Chris carefully laid down the cards in his right hand and stretched it to the bottle. He lifted it in a sudden jerk and flung it across the table at Shane.

So fast Shane moved, Ed Howells said, that the bottle was still in the air when he had dodged, lunged forward, grabbed Chris by the shirtfront and hauled him right out of his chair and over the table. As Chris struggled to get his feet under him, Shane let go the shirt and slapped him, sharp and stinging, three times, the hand flicking back and forth so quick you could hardly see it, the slaps sounding like pistol shots.

Shane stepped back and Chris stood swaying a little and shaking his head to clear it. He was a game one and mad down to his boots. He plunged in, fists smashing, and Shane let him come, slipping inside the flailing arms and jolting a powerful blow into his stomach. As Chris gasped and his head came down, Shane brought his right hand up, open, and with the heel of it caught Chris full on the mouth, snapping his head back and raking up over the nose and eyes.

The force of it knocked Chris off balance and he staggered badly. His lips were crushed. Blood was dripping over them from his battered nose. His eyes were red and watery and he was having trouble seeing with them. His face, Ed Howells said, and shook a little as he said it, looked like a horse had stomped it. But he drove in again, swinging wildly.

Shane ducked under, caught one of the flying wrists, twisted the arm to lock it and keep it from bending, and swung his shoulder into the armpit. He yanked hard on the wrist and Chris went up and over him. As the body hurtled over, Shane kept hold of the arm and wrenched it sideways and let the weight bear on it and you could hear the bone crack as Chris crashed to the floor.

A long sobbing sigh came from Chris and that died away and there was not a sound in the room. Shane never looked at the crumpled figure. He was straight and deadly and still. Every line of him was alive and eager. But he stood motionless. Only his eyes shifted to search the faces of the others at the table. They stopped on Red Marlin and Red seemed to dwindle lower in his chair.

'Perhaps,' Shane said softly, and the very softness of his voice sent shivers through Ed Howells, 'perhaps you have something to say about soda pop or pigs.'

Red Marlin sat quiet like he was trying not even to breathe. Tiny drops of sweat appeared on his forehead. He was frightened, maybe for the first time in his life, and the others knew it and he knew they knew and he did not care. And none of them blamed him at all.

Then, as they watched, the fire in Shane smouldered down and out. He seemed to withdraw back within himself. He forgot them all and turned towards Chris unconscious on the floor, and a sort of sadness, Ed Howells said, crept over him and held him. He bent and scooped the sprawling figure up in his arms and carried it to one of the other tables. Gently he set it down, the legs falling limp over the edge. He crossed to the bar and took the rag Will used to wipe it and returned to the table and tenderly cleared the blood from the face. He felt carefully along the broken arm and nodded to himself at what he felt.

All this while no one said a word. Not a one of them would have interfered with that man for a year's top wages. He spoke and his voice rang across the room at Red Marlin. 'You'd better tote him home and get that arm fixed. Take right good care of him. He has the makings of a good man.' Then he forgot them all again and looked at Chris and went on speaking as if to that limp figure that could not hear him. 'There's only one thing really wrong with you. You're young. That's the one thing time can always cure.'

The thought hurt him and he strode to the swinging doors and through them into the night. That was what Ed Howells told. 'The whole business,' he finished, 'didn't take five minutes. It was maybe thirty seconds from the time he grabbed holt of Chris till Chris was out cold on the floor. In my opinion that Shane is the most dangerous man I've ever seen. I'm glad he's working for Joe here and not for Fletcher.'

Father levelled a triumphant look at Henry Shipstead. 'So I've made a mistake, have I?'

Before anyone else could push in a word, mother was speaking. I was surprised, because she was upset and her voice was a little shrill. 'I wouldn't be too sure about that, Joe Starrett. I think you've made a bad mistake.'

'Marian, what's got into you?'

'Look what you've done just because you got him to stay on here and get mixed up in this trouble with Fletcher!'

Father was edging towards being peeved himself. 'Women never do understand these things. Lookahere, Marian. Chris will be all right. He's young and he's healthy. Soon as that arm is mended, he'll be in as good shape as he ever was.'

'Oh, Joe, can't you see what I'm talking about? I don't mean

what you've done to Chris. I mean what you've done to
Shane.'

8

This time mother was right. Shane was changed. He tried to
keep things as they had been with us and on the surface nothing was different. But he had lost the serenity that had seeped
into him through the summer. He would no longer sit around
and talk with us as much as he had. He was restless with some
far hidden desperation.

At times, when it rode him worst, he would wander alone
about our place, and this was the one thing that seemed to
soothe him. I used to see him, when he thought no one was
watching, run his hands along the rails of the corral he had
fastened, test with a tug the posts he had set, pace out past
the barn looking up at the bulging loft and stride out where the
tall corn was standing in big shocks to dig his hands in the loose
soil and lift some of it and let it run through his fingers.

He would lean on the pasture fence and study our little herd
like it meant more to him than lazy steers to be fattened for
market. Sometimes he would whistle softly, and his horse,
filled out now so you could see the quality of him and moving
with a quiet sureness and power that made you think of Shane
himself, would trot to the fence and nuzzle at him.

Often he would disappear from the house in the early evening after supper. More than once, the dishes done, when I
managed to slip past mother, I found him far back in the pasture alone with the horse. He would be standing there, one
arm on the smooth arc of the horse's neck, the fingers
gently rubbing around the ears, and he would be looking out
over our land where the last light of the sun, now out of
sight, would be flaring up the far side of the mountains, cap-
ping them with a deep glow and leaving a mystic gloaming in
the valley.

Some of the assurance that was in him when he came was
gone now. He seemed to feel that he needed to justify himself
even to me, to a boy tagging his heels.

'Could you teach me,' I asked him, ' to throw somebody the way you threw Chris?'

He waited so long I thought he would not answer. 'A man doesn't learn things like that,' he said at last. 'You know them and that's all.' Then he was talking rapidly to me, as close to pleading as he could ever come. 'I tried. You can see that, can't you, Bob? I let him ride me and I gave him his chance. A man can keep his self-respect without having to cram it down another man's throat. Surely you can see that, Bob?'

I could not see it. What he was trying to explain to me was beyond my comprehension then. And I could think of nothing to say.

'I left it up to him. He didn't have to jump me that second time. He could have called it off without crawling. He could have if he was man enough. Can't you see that, Bob?'

And still I could not. But I said I could. He was so earnest and he wanted me to so badly. It was a long, long time before I did see it and then I was a man myself and Shane was not there for me to tell. . . .

I was not sure whether father and mother were aware of the change in him. They did not talk about it, not while I was around anyway. But one afternoon I overheard something that showed mother knew.

I had hurried home from school and put on my old clothes and started out to see what father and Shane were doing in the cornfield, when I thought of a trick that had worked several times. Mother was firm set against eating between meals. That was a silly notion. I had my mind set on the cookies she kept in a tin box on a shelf by the stove. She was settled on the porch with a batch of potatoes to peel, so I slipped up to the back of the house, through the window of my little room, and tiptoed into the kitchen. Just as I was carefully putting a chair under the shelf, I heard her call to Shane.

He must have come to the barn on some errand, for he was there by the porch in only a moment. I peeped out the front window and saw him standing close in, his hat in his hand, his face tilted up slightly to look at her leaning forward in her chair.

'I've been wanting to talk to you when Joe wasn't around.'

'Yes, Marian.' He called her that the same as father did, familiar yet respectful, just as he always regarded her with a tenderness in his eyes he had for no one else.

'You've been worrying, haven't you, about what may happen in this Fletcher business? You thought it would just be a case of not letting him scare you away and of helping us through a hard time. You didn't know it would come to what it has. And now you're worried about what you might do if there's any more fighting.'

'You're a discerning woman, Marian.'

'You've been worrying about something else too.'

'You're a mighty discerning woman, Marian.'

'And you've been thinking that maybe you'll be moving on.'

'And how did you know that?'

'Because it's what you ought to do. For your own sake. But I'm asking you not to.' Mother was intense and serious, as lovely there with the light striking through her hair as I had ever seen her. 'Don't go, Shane. Joe needs you. More than ever now. More than he would ever say.'

'And you?' Shane's lips barely moved and I was not sure of the words.

Mother hesitated. Then her head went up. 'Yes. It's only fair to say it. I need you too.'

'So-o-o,' he said softly, the word lingering on his lips. He considered her gravely. 'Do you know what you're asking, Marian?'

'I know. And I know that you're the man to stand up to it. In some ways it would be easier for me, too, if you rode out of this valley and never came back. But we can't let Joe down. I'm counting on you not ever to make me do that. Because you've got to stay, Shane, no matter how hard it is for us. Joe can't keep this place without you. He can't buck Fletcher alone.'

Shane was silent, and it seemed to me that he was troubled and hard pressed in his mind. Mother was talking straight to him, slow and feeling for the words, and her voice was beginning to tremble.

'It would just about kill Joe to lose this place. He's too old to start in again somewhere else. Oh, we would get along and might even do real well. After all, he's Joe Starrett. He's all man and he can do what has to be done. But he promised me this place when we were married. He had it in his mind for all the first years. He did two men's work to get the extra money for the things we would need. When Bob was big enough to walk and help some and he could leave us, he came on here and filed his claim and built this house with his own hands, and when he brought us here it was home. Nothing else would ever be the same.'

Shane drew a deep breath and let it ease out slowly. He smiled at her and yet, somehow, as I watched him, my heart ached for him. 'Joe should be proud of a wife like you. Don't fret any more, Marian. You'll not lose this place.'

Mother dropped back in her chair. Her face, the side I could see from the window, was radiant. Then, womanlike, she was talking against herself. 'But that Fletcher is a mean and tricky man. Are you sure it will work out all right?'

Shane was already starting towards the barn. He stopped and turned to look at her again. 'I said you won't lose this place.' You knew he was right because of the way he said it and because he said it.

9

Another period of peace had settled over our valley. Since the night Shane rode into town, Fletcher's cowboys had quit using the road past the homesteads. They were not annoying us at all and only once in a while was there a rider in view across the river. They had a good excuse to let us be. They were busy fixing the ranch buildings and poleing a big new corral in preparation for the spring drive of new cattle Fletcher was planning.

Just the same, I noticed that father was as watchful as Shane now. The two of them worked always together. They did not split any more to do separate jobs in different parts of the farm. They worked together, rode into town together when anything was needed. And father took to wearing his gun all the time, even in the fields. He strapped it on after breakfast the first morning following the fight with Chris, and I saw him catch

Shane's eye with a questioning glance as he buckled the belt. But Shane shook his head and father nodded, accepting the decision, and they went out together without saying a word.

Those were beautiful fall days, clear and stirring, with the coolness in the air just enough to set one atingling, not yet mounting to the bitter cold that soon would come sweeping down out of the mountains. It did not seem possible that in such a harvest season, giving a lift to the spirit to match the well-being of the body, violence could flare so suddenly and swiftly.

Saturday evenings all of us would pile into the light work wagon, father and mother on the seat, Shane and I swinging legs at the rear, and go into town. It was the break in routine we looked forward to all week.

There was always a bustle in Grafton's store with people we knew coming and going. Mother would lay in her supplies for the week ahead, taking a long time about it and chatting with the womenfolk. She and the wives of the other homesteaders were great ones for swapping recipes and this was their bartering ground. Father would give Mr Grafton his order for what he wanted and go direct for the mail. He was always getting catalogues of farm equipment and pamphlets from Washington. He would flip through their pages and skim through any letters, then settle on a barrel and spread out his newspaper. But like as not he would soon be bogged down in an argument with almost any man handy about the best crops for the Territory and it would be Shane who would really work his way into the newspaper.

I used to explore the store, filling myself with crackers from the open barrel at the end of the main counter, playing hide and seek with Mr Grafton's big and knowing old cat that was a whiz of a mouser. Many a time, turning up boxes, I chased out fat furry ones for her to pounce on. If mother was in the right mood, I would have a bag of candy in my pocket.

This time we had a special reason for staying longer than usual, a reason I did not like. Our schoolteacher, Jane Grafton, had made me take a note home to mother asking her to stop in for a talk. About me. I never was too smart at formal schooling to begin with. Being all excited over the doings at the big ranch and what they might mean to us had not helped any. Miss

Grafton, I guess, just sort of endured me under the best of conditions. But what tipped her into being downright annoyed and writing to mother was the weather. No one could expect a boy with any spirit in him to be shut up in a schoolroom in weather like we had been having. Twice that week I had persuaded Ollie Johnson to sneak away with me after the lunch hour to see if the fish were still biting in our favourite pool below town.

Mother finished the last item on her list, looked around at me, sighed a little, and stiffened her shoulders. I knew she was going to the living quarters behind the store and talk to Miss Grafton. I squirmed and pretended I did not notice her. Only a few people were left in the store, though the saloon in the adjoining big room was doing fair business. She went over to where father was leafing through a catalogue and tapped him.

'Come along, Joe. You should hear this, too. I declare, that boy is getting too big for me to handle.'

Father glanced quickly over the store and paused, listening to the voices from the next room. We had not seen any of Fletcher's men all evening and he seemed satisfied. He looked at Shane, who was folding the newspaper.

'This won't take long. We'll be out in a moment.'

As they passed through the door at the rear of the store, Shane strolled to the saloon opening. He took in the whole room in his easy, alert way and stepped inside. I followed. But I was supposed not ever to go in there, so I stopped at the entrance. Shane was at the bar, joshing Will Atkey with a grave face that he didn't think he'd have soda pop tonight. It was a scattered group in the room, most of them from around town and familiar to me by sight at least. Those close to Shane moved a little away, eyeing him curiously. He did not appear to notice.

He picked up his drink and savoured it, one elbow on the bar, not shoving himself forward into the room's companionship and not withdrawing either, just ready to be friendly if anyone wanted that and unfriendly if anyone wanted that too.

I was letting my eyes wander about, trying to tag names to faces, when I saw that one of the swinging doors was partly open and Red Marlin was peeking in. Shane saw it too. But he could not see that more men were out on the porch, for they were close by the building wall and on the store side. I could sense them through the window near me, hulking shapes in the darkness. I was so frightened I could scarcely move.

But I had to. I had to go against mother's rule. I scrambled into the saloon and to Shane and I gasped: 'Shane! There's a lot of them out front!'

I was too late. Red Marlin was inside and the others were hurrying in and fanning out to close off the store opening. Morgan was one of them, his flat face sour and determined, his huge shoulders almost filling the doorway as he came through. Behind him was the cowboy they called Curly because of his shock of unruly hair. He was stupid and slow-moving, but he was thick and powerful and he had worked in harness with Chris for several years. Two others followed them, new men to me, with the tough experienced look of old herd hands.

There was still the back office with its outside door opening on a side stoop and the rear alley. My knees were shaking and I tugged at Shane and tried to say something about it. He stopped me with a sharp gesture. His face was clear, his eyes bright. He was somehow happy, not in the pleased and laughing way, but happy that the waiting was over and what had been ahead was here and seen and realized and he was ready for it. He put one hand on my head and rocked it gently, the fingers feeling through my hair.

'Bobby boy, would you have me run away?'

Love for that man raced through me and the warmth ran down and stiffened my legs and I was so proud of being there with him that I could not keep the tears from my eyes. I could see the rightness of it and I was ready to do as he told me when he said: 'Get out of here, Bob. This isn't going to be pretty.'

But I would go no farther than my perch just inside the store where I could watch most of the big room. I was so bound in the moment that I did not even think of running for father.

Morgan was in the lead now with his men spread out behind him. He came about half-way to Shane and stopped. The room was quiet except for the shuffling of feet as the men by the bar and the nearest tables hastened over to the far wall and some of them ducked out the front doors. Neither Shane nor Morgan gave any attention to them. They had attention only for each other. They did not look aside even when Mr Grafton, who could smell trouble in his place from any distance, stalked in from the store, planting his feet down firmly, and pushed past Will Atkey behind the bar. He had a resigned expression on his face and he reached under the counter, his hands reappearing with a short-barrelled shotgun. He laid it before him on the bar and he said in a dry, disgusted voice: 'There will be no gun-play, gentlemen. And all damage will be paid for.'

Morgan nodded curtly, not taking his eyes from Shane. He came closer and stopped again little more than an arm's length away. His head was thrust forward. His big fists were clenched at his sides.

'No one messes up one of my boys and gets away with it. We're riding you out of this valley on a rail, Shane. We're going to rough you a bit and ride you out and you'll stay out.'

'So you have it all planned,' Shane said softly. Even as he was speaking, he was moving. He flowed into action so swift you could hardly believe what was happening. He scooped up his half-filled glass from the bar, whipped it and its contents into Morgan's face, and when Morgan's hands came up reaching or striking for him, he grasped the wrists and flung himself backwards, dragging Morgan with him. His body rolled to meet the floor and his legs doubled and his feet, catching Morgan just below the belt, sent him flying on and over to fall flat in a grotesque spraddle and slide along the boards in a tangle of chairs and a table.

The other four were on Shane in a rush. As they came he whirled to his hands and knees and leaped up and behind the nearest table, tipping it in a strong heave among them. They scattered, dodging, and he stepped, fast and light, around the end and drove into the tail man, one of the new men, now nearest to him. He took the blows at him straight on to get in close and I saw his knee surge up and into the man's groin. A high scream was literally torn from the man and he collapsed to the floor and dragged himself towards the doors.

Morgan was on his feet, wavering, rubbing a hand across his face, staring hard as if trying to focus again on the room about him. The other three were battering at Shane, seeking to box him between them. They were piling blows into him, crowding in. Through that blur of movement he was weaving, quick and confident. It was incredible, but they could not hurt him. You could see the blows hit, hear the solid chunk of knuckles on flesh. But they had no effect. They seemed only to feed that fierce energy. He moved like a flame among them. He would burst out of the mêlée and whirl and plunge back, the one man actually pressing the three. He had picked the second new man and was driving always directly at him.

Curly, slow and clumsy, grunting with exasperation, grabbed at Shane to grapple with him and hold down his arms. Shane dropped one shoulder and as Curly hugged tighter brought it up under his jaw with a jolt that knocked him loose and away.

They were wary now and none too eager to let him get close to any of them. Then Red Marlin came at him from one side, forcing him to turn that way, and at the same time the second new man did a strange thing. He jumped high in the air, like a jack rabbit in a spy hop, and lashed out viciously with one boot at Shane's head. Shane saw it coming, but could not avoid it, so he rolled his head with the kick, taking it along the side. It shook him badly. But it did not block the instant response. His hands shot up and seized the foot and the man crashed down to land on the small of his back. As he hit, Shane twisted the whole leg and threw his weight on it. The man buckled on the floor like a snake when you hit it and groaned sharply and hitched himself away, the leg dragging, the fight gone out of him.

But the swing to bend down on the leg had put Shane's back to Curly and the big man was ploughing at him. Curly's arms clamped around him, pinning his arms to his body. Red Marlin leaped to help and the two of them had Shane caught tight between them.

'Hold him!' That was Morgan, coming forward with the hate plain in his eyes. Even then, Shane would have broke away. He stomped one heavy work shoe, heel edged and with all the strength he could get in quick leverage, on Curly's near foot. As Curly winced and pulled it back and was unsteady, Shane strained with his whole body in a powerful arch and you could see their arms slipping and loosening. Morgan, circling in, saw it too. He swept a bottle off the bar and brought it smashing down from behind on Shane's head.

Shane slumped and would have fallen if they had not been holding him. Then, as Morgan stepped around in front of him and watched, the vitality pumped through him and his head came up.

'Hold him!' Morgan said again. He deliberately flung a huge fist to Shane's face. Shane tried to jerk aside and the fist missed the jaw, tearing along the cheek, the heavy ring on one finger slicing deep. Morgan pulled back for another blow. He never made it.

Nothing, I would have said, could have drawn my attention from those men. But I heard a kind of choking sob beside me and it was queer and yet familiar and it turned me instantly.

Father was there in the entranceway!

He was big and terrible and he was looking across the overturned table and scattered chairs at Shane, at the dark purplish bruise along the side of Shane's head and the blood running down his cheek. I had never seen father like this. He was past anger. He was filled with a fury that was shaking him almost beyond endurance.

I never thought he could move so fast. He was on them before they even knew he was in the room. He hurtled into Morgan with ruthless force, sending that huge man reeling across the room. He reached out one broad hand and grabbed Curly by the shoulder and you could see the fingers sink into the flesh. He took hold of Curly's belt with the other hand and ripped him loose from Shane and his own shirt shredded down the back and the great muscles there knotted and bulged as he lifted Curly right up over his head and hurled the threshing body from him. Curly spun through the air, his limbs waving wildly, and crashed on the top of a table way over by the wall. It cracked under him, collapsing in splintered pieces, and the man and the wreckage smacked against the wall. Curly tried to rise, pushing himself with hands on the floor, and fell back and was still.

Shane must have exploded into action the second father yanked Curly away, for now there was another noise. It was Red Marlin, his face contorted, flung against the bar and catching at it to keep himself from falling. He staggered and caught his balance and ran for the front doorway. His flight was frantic, headlong. He tore through the swinging doors without slowing to push them. They flapped with a swishing sound and my eyes shifted quickly to Shane, for he was laughing.

He was standing there, straight and superb, the blood on his face bright like a badge, and he was laughing.

It was a soft laugh, soft and gentle, not in amusement at Red Marlin or any single thing, but in the joy of being alive and released from long discipline and answering the urge in mind and body. The lithe power in him, so different from father's sheer strength, was singing in every fibre of him.

Morgan was in the rear corner, his face clouded and uncertain. Father, his fury eased by the mighty effort of throwing Curly, had looked around to watch Red Marlin's run and now was starting towards Morgan. Shane's voice stopped him.

'Wait, Joe. The man's mine.' He was at father's side and he put a hand on father's arm. 'You'd better get them out of here.' He nodded in my direction and I noticed with surprise that mother was near and watching. She must have followed father and have been there all this while. Her lips were parted. Her eyes were glowing, looking at the whole room, not at anyone or anything in particular, but at the whole room.

Father was disappointed. 'Morgan's more my size,' he said, grumbling fashion. He was not worried about Shane. He was thinking of an excuse to take Morgan himself. But he went no further. He looked at the men over by the wall. 'This is Shane's play. If a one of you tries to interfere he'll have me to reckon with.' His tone showed that he was not mad at them, that he was not even really warning them. He was simply making the play plain. Then he came to us and looked down at mother. 'You wait out at the wagon, Marian. Morgan's had this coming to him for quite a long time now and it's not for a woman to see.'

Mother shook her head without moving her eyes now from Shane. 'No, Joe. He's one of us. I'll see this through.' And the three of us stayed there together and that was right, for he was Shane.

He advanced towards Morgan, as flowing and graceful as the old mouser in the store. He had forgotten us and the battered men on the floor and those withdrawn by the wall and Mr Grafton and Will Atkey crouched behind the bar. His whole being was concentrated on the big man before him.

Morgan was taller, half again as broad, with a long reputa-tion as a bullying fighter in the valley. But he did not like this and he was desperate. He knew better than to wait. He rushed at Shane to overwhelm the smaller man with his weight. Shane faded from in front of him and as Morgan went past hooked a sharp blow to his stomach and another to the side of his jaw. They were short and quick, flicking in so fast they were just a blur of movement. Yet each time at the instant of impact Mor-gan's big frame shook and halted in its rush for a fraction of a second before the momentum carried him forward. Again and again he rushed, driving his big fists ahead. Always Shane slip-ped away, sending in those swift hard punches.

Breathing heavily, Morgan stopped, grasping the futility of straight fighting. He plunged at Shane now, arms wide, trying to get hold of him and wrestle him down. Shane was ready and let him come without dodging, disregarding the arms stretch-ing to encircle him. He brought up his right hand, open, just as Ed Howells had told us, and the force of Morgan's own lunge as the hand met his mouth and raked upwards snapped back his head and sent him staggering.

Morgan's face was puffy and red-mottled. He bellowed some insane sound and swung up a chair. Holding it in front of him, legs forward, he rushed again at Shane, who sidestepped neatly. Morgan was expecting this and halted suddenly, swinging the chair in a swift arc to strike Shane with it full on the side. The chair shattered and Shane faltered, and then, queerly for a man usually so sure on his feet, he seemed to slip and fall to the floor.

Forgetting all caution, Morgan dived at him – and Shane's legs bent and he caught Morgan on his heavy work shoes and sent him flying back and against the bar with a crash that shook the whole length of it.

Shane was up and leaping at Morgan as if there had been springs under him there on the floor. His left hand, palm out, smacked against Morgan's forehead, pushing the head back, and his right fist drove straight to Morgan's throat. You could see the agony twist the man's face and the fear widen his eyes. And Shane, using his right fist now like a club and lining his whole body behind it, struck him on the neck below and back of the ear. It made a sickening, dull sound and Morgan's eyes rolled white and he went limp all over, sagging slowly and forward to the floor.

10

In the hush that followed Morgan's fall, the big bar-room was so quiet again that the rustle of Will Atkey straightening from below the bar level was loud and clear and Will stopped moving, embarrassed and a little frightened.

Shane looked neither at him nor at any of the other men staring from the wall. He looked only at us, at father and mother and me, and it seemed to me that it hurt him to see us there.

He breathed deeply and his chest filled and he held it, held it long and achingly, and released it slowly and sighing. Suddenly you were impressed by the fact that he was quiet, that he was still. You saw how battered and bloody he was. In the moments before you saw only the splendour of movement, the flowing brute beauty of line and power in action. The man, you felt, was tireless and indestructible. Now that he was still and the fire in him banked and subsided, you saw, and in the seeing remembered, that he had taken bitter punishment.

His shirt collar was dark and sodden. Blood was soaking into it, and this came only in part from the cut on his cheek. More was oozing from the matted hair where Morgan's bottle had hit. Unconsciously he put up one hand and it came away smeared and sticky. He regarded it grimly and wiped it clean on his shirt. He swayed slightly and when he started towards us, his feet dragged and he almost fell forward.

One of the townsmen, Mr Weir, a friendly man who kept the stage post, pushed out from the wall, clucking sympathy, as though to help him. Shane pulled himself erect. His eyes blazed refusal. Straight and superb, not a tremor in him, he came to us and you knew that the spirit in him would sustain him thus alone for the farthest distance and for ever.

But there was no need. The one man in our valley, the one man, I believe, in all the world whose help he would take, not to whom he would turn but whose help he would take, was there and ready. Father stepped to meet him and put out a big arm reaching for his shoulders. 'All right, Joe,' Shane said, so softly I doubt whether the others in the room heard. His eyes closed and he leaned against father's arm, his body relaxing and his head dropping sideways. Father bent and fitted his other arm under Shane's knees and picked him up like he did me when I stayed up too late and got all drowsy and had to be carried to bed.

Father held Shane in his arms and looked over him at Mr Grafton. 'I'd consider it a favour, Sam, if you'd figure the damage and put it on my bill.'

For a man strict about bills and keen for a bargain, Mr Grafton surprised me. 'I'm marking this to Fletcher's account. I'm seeing that he pays.'

Mr Weir surprised me even more. He spoke promptly and he was emphatic about it. 'Listen to me, Starrett. It's about time this town worked up a little pride. Maybe it's time, too, we got to be more neighbourly with you homesteaders. I'll take a collection to cover this. I've been ashamed of myself ever since it started tonight, standing here and letting five of them jump that man of yours.'

Father was pleased. But he knew what he wanted to do. 'That's mighty nice of you, Weir. But this ain't your fight. I wouldn't worry, was I you, about keeping out of it.' He looked down at Shane and the pride was plain busting out of him. 'Matter of fact, I'd say the odds tonight, without me butting in, too, was mighty close to even.' He looked again at Mr Grafton. 'Fletcher ain't getting in on this with a nickel, I'm paying.' He tossed back his head. 'No, by Godfrey! We're paying. Me and Shane.'

He went to the swinging doors, turning sideways to push them open. Mother took my hand and we followed. She always knew when to talk and when not to talk, and she said no word while we watched father lift Shane to the wagon seat, climb beside him, hoist him to sitting position with one arm around him and take the reins in the other hand. Will Atkey trotted out with our things and stowed them away. Mother and I perched on the back of the wagon, father chirruped to the team, and we were started home.

There was not a sound for quite a stretch except the clop of hoofs and the little creakings of the wheels. Then I heard a chuckle up front. It was Shane. The cool air was reviving him and he was sitting straight, swaying with the wagon's motion.

'What did you do with the thick one, Joe? I was busy with the redhead.'

'Oh, I just kind of tucked him out of the way.' Father wanted to let it go at that. Not mother.

'He picked him up like – like a bag of potatoes and threw him clear across the room.' She did not say it to Shane, not to any person. She said it to the night, to the sweet darkness around us, and her eyes were shining in the starlight.

We turned in at our place and father shooed the rest of us into the house while he unhitched the team. In the kitchen mother set some water to heat on the stove and chased me to bed. Her back was barely to me after she tucked me in before I was peering around the door jamb. She got several clean rags, took the water from the stove, and went to work on Shane's head. She was tender as could be, crooning like to herself under her breath the while. It pained him plenty as the warm water soaked into the gash under the matted hair and as she washed the clotted blood from his cheek. But it seemed to pain her more, for her hand shook at the worst moments, and she was the one who flinched while he sat there quietly and smiled reassuringly at her.

Father came in and sat by the stove, watching them. He pulled out his pipe and made a very careful business of packing it and lighting it.

She finished. Shane would not let her try a bandage. 'This air is the best medicine,' he said. She had to be content with cleaning the cuts thoroughly and making certain all bleeding had stopped. Then it was father's turn.

'Get that shirt off, Joe. It's torn all down the back. Let me see what I can do with it.' Before he could rise, she had changed her mind. 'No. We'll keep it just like it is. To remember to-night by. You were magnificent, Joe, tearing that man away and –'

'Shucks,' said father. 'I was just peeved. Him holding Shane so Morgan could pound him.'

'And you, Shane.' Mother was in the middle of the kitchen,

looking from one to the other. 'You were magnificent, too. Morgan was so big and horrible and yet he didn't have even a chance. You were so cool and quick and – and dangerous and –'

'A woman shouldn't have to see things like that.' Shane interrupted her, and he meant it. But she was talking right ahead.

'You think I shouldn't because it's brutal, and nasty and not just fighting to see who is better at it, but mean and vicious and to win by any way, but to win. Of course it is. But you didn't start it. You didn't want to do it. Not until they made you anyway. You did it because you had to.'

Her voice was climbing and she was looking back and forth and losing control of herself. 'Did ever a woman have two such men?' And she turned from them and reached out blindly for a chair and sank into it and dropped her face into her hands and the tears came.

The two men stared at her and then at each other in that adult knowledge beyond my understanding. Shane rose and stepped over by mother. He put a hand gently on her head and I felt again his fingers in my hair and the affection flooding through me. He walked quietly out the door and into the night.

Father drew on his pipe. It was out and absently he lit it. He rose and went to the door and out on the porch. I could see him there dimly in the darkness, gazing across the river.

Gradually mother's sobs died down. She raised her head and wiped away the tears.

'Joe.'

He turned and started in and waited then by the door. She stood up. She stretched her hands towards him and he was there and had her in his arms.

'Do you think I don't know, Marian?'

'But you don't. Not really. You can't. Because I don't know myself.'

Father was staring over her head at the kitchen walls not seeing anything there. 'Don't fret yourself, Marian. I'm man enough to know a better when his trail meets mine. Whatever happens will be all right.'

'Oh, Joe ... Joe! Kiss me. Hold me tight and don't ever let go.'

I I

What happened in our kitchen that night was beyond me in those days. But it did not worry me because father had said it would be all right, and how could anyone, knowing him, doubt that he would make it so.

And we were not bothered by Fletcher's men any more at all. There might not have been a big ranch on the other side of the river, sprawling up the valley and over on our side above Ernie Wright's place, for all you could tell from our house. They left us strictly alone and were hardly ever seen now even in town. Fletcher himself, I heard from kids at school, was gone again. He went on the stage to Cheyenne and maybe farther, and nobody seemed to know why he went.

Yet father and Shane were more wary than they had been before. They stayed even closer together, and they spent no more time than they had to in the fields. There was no more talking on the porch in the evenings, though the nights were so cool and lovely they called you to be out and under the winking stars. We kept to the house, and father insisted on having the lamps well shaded and he polished his rifle and hung it, ready loaded, on a couple of nails by the kitchen door.

All this caution failed to make sense to me. So at dinner about a week later I asked: 'Is there something new that's wrong? That stuff about Fletcher is finished, isn't it?'

'Finished?' said Shane, looking at me over his coffee cup. 'Bobby boy, it's only begun.'

'That's right,' said father. 'Fletcher's gone too far to back out now. It's a case of now or never with him. If he can make us run, he'll be setting pretty for a long stretch. If he can't it'll be only a matter o' time before he's shoved smack out of this valley. There's three or four of the men who looked through here last year ready right now to sharpen stakes and move in as soon they think it's safe. I'll bet Fletcher feels he got aholt of a bear by the tail and it'd be nice to be able to let go.'

'Why doesn't he do something, then?' I asked. 'Seems to me mighty quiet around here lately.'

'Seems to you, eh?' said father. 'Seems to me you're mighty young to be doing much seemsing. Don't you worry, son. Fletcher is fixing to do something. The grass that grows under his feet won't feed any cow. I'd be easier in my mind if I knew what he's up to.'

'You see, Bob' – Shane was speaking to me the way I liked, as if maybe I was a man and could understand all he said – 'by talking big and playing it rough, Fletcher has made this a straight win or lose deal. It's the same as if he'd kicked loose a stone that starts a rockslide and all he can do is hope to ride it down and hit bottom safe. Maybe he doesn't realize that yet. I think he does. And don't let things being quiet fool you. When there's noise, you know where to look and what's happening. When things are quiet, you've got to be most careful.'

Mother sighed. She was looking at Shane's cheek where the cut was healing into a scar like a thin line running back from near the mouth corner. 'I suppose you two are right. But does there have to be any more fighting?'

'Like the other night?' asked father. 'No, Marian. I don't think so. Fletcher knows better now.'

'He knows better,' Shane said, 'because he knows it won't work. If he's the man I think he is, he's known that since the first time he sicced Chris on me. I doubt that was his move the other night. That was Morgan's. Fletcher'll be watching for some way that has more finesse – and will be more final.'

'Hm-m-m,' said father, a little surprised. 'Some legal trick, eh?'

'Could be. If he can find one. If not – ' Shane shrugged and gazed out the window. 'There are other ways. You can't call a man like Fletcher on things like that. Depends on how far he's willing to go. But whatever he does, once he's ready, he'll do it speedy and sure.'

'Hm-m-m,' said father again. 'Now you put it thataway, I see you're right. That's Fletcher's way. Bet you've bumped against someone like him before.' When Shane did not answer, just kept staring out the window, he went on, 'Wish I could be as patient about it as you. I don't like this waiting.'

But we did not have to wait long. It was the next day, a Friday, when we were finishing supper, that Lew Johnson and Henry Shipstead brought us the news. Fletcher was back and he had not come back alone. There was another man with him.

Lew Johnson saw them as they got off the stage. He had a good chance to look the stranger over while they waited in front of the post for horses to be brought in from the ranch. Since it was beginning to get dark, he had not been able to make out the stranger's face too well. The light striking through the post window, however, was enough for him to see what kind of man he was.

He was tall, rather broad in the shoulders and slim in the waist. He carried himself with a sort of swagger. He had a moustache that he favoured and his eyes, when Johnson saw them reflecting the light from the window, were cold and had a glitter that bothered Johnson.

This stranger was something of a dude about his clothes. Still, that did not mean anything. When he turned, the coat he wore matching his pants flapped open and Johnson could see what had been half-hidden before. He was carrying two guns, big capable forty-fives, in holsters hung fairly low and forward. Those holsters were pegged down at the tips with thin straps fastened around the man's legs. Johnson said he saw the tiny buckles when the light flashed on them.

Wilson was the man's name. That was what Fletcher called him when a cowboy rode up leading a couple of horses. A funny other name. Stark. Stark Wilson. And that was not all.

Lew Johnson was worried and went into Grafton's to find Will Atkey, who always knew more than anyone else about people apt to be coming along the road because he was constantly picking up information from the talk of men drifting in to the bar. Will would not believe it at first when Johnson told him the name. What would he be doing here, Will kept saying. Then Will blurted out that this Wilson was a bad one, a killer. He was a gun-fighter said to be just as good with either hand and as fast on the draw as the best of them. He came to Cheyenne from Kansas, Will claimed he had heard, with a reputation for killing three men there and nobody knew how many more down in the south-west territories where he used to be.

Lew Johnson was rattling on, adding details as he could think of them. Henry Shipstead was slumped in a chair by the stove. Father was frowning at his pipe, absently fishing in a pocket for a match. It was Shane who shut off Johnson with a suddenness that startled the rest of us. His voice was sharp and clear and it seemed to crackle in the air. You could feel him taking charge of that room and all of us in it.

'When did they hit town?'

'Last night.'

'And you waited till now to tell it!' There was disgust in Shane's voice. 'You're a farmer all right, Johnson. That's all you ever will be.' He whirled on father. 'Quick, Joe. Which one has the hottest head? Which one's the easiest to prod into being a fool? Torrey is it? Or Wright?'

'Ernie Wright,' father said slowly.

'Get moving, Johnson. Get out there on your horse and make it to Wright's in a hurry. Bring him here. Pick up Torrey, too. But get Wright first.'

'He'll have to go into town for that,' Henry Shipstead said heavily. 'We passed them both down the road riding in.'

Shane jumped to his feet. Lew Johnson was shuffling reluctantly towards the door. Shane brushed him aside. He strode to the door himself, yanked it open, started out. He stopped, leaning forward and listening.

'Hell, man,' Henry Shipstead was grumbling, 'what's your hurry? We told them about Wilson. They'll stop here on their way back.' His voice ceased. All of us could hear it now, a horse pounding up the road at full gallop.

Shane turned back into the room. 'There's your answer,' he said bitterly. He swung the nearest chair to the wall and sat down. The fire blazing in him a moment before was gone. He was withdrawn into his own thoughts, and they were dark and not pleasant.

We heard the horse sliding to a stop out front. The sound was so plain you could fairly see the forelegs bracing and the hoofs digging into the ground. Frank Torrey burst into the doorway. His hat was gone, his hair blowing wild. His chest heaved like he had been running as hard as the horse. He put his hands on the doorposts to hold himself steady and his voice was a hoarse whisper, though he was trying to shout across the room at father.

'Ernie's shot! They've killed him!'

The words jerked us to our feet and we stood staring. All but Shane. He did not move. You might have thought he was not even interested in what Torrey had said.

Father was the one who took hold of the scene. 'Come in, Frank,' he said quietly. 'I take it we're too late to help Ernie now. Sit down and talk and don't leave anything out.' He led Frank Torrey to a chair and pushed him into it. He closed the door and returned to his own chair. He looked older and tired.

It took Frank Torrey quite a while to pull himself together and tell his story straight. He was frightened. The fear was bedded deep in him and he was ashamed of himself for it.

He and Ernie Wright, he told us, had been to the stage office asking for a parcel Ernie was expecting. They dropped into Grafton's for a freshener before starting back. Since things had been so quiet lately, they were not thinking of any trouble even though Fletcher and the new man, Stark Wilson, were in the poker game at the big table. But Fletcher and Wilson must have been watching for a chance like that. They chucked in their hands and came over to the bar.

Fletcher was nice and polite as could be, nodding to Torrey and singling out Ernie for talk. He said he was sorry about it, but he really needed the land Ernie had filed on. It was the right place to put up winter wind-shelters for the new herd he was bringing in soon. He knew Ernie had not proved up on it yet. Just the same, he was willing to pay a fair price.

'I'll give you three hundred dollars,' he said, 'and that's more than the lumber in your buildings will be worth to me.'

Ernie had more than that of his money in the place already. He had turned Fletcher down three or four times before. He was mad, the way he always was when Fletcher started his smooth talk.

'No,' he said shortly. 'I'm not selling. Not now or ever.'

Fletcher shrugged like he had done all he could and slipped a quick nod at Stark Wilson. This Wilson was half-smiling at Ernie. But his eyes, Frank Torrey said, had nothing like a smile in them.

'I'd change my mind if I were you,' he said to Ernie. 'That is, if you have a mind to change.'

'Keep out of this,' snapped Ernie. 'It's none of your business.'

'I see you haven't heard,' Wilson said softly. 'I'm Mr Fletcher's new business agent. I'm handling his business affairs for him. His business with stubborn jackasses like you.' Then he said what showed Fletcher had coaxed him to it. 'You're a damn fool, Wright. But what can you expect from a breed?'

'That's a lie!' shouted Ernie. 'My mother wasn't no Indian!'

'Why, you crossbred squatter,' Wilson said, quick and sharp, 'are you telling me I'm wrong?'

'I'm telling you you're a God-damned liar!'

The silence that shut down over the saloon was so complete, Frank Torrey told us, that he could hear the ticking of the old alarum clock on the shelf behind the bar. Even Ernie, in the second his voice stopped, saw what he had done. But he was mad clear through and he glared at Wilson, his eyes reckless.

'So o o o,' said Wilson, satisfied now and stretching out the word with ominous softness. He flipped back his coat on the right side in front and the holster there was free with the gun grip ready for his hand.

'You'll back that, Wright. Or you'll crawl out of here on your belly.'

Ernie moved out a step from the bar, his arms stiff at his sides. The anger in him held him erect as he beat down the terror tearing at him. He knew what this meant, but he met it straight. His hand was firm on his gun and pulling up when Wilson's first bullet hit him and staggered him. The second spun him halfway around and a faint froth appeared on his lips and all expression died from his face and he sagged to the floor.

While Frank Torrey was talking, Jim Lewis and a few minutes later Ed Howells had come in. Bad news travels fast and they seemed to know something was wrong. Perhaps they had heard that frantic galloping, the sound carrying far in the still night air. They were all in our kitchen now and they were more shaken and sober than I had ever seen them.

I was pressed close to mother, grateful for her arms around me. I noticed that she had little attention for the other men. She was watching Shane, bitter and silent across the room.

'So that's it,' father said grimly. 'We'll have to face it. We sell and at his price or he slips the leash on his hired killer. Did Wilson make a move towards you, Frank?'

'He looked at me.' Simply recalling that made Torrey shiver through. 'He looked at me and said, "Too bad, isn't it, mister, that Wright didn't change his mind?" '

'Then what?'

'I got out of there quick as I could and came here.'

Jim Lewis had been fidgeting on his seat, more nervous every minute. Now he jumped up, almost shouting. 'But damn it, Joe! A man can't just go around shooting people!'

'Shut up, Jim,' growled Henry Shipstead. 'Don't you see the set-up? Wilson badgered Ernie into getting himself in a spot where he had to go for his gun. Wilson can claim he shot in self-defence. He'll try the same thing on each of us.'

'That's right, Jim,' put in Lew Johnson. 'Even if we tried to get a marshal in here, he couldn't hold Wilson. It was an even break and the faster man won is the way most people will figure it and plenty of them saw it. A marshal couldn't get here in time anyway.'

'But we've got to stop it!' Lewis was really shouting now. 'What chance have any of us got against Wilson? We're not gunmen. We're just a bunch of old cowhands and farmers. Call it anything you want. I call it murder.'

'Yes!'

The word sliced through the room. Shane was up and his face was hard with the rock ridges running along his jaw. 'Yes. It's murder. Trick it out as self-defence or with fancy words about an even break for a fair draw and it's still murder.' He looked at father and the pain was deep in his eyes. But there was only contempt in his voice as he turned to the others.

'You five can crawl back in your burrows. You don't have to worry – yet. If the time comes, you can always sell and run. Fletcher won't bother with the likes of you now. He's going the limit and he knows the game. He picked Wright to make the play plain. That's done. Now he'll head straight for the one real man in this valley, the man who's held you here and will go on trying to hold you and keep for you what's yours as long as there's life in him. He's standing between you and Fletcher and Wilson this minute and you ought to be thankful that once in a while this country turns out a man like Joe Starrett.'

And a man like Shane. ... Were those words only in my mind or did I hear mother whisper them? She was looking at him and then at father and she was both frightened and proud at once. Father was fumbling with his pipe, packing it and making a fuss with it like it needed his whole attention.

The others stirred uneasily. They were reassured by what Shane said and yet shamed that they should be. And they did not like the way he said it.

'You seem to know a lot about that kind of dirty business,' Ed Howells said, with maybe an edge of malice to his voice.

'I do.'

Shane let the words lie there, plain and short and ugly. His face was stern and behind the hard front of his features was a sadness that fought to break through. But he stared levelly at Howells and it was the other man who dropped his eyes and turned away.

Father had his pipe going. 'Maybe it's a lucky break for the rest of us,' he said mildly, 'that Shane here has been around a bit. He can call the cards for us plain. Ernie might still be alive, Johnson, if you had had the sense to tell us about Wilson right off. It's a good thing Ernie wasn't a family man.' He turned to Shane. 'How do you rate Fletcher now he's shown his hand?'

You could see that the chance to do something, even just to talk at the problem pressing us, eased the bitterness in Shane.

'He'll move in on Wright's place first thing tomorrow. He'll have a lot of men busy on this side of the river from now on, probably push some cattle around behind the homesteads, to keep the pressure plain on all of you. How quick he'll try you, Joe, depends on how he reads you. If he thinks you might crack, he'll wait and let knowing what happened to Wright work on you. If he really knows you, he'll not wait more than a day or two to make sure you've had time to think it over and then he'll grab the first chance to throw Wilson at you. He'll want it, like with Wright, in a public place where there'll be plenty of witnesses. If you don't give him a chance, he'll try to make one.'

'Hm-m-m,' father said soberly. 'I was sure you'd give it to me straight and that rings right.' He pulled on his pipe for a moment. 'I reckon, boys, this will be a matter of waiting for the next few days. There's no immediate danger right off any-way. Grafton will take care of Ernie's body tonight. We can meet in town in the morning to fix him a funeral. After that, we'd better stay out of town and stick close home as much as possible. I'd suggest you all study on this and drop in again tomorrow night. Maybe we can figure out something. I'd like to see how the town's taking it before I make up my mind on anything.'

They were ready to leave it at that. They were ready to leave it to father. They were decent men and good neighbours. But not a one of them, were the decision his, would have stood up to Fletcher now. They would stay as long as father was there. With him gone, Fletcher would have things his way. That was how they felt as they muttered their good nights and bunched out to scatter up and down the road.

Father stood in the doorway and watched them go. When he came back to his chair, he walked slowly and he seemed hag-gard and worn. 'Somebody will have to go to Ernie's place tomorrow,' he said, 'and gather up his things. He's got relatives somewhere in Iowa.'

'No.' There was finality in Shane's tone. 'You'll not go near the place. Fletcher might be counting on that. Grafton can do it.'

'But Ernie was my friend,' father said simply.

'Ernie's past friendship. Your debt is to the living.'

Father looked at Shane and this brought him again into the immediate moment and cheered him. He nodded assent and turned to mother, who was hurrying to argue with him.

'Don't you see, Joe? If you can stay away from any place where you might meet Fletcher and – and that Wilson, things will work out. He can't keep a man like Wilson in this little valley forever.'

She was talking rapidly and I knew why. She was not really trying to convince father as much as she was trying to convince herself. Father knew it, too.

'No, Marian. A man can't crawl into a hole somewhere and hide like a rabbit. Not if he has any pride.'

'All right, then. But can't you keep quiet and not let him ride you and drive you into any fight?'

'That won't work either.' Father was grim, but he was better and facing up to it. 'A man can stand for a lot of pushing if he has to. Specially when he has his reasons.' His glance shifted briefly to me. 'But there are some things a man can't take. Not if he's to go on living with himself.'

I was startled as Shane suddenly sucked in his breath with a long breaking intake. He was battling something within him, that old hidden desperation, and his eyes were dark and tormented against the paleness of his face. He seemed unable to look at us. He strode to the door and went out. We heard his footsteps fading towards the barn.

I was startled now at father. His breath, too, was coming in long, broken sweeps. He was up and pacing back and forth. When he swung on mother and his voice battered at her, almost fierce in its intensity, I realized that he knew about the change in Shane and that the knowing had been cankering in him all the past weeks.

'That's the one thing I can't stand, Marian. What we're doing to him. What happens to me doesn't matter too much. I talk big and I don't belittle myself. But my weight in any kind of scale won't match his and I know it. If I understood him then as I do now, I'd never have got him to stay on here. But I didn't figure Fletcher would go this far. Shane won his fight before ever he came riding into this valley. It's been tough enough on him already. Should we let him lose just because of us? Fletcher can have his way. We'll sell out and move on.'

I was not thinking. I was only feeling. For some strange reason I was feeling Shane's fingers in my hair, gently rocking my head. I could not help what I was saying, shouting across the room. 'Father! Shane wouldn't run away! He wouldn't run away from anything!'

Father stopped pacing, his eyes narrowed in surprise. He stared at me without really seeing me. He was listening to mother.

'Bob's right, Joe. We can't let Shane down.' It was queer, hearing her say the same thing to father she had said to Shane, the same thing with only the name different. 'He'd never forgive us if we ran away from this. That's what we'd be doing. This isn't just a case of bucking Fletcher any more. It isn't just a case of keeping a piece of ground Fletcher wants for his range. We've got to be the kind of people Shane thinks we are. Bob's right. He wouldn't run away from anything like that. And that's the reason we can't.'

'Lookahere, Marian, you don't think I want to do any running? No. You know me better than that. It'd go against everything in me. But what's my fool pride and this place and any plans we've had alongside of a man like that?'

'I know, Joe. But you don't see far enough.' They were both talking earnestly, not breaking in, hearing each other out, and sort of groping to put their meaning plain. 'I can't really explain it, Joe. But I just know that we're bound up in something bigger than any one of us, and that running away is the one thing that would be worse than whatever might happen to us. There wouldn't be anything real ahead for us, any of us, maybe even for Bob, all the rest of our lives.'

'Humph,' said father. 'Torrey could do it. And Johnson. All the rest of them. And it wouldn't bother them too much.'

'Joe! Joe Starrett! Are you trying to make me mad? I'm not talking about them. I'm talking about us.'

'Hm-m-m,' said father softly, musing like to himself. 'The salt would be done. There just wouldn't be any flavour. There wouldn't be much meaning left.'

'Oh, Joe! Joe! That's what I've been trying to say. And I know this will work out some way. I don't know how. But it will, if we face it and stand up to it and have faith in each other. It'll work out. Because it's got to.'

'That's a woman's reason, Marian. But you're part right anyway. We'll play this game through. It'll need careful watching and close figuring. But maybe we can wait Fletcher out and make him overplay his hand. The town won't take much to this Wilson deal. Men like that fellow Weir have minds of their own.'

Father was more cheerful now that he was beginning to get his thoughts straightened out. He and mother talked low in the kitchen for a long time after they sent me to bed, and I lay in my little room and saw through the window the stars wheeling distantly in the far outer darkness until I fell asleep at last.

12

The morning sun brightened our house and everything in the world outside. We had a good breakfast, father and Shane taking their time because they had routed out early to get the chores done and were waiting to go to town. They saddled up presently and rode off, and I moped in front of the house, not able to settle to any kind of playing.

After she bustled through the dishes, mother saw me standing and staring down the road and called me to the porch. She got our tattered old parchesi board and she kept me humping to beat her. She was a grand one for games like that. She would be as excited as a kid, squealing at the big numbers and doubles and counting proudly out loud as she moved her markers ahead.

When I had won three games running, she put the board away and brought out two fat apples and my favourite of the books she had from the time she taught school. Munching on her apple, she read to me and before I knew it the shadows were mighty short and she had to skip in to get dinner and father and Shane were riding up to the barn.

They came in while she was putting the food on the table. We sat down and it was almost like a holiday, not just because it was not a work day, but because the grown folks were talking lightly, were determined not to let this Fletcher business spoil our good times. Father was pleased at what had happened in town.

'Yes, sir,' he was saying as we were finishing dinner. 'Ernie had a right good funeral. He would have appreciated it. Grafton made a nice speech and, by Godfrey, I believe he meant it. That fellow Weir had his clerk put together a really fine coffin. Wouldn't take a cent for it. And Sims over at the mine is knocking out a good stone. He wouldn't take a cent either. I was surprised at the crowd, too. Not a good word for Fletcher among them. And there must have been thirty people there.'

'Thirty-four,' said Shane. 'I counted 'em. They weren't just paying their respects to Wright, Marian. That wouldn't have brought in some of those I checked. They were showing their opinion of a certain man named Starrett, who made a pretty fair speech himself. This husband of yours is becoming quite a respected citizen in these parts. Soon as the town gets grown up and organized, he's likely to start going places. Give him time and he'll be mayor.'

Mother caught her breath with a little sob. 'Give ... him ... time,' she said slowly. She looked at Shane and there was panic in her eyes. The lightness was gone and before anyone could say more, we heard the horses turning into our yard.

I dashed to the window to peer out. It struck me strange that Shane, usually so alert, was not there ahead of me. Instead he pushed back his chair and spoke gently, still sitting in it. 'That will be Fletcher, Joe. He's heard how the town is taking this and knows he has to move fast. You take it easy. He's playing against time now, but he won't push anything here.'

Father nodded at Shane and went to the door. He had taken off his gunbelt when he came in and now passed it to lift the rifle from its nails on the wall. Holding it in his right hand, barrel down, he opened the door and stepped out on the porch, clear to the front edge. Shane followed quietly and leaned in the doorway, relaxed and watchful. Mother was beside me at the window, staring out, crumpling her apron in her hand.

There were four of them, Fletcher and Wilson in the lead, two cowboys tagging. They had pulled up about twenty feet from the porch. This was the first time I had seen Fletcher for nearly a year. He was a tall man who must once have been a handsome figure in the fine clothes he always wore and with his arrogant air and his finely chiselled face set off by his short-cropped black beard and brilliant eyes. Now a heaviness was setting in about his features and a fatty softness was beginning to show in his body. His face had a shrewd cast and a kind of reckless determination was on him that I did not remember ever noticing before.

Stark Wilson, for all the dude look Frank Torrey had mentioned, seemed lean and fit. He was sitting idly in his saddle, but the pose did not fool you. He was wearing no coat and the two guns were swinging free. He was sure of himself, serene and deadly. The curl of his lip beneath his moustache was a combination of confidence in himself and contempt for us.

Fletcher was smiling and affable. He was certain he held the cards and was going to deal them as he wanted. 'Sorry to bother you, Starrett, so soon after that unfortunate affair last night. I wish it could have been avoided. I really do. Shooting is so unnecessary in these things, if only people would show sense. But Wright never should have called Mr Wilson here a liar. That was a mistake.'

'It was,' father said curtly. 'But then Ernie always did believe in telling the truth.' I could see Wilson stiffen and his lips tighten. Father did not look at him. 'Speak your piece, Fletcher, and get off my land.'

Fletcher was still smiling. 'There's no call for us to quarrel, Starrett. What's done is done. Let's hope there's no need for anything like it to be done again. You've worked cattle on a big ranch and you can understand my position. I'll be wanting all the range I can get from now on. Even without that, I can't let a bunch of nesters keep coming in here and choke me off from my water rights.'

'We've been over that before,' father said. 'You know where I stand. If you have more to say, speak up and be done with it.'

'All right, Starrett. Here's my proposition. I like the way you do things. You've got some queer notions about the cattle business, but when you tackle a job, you take hold and do it thoroughly. You and that man of yours are a combination I could use. I want you on my side of the fence. I'm getting rid of Morgan and I want you to take over as foreman. From what I hear your man would make one hell of a driving trail boss. The spot's his. Since you've proved up on this place, I'll buy it from you. If you want to go on living here, that can be arranged. If you want to play around with that little herd of yours, that can be arranged too. But I want you working for me.'

Father was surprised. He had not expected anything quite like this. He spoke softly to Shane behind him. He did not turn or look away from Fletcher, but his voice carried clearly.

'Can I call the turn for you, Shane?'

'Yes, Joe.' Shane's voice was just as soft, but it, too, carried clearly and there was a little note of pride in it.

Father stood taller there on the edge of the porch. He stared straight at Fletcher. 'And the others,' he said slowly. 'Johnson, Shipstead, and the rest. What about them?'

'They'll have to go.'

Father did not hesitate. 'No.'

'I'll give you a thousand dollars for this place as it stands and that's my top offer.'

'No.'

The fury in Fletcher broke over his face and he started to turn in the saddle towards Wilson. He caught himself and forced again that shrewd smile. 'There's no percentage in being hasty, Starrett. I'll boost the ante to twelve hundred. That's a lot better than what might happen if you stick to being stubborn. I'll not take an answer now. I'll give you till tonight to think it over. I'll be waiting at Grafton's to hear you talk sense.'

He swung his horse and started away. The two cowboys turned to join him by the road. Wilson did not follow at once. He leaned forward in his saddle and drove a sneering look at father.

'Yes, Starrett. Think it over. You wouldn't like someone else to be enjoying this place of yours – and that woman there in the window.'

He was lifting his reins with one hand to pull his horse around and suddenly he dropped them and froze to attention. It must have been what he saw in father's face. We could not see it, mother and I, because father's back was to us. But we could see his hand tightening on the rifle at his side.

'Don't, Joe!'

Shane was beside father. He slipped past, moving smooth and steady, down the steps and over to one side to come at Wilson on his right hand and stop not six feet from him. Wilson was puzzled and his right hand twitched and then was still as Shane stopped and as he saw that Shane carried no gun.

Shane looked up at him and Shane's voice flicked in a whiplash of contempt. 'You talk like a man because of that flashy hardware you're wearing. Strip it away and you'd shrivel down to boy size.'

The very daring of it held Wilson motionless for an instant and father's voice cut into it. 'Shane! Stop it!'

The blackness faded from Wilson's face. He smiled grimly at Shane. 'You do need someone to look after you.' He whirled

94

his horse and put it to a run to join Fletcher and the others in the road.

It was only then that I realized mother was gripping my shoulders so that they hurt. She dropped on a chair and held me to her. We could hear father and Shane on the porch.

'He'd have drilled you, Joe, before you could have brought the gun up and pumped in a shell.'

'But you, you crazy fool!' Father was covering his feelings with a show of exasperation. 'You'd have made him plug you just so I'd have a chance to get him.'

Mother jumped up. She pushed me aside. She flared at them from the doorway. 'And both of you would have acted like fools just because he said that about me. I'll have you two know that if it's got to be done, I can take being insulted just as much as you can.'

Peering around her, I saw them gaping at her in astonishment. 'But Marian,' father objected mildly, coming to her. 'What better reason could a man have?'

'Yes,' said Shane gently. 'What better reason?' He was not looking just at mother. He was looking at the two of them.

13

I do not know how long they would have stood there on the porch in the warmth of that moment. I shattered it by asking what seemed to me a simple question until after I had asked it and the significance hit me.

'Father, what are you going to tell Fletcher tonight?'

There was no answer. There was no need for one. I guess I was growing up. I knew what he would tell Fletcher. I knew what he would say. I knew, too, that because he was father he would have to go to Grafton's and say it. And I understood why they could no longer bear to look at one another, and the breeze blowing in from the sun-washed fields was suddenly so chill and cheerless.

They did not look at each other. They did not say a word to each other. Yet somehow I realized that they were closer together in the stillness there on the porch than they had ever been. They knew themselves and each of them knew that the other grasped the situation whole. They knew that Fletcher had dealt himself a winning hand, had caught father in the one play that he could not avoid because he would not avoid it. They knew that talk is meaningless when a common knowledge is already there. The silence bound them as no words ever could.

Father sat on the top porch step. He took out his pipe and drew on it as the match flamed and fixed his eyes on the horizon, on the mountains far across the river. Shane took the chair I had used for the games with mother. He swung it to the house wall and bent into it in that familiar unconscious gesture and he, too, looked into the distance. Mother turned into the kitchen and went about clearing the table as if she was not really aware of what she was doing. I helped her with the dishes and the old joy of sharing with her in the work was gone and there was no sound in the kitchen except the drip of the water and the chink of dish on dish.

When we were done, she went to father. She sat beside him on the step, her hand on the wood between them, and his covered hers and the moments merged in the slow, dwindling procession of time.

Loneliness gripped me. I wandered through the house, finding nothing there to do, and out on the porch and past those three and to the barn. I searched around and found an old shovel handle and started to whittle me a play sabre with my knife. I had been thinking of this for days. Now the idea held no interest. The wood curls dropped to the barn floor, and after a while I let the shovel handle drop among them. Everything that had happened before seemed far off, almost like another existence. All that mattered was the length of the shadows creeping across the yard as the sun drove down the afternoon sky.

I took a hoe and went into mother's garden where the ground was caked around the turnips, the only things left unharvested. But there was scant work in me. I kept at it for a couple of rows, then the hoe dropped and I let it lie. I went to the front of the house, and there they were sitting, just as before.

I sat on the step below father and mother, between them, and their legs on each side of me made it seem better. I felt father's hand on my head.

'This is kind of tough on you, Bob.' He could talk to me because I was only a kid. He was really talking to himself.

'I can't see the full finish. But I can see this. Wilson down and there'll be an end to it. Fletcher'll be done. The town will see to that. I can't beat Wilson on the draw. But there's strength enough in this clumsy body of mine to keep me on my feet till I get him, too.' Mother stirred and was still, and his voice went on. 'Things could be worse. It helps a man to know that if anything happens to him, his family will be in better hands than his own.'

There was a sharp sound behind us on the porch. Shane had risen so swiftly that his chair had knocked against the wall. His hands were clenched tightly and his arms were quivering. His face was pale with the effort shaking him. He was desperate with an inner torment, his eyes tortured by thoughts that he could not escape, and the marks were obvious on him and he did not care. He strode to the steps, down past us and around the corner of the house.

Mother was up and after him, running headlong. She stopped abruptly at the house corner, clutching at the wood, panting and irresolute. Slowly she came back, her hands outstretched as if to keep from falling. She sank again on the step, close against father, and he gathered her to him with one great arm.

The silence spread and filled the whole valley and the shadows crept across the yard. They touched the road and began to merge in the deeper shading that meant the sun was dipping below the mountains far behind the house. Mother straightened, and as she stood up, father rose, too. He took hold of her two arms and held her in front of him. 'I'm counting on you, Marian, to help him win again. You can do it, if anyone can.' He smiled a strange little sad smile and he loomed up there above me the biggest man in all the world. 'No supper for me now, Marian. A cup of your coffee is all I want.' They passed through the doorway together.

Where was Shane? I hurried towards the barn. I was almost to it when I saw him out by the pasture. He was staring over it and the grazing steers at the great lonely mountains tipped with the gold of the sun now rushing down behind them. As I watched, he stretched his arms up, the fingers reaching to their utmost limits, grasping and grasping, it seemed, at the glory glowing in the sky.

He whirled and came straight back, striding with long, steady steps, his head held high. There was some subtle, new, unchangeable certainty in him. He came close and I saw that his face was quiet and untroubled and that little lights danced in his eyes.

'Skip into the house, Bobby boy. Put on a smile. Everything is going to be all right.' He was past me, without slowing, swinging into the barn.

But I could not go into the house. And I did not dare follow him, not after he had told me to go. A wild excitement was building up in me while I waited by the porch, watching the barn door.

The minutes ticked past and the twilight deepened and a patch of light sprang from the house as the lamp in the kitchen was lit. And still I waited. Then he was coming swiftly towards me and I stared and stared and broke and ran into the house with the blood pounding in my head.

'Father! Father! Shane's got his gun!'

He was close back of me. Father and mother barely had time to look up from the table before he was framed in the doorway. He was dressed as he was that first day when he rode into our lives, in that dark and worn magnificence from the black hat with its wide curling brim to the soft black boots. But what caught your eye was the single flash of white, the outer ivory plate on the grip of the gun, showing sharp and distinct against the dark material of the trousers. The tooled cartridge belt nestled around him, riding above the hip on the left, sweeping down on the right to hold the holster snug along the thigh, just as he had said, the gun handle about half-way between the wrist and elbow of his right arm hanging there relaxed and ready.

Belt and holster and gun.... These were not things he was wearing or carrying. They were part of him, part of the man, of the full sum of the integrate force that was Shane. You could see now that for the first time this man who had been living with us, who was one of us, was complete, was himself in the final effect of his being.

Now that he was no longer in his crude work clothes, he seemed again slender, almost slight, as he did that first day. The change was more than that. What had been seeming iron was again steel. The slenderness was that of a tempered blade and a razor edge was there. Slim and dark in the doorway, he seemed somehow to fill the whole frame.

This was not our Shane. And yet it was. I remembered Ed Howells saying that this was the most dangerous man he had ever seen. I remembered in the same rush that father had said he was the safest man we ever had in our house. I realized that both were right and that this, this at last, was Shane.

He was in the room now and he was speaking to them both in that bantering tone he used to have only for mother. 'A fine pair of parents you are. Haven't even fed Bob yet. Stack him full of a good supper. Yourselves, too. I have a little business to tend to in town.'

Father was looking fixedly at him. The sudden hope that had sprung in his face had as quickly gone. 'No, Shane. It won't do. Even your thinking of it is the finest thing any man ever did for me. But I won't let you. It's my stand. Fletcher's making his play against me. There's no dodging. It's my business.'

'There's where you're wrong, Joe,' Shane said gently. 'This is my business. My kind of business. I've had fun being a farmer. You've shown me new meaning in the word, and I'm proud that for a while maybe I qualified. But there are a few things a farmer can't handle.'

The strain of the long afternoon was telling on father. He pushed up from the table. 'Damn it, Shane, be sensible. Don't make it harder for me. You can't do this.'

Shane stepped near, to the side of the table, facing father across a corner. 'Easy does it, Joe. I'm making this my business.'

'No. I won't let you. Suppose you do put Wilson out of the way. That won't finish anything. It'll only even the score and swing things back worse than ever. Think what it'll mean to you. And where will it leave me? I couldn't hold my head up around here any more. They'd say I ducked and they'd be right. You can't do it and that's that.'

'No!' Shane's voice was even more gentle, but it had a quiet, inflexible quality that had never been there before. 'There's no man living can tell me what I can't do. Not even you, Joe. You forget there is still a way.'

He was talking to hold father's attention. As he spoke the gun was in his hand and before father could move he swung it, swift and sharp, so the barrel lined flush along the side of father's head, back of the temple, above the ear. Strength was in the blow and it thudded dully on the bone and father folded over the table and as it tipped with his weight slid towards the floor. Shane's arm was under him before he hit and Shane pivoted father's loose body up and into his chair and righted the table while the coffee cups rattled on the floor boards. Father's head lolled back and Shane caught it and eased it and the big shoulders forward till they rested on the table, the face down and cradled in the limp arms.

Shane stood erect and looked across the table at mother. She had not moved since he appeared in the doorway, not even when father fell and the table teetered under her hands on its edge. She was watching Shane, her throat curving in a lovely proud line, her eyes wide with a sweet warmth shining in them.

Darkness had shut down over the valley as they looked at each other across the table and the only light now was from the lamp swinging ever so slightly above them, circling them with its steady glow. They were alone in a moment that was all their own. Yet, when they spoke, it was of father.

'I was afraid,' Shane murmured, 'that he would take it that way. He couldn't do otherwise and be Joe Starrett.'

'I know.'

'He'll rest easy and come out maybe a little groggy but all right. Tell him, Marian. Tell him no man need be ashamed of being beat by Shane.'

The name sounded queer like that, the man speaking of himself. It was the closest he ever came to boasting. And then you understood that there was not the least hint of a boast. He was stating a fact, simple and elemental as the power that dwelled in him.

'I know,' she said again. 'I don't need to tell him. He knows, too.' She was rising, earnest and intent. 'But there is something else I must know. We have battered down words that might have been spoken between us and that was as it should be. But I have a right to know now. I am part of this, too. And what I do depends on what you tell me now. Are you doing this just for me?'

Shane hesitated for a long, long moment. 'No, Marian.' His gaze seemed to widen and encompass us all, mother and the still figure of father and me huddled on a chair by the window, and somehow the room and the house and the whole place. Then he was looking only at mother and she was all that he could see.

'No, Marian. Could I separate you in my mind and afterwards be a man?'

He pulled his eyes from her and stared into the night beyond the open door. His face hardened, his thoughts leaping to what lay ahead in town. So quiet and easy you were scarce aware that he was moving, he was gone into the outer darkness.

14

Nothing could have kept me there in the house that night. My mind held nothing but the driving desire to follow Shane. I waited, hardly daring to breathe while mother watched him go. I waited until she turned to father, bending over him, then I slipped around the door-post out to the porch. I thought for a moment she had noticed me, but I could not be sure and she did not call to me. I went softly down the steps and into the freedom of the night.

Shane was nowhere in sight. I stayed in the darker shadows, looking about, and at last I saw him emerging once more from the barn. The moon was rising low over the mountains, a clean, bright crescent. Its light was enough for me to see him plainly in outline. He was carrying his saddle and a sudden pain stabbed through me as I saw that with it was his saddle-roll. He went towards the pasture gate, not slow, not fast, just firm and steady. There was a catlike certainty in his every movement, a silent, inevitable deadliness. I heard him, there by the gate, give his low whistle and the horse came out of the shadows at the far end of the pasture, its hooves making no noise in the deep grass, a dark and powerful shape etched in the moonlight drifting across the field straight to the man.

I knew what I would have to do. I crept along the corral

fence, keeping tight to it, until I reached the road. As soon as I was around the corner of the corral with it and the barn between me and the pasture, I started to run as rapidly as I could towards town, my feet plumping softly in the thick dust of the road. I walked this every school day and it had never seemed long before. Now the distance stretched ahead, lengthening in my mind as if to mock me.

I could not let him see me. I kept looking back over my shoulder as I ran. When I saw him swinging into the road, I was well past Johnson's, almost past Shipstead's, striking into the last open stretch to the edge of town. I scurried to the side of the road and behind a clump of bulberry bushes. Panting to get my breath, I crouched there and waited for him to pass. The hoofbeats swelled in my ears, mingled with the pounding beat of my own blood. In my imagination he was galloping furiously and I was positive he was already rushing past me. But when I parted the bushes and pushed forward to peer out, he was moving at a moderate pace and was only almost abreast of me.

He was tall and terrible there in the road, looming up gigantic in the mystic half-light. He was the man I saw that first day, a stranger, dark and forbidding, forging his lone way out of an unknown past in the utter loneliness of his own immovable and instinctive defiance. He was the symbol of all the dim, formless imaginings of danger and terror in the untested realm of human potentialities beyond my understanding. The impact of the menace that marked him was like a physical blow.

I could not help it. I cried out and stumbled and fell. He was off his horse and over me before I could right myself, picking me up, his grasp strong and reassuring. I looked at him, tearful and afraid, and the fear faded from me. He was no stranger. That was some trick of the shadows. He was Shane. He was shaking me gently and smiling at me.

'Bobby boy, this is no time for you to be out. Skip along home and help your mother. I told you everything would be all right.'

He let go of me and turned slowly, gazing out across the far sweep of the valley silvered in the moon's glow. 'Look at it, Bob. Hold it in your mind like this. It's a lovely land, Bob. A good place to be a boy and grow straight inside as a man should.'

My gaze followed his, and I saw our valley as though for the first time and the emotion in me was more than I could stand. I choked and reached out for him and he was not there.

He was rising into the saddle and the two shapes, the man and the horse, became one and moved down the road towards the yellow squares that were the patches of light from the windows of Grafton's building a quarter of a mile away. I wavered a moment, but the call was too strong. I started after him, running frantic in the middle of the road.

Whether he heard me or not, he kept right on. There were several men on the long porch of the building by the saloon doors. Red Marlin's hair made him easy to spot. They were scanning the road intently. As Shane hit the panel of light from the near big front window, the store window, they stiffened to attention. Red Marlin, a startled expression on his face, dived quickly through the doors.

Shane stopped, not by the rail but by the steps on the store side. When he dismounted, he did not slip the reins over the horse's head as the cowboys always did. He left them looped over the pommel of the saddle and the horse seemed to know what this meant. It stood motionless, close by the steps, head up, waiting, ready for whatever swift need.

Shane went along the porch and halted briefly, fronting the two men still there.

'Where's Fletcher?'

They looked at each other and at Shane. One of them started to speak. 'He doesn't want –' Shane's voice stopped him. It slapped at them, low and with an edge that cut right into your mind. 'Where's Fletcher?'

One of them jerked a hand towards the doors and then, as they moved to shift out of his way, his voice caught them.

'Get inside. Go clear to the bar before you turn.'

They stared at him and stirred uneasily and swung together to push through the doors. As the doors came back, Shane grabbed them, one with each hand, and pulled them out and wide open and he disappeared between them.

Clumsy and tripping in my haste, I scrambled up the steps and into the store. Sam Grafton and Mr Weir were the only persons there and they both hurrying to the entrance to the saloon, so intent that they failed to notice me. They stopped in the opening. I crept behind them to my familiar perch on my box where I could see past them.

The big room was crowded. Almost everyone who could be seen regularly around town was there, everyone but our homestead neighbours. There were many others who were new to me. They were lined up elbow to elbow nearly the entire length of the bar. The tables were full and more men were lounging along the far wall. The big round poker table at the back between the stairway to the little balcony and the door to Grafton's office was littered with glasses and chips. It seemed strange, for all the men standing, that there should be an empty chair at the far curve of the table. Someone must have been in that chair, because chips were at the place and a half-smoked cigar, a wisp of smoke curling up from it, was by them on the table.

Red Marlin was leaning against the back wall, behind the chair. As I looked, he saw the smoke and appeared to start a little. With a careful show of casualness he slid into the chair and picked up the cigar.

A haze of thinning smoke was by the ceiling over them all, floating in involved streamers around the hanging lamps. This was Grafton's saloon in the flush of a banner evening's business. But something was wrong, was missing. The hum of activity, the whirr of voices, that should have risen from the scene, been part of it, was stilled in a hush more impressive than any noise could be. The attention of everyone in the room, like a single sense, was centred on that dark figure just inside the swinging doors, back to them and touching them.

This was the Shane of the adventures I had dreamed for him, cool and competent, facing that room full of men in the simple solitude of his own invincible completeness.

His eyes searched the room. They halted on a man sitting at a small table in the front corner with his hat on low over his forehead. With a thump of surprise I recognized it was Stark Wilson and he was studying Shane with a puzzled look on his face. Shane's eyes swept on, checking off each person. They stopped again on a figure over by the wall and the beginnings of a smile showed in them and he nodded almost imperceptibly. It was Chris, tall and lanky, his arm in a sling, and as he caught the nod he flushed a little and shifted his weight from one foot to the other. Then he straightened his shoulders and over his face came a slow smile, warm and friendly, the smile of a man who knows his own mind at last.

But Shane's eyes were already moving on. They narrowed as they rested on Red Marlin. Then they jumped to Will Atkey trying to make himself small behind the bar.

'Where's Fletcher?'

Will fumbled with the cloth in his hands. 'I – I don't know. He was here a while ago.' Frightened at the sound of his own voice in the stillness, Will dropped the cloth, started to stoop for it, and checked himself, putting his hands to the inside rim of the bar to hold himself steady.

Shane tilted his head slightly so his eyes could clear his hat brim. He was scanning the balcony across the rear of the room. It was empty and the doors there were closed. He stepped forward, disregarding the men by the bar, and walked quietly past them the long length of the room. He went through the doorway to Grafton's office and into the semi-darkness beyond.

And still the hush held. Then he was in the office doorway again and his eyes bored towards Red Marlin.

'Where's Fletcher?'

The silence was taut and unendurable. It had to break. The sound was that of Stark Wilson coming to his feet in the far front corner. His voice, lazy and insolent, floated down the room.

'Where's Starrett?'

While the words yet seemed to hang in the air, Shane was moving towards the front of the room. But Wilson was moving, too. He was crossing towards the swinging doors and he took his stand just to the left of them, a few feet out from the wall. The position gave him command of the wide aisle running back between the bar and the tables and Shane coming forward in it.

Shane stopped about three-quarters of the way forward, about five yards from Wilson. He cocked his head for one quick sidewise glance again at the balcony and then he was looking only at Wilson. He did not like the set-up. Wilson had the front wall and he was left in the open of the room. He understood the fact, assessed it, accepted it.

They faced each other in the aisle and the men along the bar jostled one another in their hurry to get to the opposite side of the room. A reckless arrogance was on Wilson, certain of himself and his control of the situation. He was not one to miss the significance of the slim deadliness that was Shane. But even now, I think, he did not believe that anyone in our valley would deliberately stand up to him.

'Where's Starrett?' he said once more, still mocking Shane but making it this time a real question.

The words went past Shane as if they had not been spoken. 'I had a few things to say to Fletcher,' he said gently. 'That can wait. You're a pushing man, Wilson, so I reckon I had better accommodate you.'

Wilson's face sobered and his eyes glinted coldly. 'I've no quarrel with you,' he said flatly, 'even if you are Starrett's man. Walk out of here without any fuss and I'll let you go. It's Starrett I want.'

'What you want, Wilson, and what you'll get are two different things. Your killing days are done.'

Wilson had it now. You could see him grasp the meaning. This quiet man was pushing him just as he had pushed Ernie Wright. As he measured Shane, it was not to his liking. Something that was not fear but a kind of wondering and baffled reluctance showed in his face. And then there was no escape, for that gentle voice was pegging him to the immediate and implacable moment.

'I'm waiting, Wilson. Do I have to crowd you into slapping leather?'

Time stopped and there was nothing in all the world but two men looking into eternity in each other's eyes. And the room rocked in the sudden blur of action indistinct in its incredible swiftness and the roar of their guns was a single sustained blast. And Shane stood, solid on his feet as a rooted oak, and Wilson swayed, his right arm hanging useless, blood beginning to show in a small stream from under the sleeve over the hand, the gun slipping from the numbing fingers.

He backed against the wall, a bitter disbelief twisting his features. His left arm hooked and the second gun was showing and Shane's bullet smashed into his chest and his knees buckled, sliding him slowly down the wall till the lifeless weight of the body toppled it sideways to the floor.

Shane gazed across the space between and he seemed to have forgotten all else as he let his gun ease into the holster. 'I gave him his chance,' he murmured out of the depths of a great sadness. But the words had no meaning for me, because I noticed on the dark brown of his shirt, low and just above the belt to one side of the buckle, the darker spot gradually widening. Then others noticed, too, and there was a stir in the air and the room was coming to life.

Voices were starting, but no one focused on them. They were snapped short by the roar of a shot from the rear of the room. A wind seemed to whip Shane's shirt at the shoulder and the glass of the front window beyond shattered near the bottom.

Then I saw it.

It was mine alone. The others were turning to stare at the back of the room. My eyes were fixed on Shane and I saw it. I saw the whole man move, all of him, in the single flashing instant. I saw the head lead and the body swing and the driving power of the legs beneath. I saw the arm leap and the hand take the gun in the lightning sweep. I saw the barrel line up like – like a finger pointing – and the flame spurt even as the man himself was still in motion.

And there on the balcony Fletcher, impaled in the act of aiming for a second shot, rocked on his heels and fell back into the open doorway behind him. He clawed at the jambs and pulled himself forward. He staggered to the rail and tried to raise the gun. But the strength was draining out of him and he collapsed over the rail, jarring it loose and falling with it.

Across the stunned and barren silence of the room Shane's voice seemed to come from a great distance. 'I expect that finishes it,' he said. Unconsciously, without looking down, he broke out the cylinder of his gun and reloaded it. The stain on his shirt was bigger now, spreading fanlike above the belt, but he did not appear to know or care. Only his movements were slow, retarded by an unutterable weariness. The hands were sure and steady, but they moved slowly and the gun dropped into the holster of its own weight.

He backed with dragging steps towards the swinging doors until his shoulders touched them. The light in his eyes was unsteady like the flickering of a candle guttering towards darkness. And then, as he stood there, a strange thing happened.

How could one describe it, the change that came over him? Out of the mysterious resources of his will the vitality came. It came creeping, a tide of strength that crept through him and fought and shook off the weakness. It shone in his eyes and they were alive again and alert. It welled up in him, sending that familiar power surging through him again until it was singing again in every vibrant line of him.

He faced that room full of men and read them all with the one sweeping glance and spoke to them in that gentle voice with that quiet, inflexible quality.

'I'll be riding on now. And there's not a one of you that will follow.'

He turned his back on them in the indifference of absolute knowledge they would do as he said. Straight and superb, he was silhouetted against the doors and the patch of night above them. The next moment they were closing with a soft swish of sound.

The room was crowded with action now. Men were clustering around the bodies of Wilson and Fletcher, pressing to the bar, talking excitedly. Not a one of them, though, approached too close to the doors. There was a cleared space by the doorway as if someone had drawn a line marking it off.

I did not care what they were doing or what they were saying. I had to get to Shane. I had to get to him in time. I had to know, and he was the only one who could ever tell me.

I dashed out the store door and I was in time. He was on his horse, already starting away from the steps.

'Shane,' I whispered desperately, loud as I dared without the men inside hearing me. 'Oh, Shane!'

He heard me and reined around and I hurried to him, standing by a stirrup and looking up.

'Bobby! Bobby boy! What are you doing here?'

'I've been here all along,' I blurted out. 'You've got to tell me. Was that Wilson –'

He knew what was troubling me. He always knew. 'Wilson,' he said, 'was mighty fast. As fast as I've ever seen.'

'I don't care,' I said, the tears starting. 'I don't care if he was the fastest that ever was. He'd never have been able to shoot you, would he? You'd have got him straight, wouldn't you – if you had been in practice?'

He hesitated a moment. He gazed down at me and into me and he knew. He knew what goes on in a boy's mind and what can help him stay clean inside through the muddled, dirtied years of growing up.

'Sure. Sure, Bob. He'd never even have cleared the holster.'

He started to bend down towards me, his hand reaching for my head. But the pain struck him like a whiplash and the hand jumped to his shirt front by the belt, pressing hard, and he reeled a little in the saddle.

The ache in me was more than I could bear. I stared dumbly at him, and because I was just a boy and helpless I turned away and hid my face against the firm, warm flank of the horse.

'Bob.'

'Yes, Shane.'

'A man is what he is, Bob, and there's no breaking the mould. I tried that and I've lost. But I reckon it was in the cards from the moment I saw a freckled kid on a rail up the road there and a real man behind him, the kind that could back him for the chance another kid never had.'

'But – but, Shane, you –'

'There's no going back from a killing, Bob. Right or wrong, the brand sticks and there's no going back. It's up to you now. Go home to your mother and father. Grow strong and straight and take care of them. Both of them.'

'Yes, Shane.'

'There's only one thing more I can do for them now.'

I felt the horse move away from me. Shane was looking down the road and on to the open plain and the horse was obeying the silent command of the reins. He was riding away and I knew that no word or thought could hold him. The big horse, patient and powerful, was already settling into the steady pace that had brought him into our valley, and the two, the man and the horse, were a single dark shape in the road as they passed beyond the reach of the light from the windows.

I strained my eyes after him, and then in the moonlight I could make out the inalienable outline of his figure receding into the distance. Lost in my loneliness, I watched him go, out of town, far down the road where it curved out to the level country beyond the valley. There were men on the porch behind me, but I was aware only of that dark shape growing small and indistinct along the far reach of the road. A cloud passed over the moon and he merged into the general shadow and I could not see him and the cloud passed on and the road was a plain thin ribbon to the horizon and he was gone.

I stumbled back to fall on the steps, my head in my arms to hide the tears. The voices of the men around me were meaningless noises in a bleak and empty world. It was Mr Weir who took me home.

15

Father and mother were in the kitchen, almost as I had left them. Mother had hitched her chair close to father's. He was sitting up, his face tired and haggard, the ugly red mark standing out plain along the side of his head. They did not come to meet us. They sat still and watched us move into the doorway.

They did not even scold me. Mother reached and pulled me to her and let me crawl into her lap as I had not done for three years or more. Father just stared at Mr Weir. He could not trust himself to speak first.

'Your troubles are over, Starrett.'

Father nodded. 'You've come to tell me,' he said wearily, 'that he killed Wilson before they got him. I know. He was Shane.'

'Wilson,' said Mr Weir. 'And Fletcher.'

Father started. 'Fletcher, too? By Godfrey, yes. He would do it right.' Then father sighed and ran a finger along the bruise on his head. 'He let me know this was one thing he wanted to handle by himself. I can tell you, Weir, waiting here is the hardest job I ever had.'

Mr Weir looked at the bruise. 'I thought so. Listen, Starrett. There's not a man in town doesn't know you didn't stay here of your own will. And there's damn few that aren't glad it was Shane came into the saloon tonight.'

The words broke from me. 'You should have seen him,

father. He was – he was' – I could not find it at first. 'He was – beautiful, father. And Wilson wouldn't even have hit him if he'd been in practice. He told me so.'

'He told you!' The table was banging over as father drove to his feet. He grabbed Mr Weir by the coat front. 'My God, man! Why didn't you tell me? He's alive?'

'Yes,' said Mr Weir. 'He's alive all right. Wilson got to him. But no bullet can kill that man.' A puzzled, faraway sort of look flitted across Mr Weir's face. 'Sometimes I wonder whether anything ever could.'

Father was shaking him. 'Where is he?'

'He's gone,' said Mr Weir. 'He's gone, alone and unfollowed as he wanted it. Out of the valley and no one knows where.'

Father's hands dropped. He slumped again into his chair. He picked up his pipe and it broke in his fingers. He let the pieces fall and stared at them on the floor. He was still staring at them when new footsteps sounded on the porch and a man pushed into our kitchen.

It was Chris. His right arm was tight in the sling, his eyes unnaturally bright and the colour high in his face. In his left hand he was carrying a bottle, a bottle of red cherry soda pop. He came straight in and righted the table with the hand holding the bottle. He smacked the bottle on the top boards and seemed startled at the noise he made. He was embarrassed and he was having trouble with his voice. But he spoke up firmly.

'I brought that for Bob. I'm a damned poor substitute, Starrett. But as soon as this arm's healed, I'm asking you to let me work for you.'

Father's face twisted and his lips moved, but no words came. Mother was the one who said it. 'Shane would like that, Chris.'

And still father said nothing. What Chris and Mr Weir saw as they looked at him must have shown them that nothing they could do or say would help at all. They turned and went out together, walking with long, quick steps.

Mother and I sat there watching father. There was nothing we could do either. This was something he had to wrestle alone. He was so still that he seemed even to have stopped breathing. Then a sudden restlessness hit him and he was up and pacing aimlessly about. He glared at the walls as if they stifled him and strode out the door into the yard. We heard his steps around the house and heading into the fields and then we could hear nothing.

I do not know how long we sat there. I know that the wick in the lamp burned low and sputtered awhile and went out and the darkness was a relief and a comfort. At last mother rose, still holding me, the big boy bulk of me, in her arms. I was surprised at the strength in her. She was holding me tightly to her and she carried me into my little room and helped me undress in the dim shadows of the moonlight through the window. She tucked me in and sat on the edge of the bed, and then, only then, she whispered to me: 'Now, Bob. Tell me everything. Just as you saw it happen.'

I told her, and when I was done, all she said in a soft little murmur was 'Thank you.' She looked out the window and murmured the words again and they were not for me and she was still looking out over the land to the great grey mountains when finally I fell asleep.

She must have been there the whole night through, for when I woke with a start, the first streaks of dawn were showing through the window and the bed was warm where she had been. The movement of her leaving must have awakened me. I crept out of bed and peeked into the kitchen. She was standing in the open outside doorway.

I fumbled into my clothes and tiptoed through the kitchen to her. She took my hand and I clung to hers and it was right that we should be together and that together we should go find father.

We found him out by the corral, by the far end where Shane had added to it. The sun was beginning to rise through the cleft in the mountains across the river, not the brilliant glory of midday but the fresh and renewed reddish brilliance of early morning. Father's arms were folded on the top rail, his head bowed on them. When he turned to face us, he leaned back against the rail as if he needed the support. His eyes were rimmed and a little wild.

'Marian, I'm sick of the sight of this valley and all that's in it. If I tried to stay here now, my heart wouldn't be in it any more. I know it's hard on you and the boy, but we'll have to pull up stakes and move on. Montana, maybe. I've heard there's good land for the claiming up that way.'

Mother heard him through. She had let go my hand and stood erect, so angry that her eyes snapped and her chin quivered. But she heard him through.

'Joe! Joe Starrett!' Her voice fairly crackled and was rich with emotion that was more than anger. 'So you'd run out on Shane just when he's really here to stay!'

'But, Marian. You don't understand. He's gone.'

'He's not gone. He's here, in this place, in this place he gave us. He's all around us and in us, and he always will be.'

She ran to the tall corner post, to the one Shane had set. She beat at it with her hands. 'Here, Joe. Quick. Take hold. Pull it down.'

Father stared at her in amazement. But he did as she said. No one could have denied her in that moment. He took hold of the post and pulled at it. He shook his head and braced his feet and strained at it with all his strength. The big muscles of his shoulders and back knotted and bulged till I thought this shirt, too, would shred. Creakings ran along the rails and the post moved ever so slightly and the ground at the base showed little cracks fanning out. But the rails held and the post stood.

Father turned from it, beads of sweat breaking on his face, a light creeping up his drawn cheeks.

'See, Joe. See what I mean. We have roots here now that we can never tear loose.'

And the morning was in father's face, shining in his eyes, giving him new colour and hope and understanding.

16

I guess that is all there is to tell. The folks in town and the kids at school liked to talk about Shane, to spin tales and speculate about him. I never did. Those nights at Grafton's became legends in the valley and countless details were added as they grew and spread just as the town, too, grew and spread up the river banks. But I never bothered, no matter how strange the tales became in the constant retelling. He belonged to me, to father and mother and me, and nothing could ever spoil that.

For mother was right. He was there. He was there in our place and in us. Whenever I needed him, he was there. I could close my eyes and he would be with me and I would see him plain and hear again that gentle voice.

I would think of him in each of the moments that revealed him to me. I would think of him most vividly in that single flashing instant when he whirled to shoot Fletcher on the balcony at Grafton's saloon. I would see again the power and grace of a co-ordinate force beautiful beyond comprehension. I would see the man and the weapon wedded in the one indivisible deadliness. I would see the man and the tool, a good man and a good tool, doing what had to be done.

And always my mind would go back at the last to that moment when I saw him from the bushes by the roadside just on the edge of town. I would see him there in the road, tall and terrible in the moonlight, going down to kill or be killed, and stopping to help a stumbling boy and to look out over the land, the lovely land, where that boy had a chance to live out his boyhood and grow straight inside as a man should.

And when I would hear the men in town talking among themselves and trying to pin him down to a definite past, I would smile quietly to myself. For a time they inclined to the notion, spurred by the talk of a passing stranger, that he was a certain Shannon who was famous as a gunman and gambler way down in Arkansas and Texas and dropped from sight without anyone knowing why or where. When that notion dwindled, others followed, pieced together in turn from scraps of information gleaned from stray travellers. But when they talked like that, I simply smiled because I knew he could have been none of these.

He was the man who rode into our little valley out of the heart of the great glowing West and when his work was done rode back whence he had come and he was Shane.

Cooter James

Cooter James rode in from the line camp blowing flakes of the first snow off his moustache and feeling sorry for himself. He was in no mood for light talk when he pulled up by the ranch-house porch and found Jess Winslow standing there watching him approach.

'Jess,' he said, 'stock's all right and camp's tight. But you'd best send another man out. Can't winter it again.'

'Trouble,' said Jess Winslow. 'I ought to know trouble's riding with you the way your moustache sags. What is it? Age getting you soft?'

Cooter James was too low to flare much at that. 'Only turned forty last year,' he said. 'Just when a man's got his growth and a bit of sense in him. Three years running I've rode that line. Not doing it again.'

'Money,' said Jess. 'That's what it is. You're hitting me for more money.'

Cooter James sighed. 'Not a matter of money. Matter of principle. Way back doing line work got worried being alone. Promised myself when I took to spooking easy and talking to myself I'd take fair warning. Last night an owl woke me shivering. This morning caught myself talking to the coffee pot. Saddled up and came straight in.'

'Letting me down,' said Jess. 'That's what you're doing. Just when I need that line rode right you're letting me down.'

'Sorry, Jess,' said Cooter. 'Man that can't keep a promise to himself's a peaked kind of mangy packrat.'

'That's how you look to me this minute now,' said Jess Winslow. 'Jumping at owls and scared of your own voice. Packrat's too nice a word.'

Cooter James sighed again. He wasn't much to look at and he knew it. Short and thickening around the middle with a limp from a bronc-thrown broken bone that never healed right. Scrambled features burnt and weathered with always-squinting, muddy-blue eyes and a hooked nose over a handle-bar moustache that drooped to hide a short upper lip. But he was a good hand on any man's ranch and he knew that too.

'Easy, Jess,' he said. 'I'm quitting. Just made myself another promise. Going to winter warm and lazy in town. Thank you for my time quick as convenient.'

Cooter James rode into town sighing soft into the drooping ends of his moustache. 'Change,' he said. 'That's what I need. Easy living for a spell.' He had money to spend and he spent it, on thorough barbering and town clothes and genteel living quarters, a room at Mrs Pearson's boarding house. Four days and he had his fill of that. The food was solid and staying, but he had an uneasy feeling that Mrs Pearson disapproved of his table manners. The bed was too bouncy and the floor was too smooth, and he had difficulty navigating among the fussy scatter rugs that gave treacherous footing for a man used to unfinished planks. He was uncomfortable in his town clothes, and he felt shorter than ever in shoes lacking the high heels of his worn old boots. And he never could remember to scrape his feet on the mat before coming in the front door.

On the evening of the fourth day, Cooter took a long look at Mr Pearson, who clerked ten hours at a stretch at the railroad freight office and came home to scrape his feet careful on the mat. Cooter sighed into what was left of his moustache and went upstairs to bed, mighty thoughtful. In the morning he rolled his town clothes into a neat bundle. He put on his old blue jeans and flannel shirt and work jacket. He struggled to get his feet again into his boots and jammed his faded stetson on his head. He left an extra five-dollar bill on the bed and went downstairs and out the front door.

Two hours' walking found him what he wanted, a sagging shed at the edge of town abandoned when the railroad section gang moved on. Three days later he was snug and settled; the shed braced and tight, a bunk rigged, a cracked stove brought from the blacksmith shop and food on shelves along one wall. He could sleep late and putter around the place with not a thing pressing. He could wander around town and toss the time of day with plenty of folks and stop at the livery stable to visit his horse. He could spend as many hours as he wanted sitting by his stove reading through the stack of old newspapers he had found in a corner of the shed. Then late one night a board squeaked and he woke shivering and got up and made a pot of coffee and started talking to it.

'What's wrong with me?' said Cooter. 'Took fair warning. Warm and lazy in town. Still there's an itch inside I can't get at. Might be I need something new to be doing.'

That was why Cooter James went to working in Silas John Unger's general store and got himself involved with a barrel of flour.

Silas John Unger knew Cooter from the time they were Circle Bar hands together. He was lean with a lantern jaw and hair lightened with streaks of grey. He was maybe ten years older, and fatherly in his feeling for Cooter James. 'Cooter boy,' he said, 'it pleases me to have you acquiring some smattering of sense at last. I'm doing well and putting money in the bank. You should be doing the same. When the sun's shining, get ready for a rainy day.'

'Rain don't bother me,' said Cooter. 'And storekeeping's not my style. Want only to wear out the winter with it. If there's work enough to warrant.'

'There's work enough,' said Silas John. 'During the selling times at least. When things are slack, we can play chequers like in the old days.'

Several weeks went by, and Cooter was twenty-nine games ahead on the chart they kept, when Silas John read a letter in one morning's mail. He chewed a pencil and made tracks on a piece of paper and came out of the cubbyhole he called his office.

'Cooter boy,' he said, 'the country hereabouts is getting thick with homesteaders and I'm thinking of adding a line of farm machinery. I'll have to go East to Chicago to tie the deal. Do you reckon you can handle things while I'm gone?'

'Reckon so,' said Cooter.

Silas John tapped his nose with the pencil. 'One thing worries me. You never had much head for figures. I like my books kept straight and neat.'

Cooter blew air through the ends of his moustache that was growing out again the way he liked. 'Set me on a corral rail,' he said. 'Drive steers past all day. Come night I'll have you the tally right with the swaybacks and bigjaws marked. Reckon I can keep figures on a cramped little store like this.'

'Steers are one thing,' said Silas John. 'Store goods another.'

'Take your trip,' said Cooter. 'Take your time. If my figures don't tot up exact, I'll teach you how to beat that chequer game of mine.'

Cooter James kept his figures clean and straight in the two books, one for cash and one for credit, and he lined down the pages neater than Silas John ever did. One day he tallied out fifteen cents ahead on the cash account. That bothered him till he undercharged a homesteader's wife fifteen cents on her winter dress goods and decided that balanced the account. Then reports came of a blizzard in the hills, and people began crowding into town by wagon to lay in quantity supplies for the hard months. He was busy as he had ever been at branding time, making up orders, packing goods into the wagons, and keeping the books posted. He was a tired man but a triumphant man when Silas John strolled in and sat down on a nail keg and set his satchel on the floor and looked around.

'You've been doing business,' said Silas John. 'My shelves look like people been buying.'

'Been putting money in the bank for you,' said Cooter. 'Been protecting my chequer game too.'

Silas John went into his cubbyhole and bent over the books. After a while he came out and looked at Cooter perched on the rear counter and shook his head and went back in and chewed a pencil. Then he began coming out and counting articles and going back in to check the books. He kept at this till Cooter was blowing his moustaches with chuckles.

'Enjoying yourself?' said Cooter. 'Remind me of a chipmunk laying up nuts in a hollow tree.' He slid off the counter and went up front to tend to a customer. When that was done he found Silas John occupying the perch on the rear counter and jutting his jaw at a high angle.

'Cooter boy,' said Silas John, 'you've lost me a barrel of flour.'

'Crazy as a cracked teapot,' said Cooter. 'Couldn't lose anything that big.'

'You could,' said Silas John. 'There were nineteen barrels out back when I left. There's four now. That means you sold fifteen. But there's only fourteen marked in the books, three cash and eleven credit.'

Cooter's moustache sagged. His jawline stiffened. 'Certain of those figures?'

Silas John slid off the counter and straightened tall. 'That I am,' he said.

'Right,' said Cooter. His jawline stiffened even more and his muddy blue eyes tightened at the corners in a serious squint. 'Take the price out of my pay.'

'That I'll not,' said Silas John. 'What's a little matter of a barrel of flour between you and me.'

'Not a little matter,' said Cooter. 'Matter of principle.'

'Pay for it, then,' said Silas John. 'I know better than to try to stop you. But I'm giving you a bonus for taking care of my store while I was gone. I make it the price of a barrel of flour. You know better than to try to stop me.'

Cooter sighed into the drooping ends of his moustache and his lips relaxed in a small smile behind it. 'Reminds me of the old days,' he said. He reached behind the counter and pulled out the battered chequerboard. 'Got another debt to pay,' he said, and began setting the chequers in place.

Two weeks went by, and Cooter James was only seven games ahead on the chart and fighting to hold his lead. That gave a mild tingle to the days, and it was pleasant wagging away the time with Silas John. It was pleasant too at his shed where he could be his own boss yet close to other folks within a nice neighbourly reach. Then early one morning a train tooted faint and far off down the track, and he woke shivering and crawled out of bed in his undershirt and made a pot of coffee and started talking to it.

'Can't get to the bottom of this,' said Cooter. 'Doing something new and enjoying myself. Still there's that itch I can't scratch. Might be I need something to occupy my mind.' That was why, in the middle of a game during the noon slack, he leaned back and looked at Silas John.

'Barrel of flour,' he said.

'Gone and forgotten,' said Silas John. 'Get on with the game.'

'Not forgotten,' said Cooter. 'Going to find what happened to it.'

It was Silas John's turn to lean back and look interested.

'Cooter boy,' he said, 'how're you planning to do that?'

'Simple,' said Cooter. 'Add a barrel of flour to every bill. Man that got it will pay. Won't know we don't know. Others'll scratch it off or complain when they stop in.'

'Sounds simple,' said Silas John. 'But simple-sounding things often ain't so.'

'This one is,' said Cooter. 'Just keep out of my way and let me make out the bills.'

Cooter James burned his kerosene lamp late over the bills and in the morning took them to the post office. 'Only a matter of time now,' he said, and went on to the store where there was plenty of work waiting. The next three days, while Silas John handled the inside business, he was busy building an open-face shed by the store for the farm machinery that was coming. The day after that he was busy uncrating the sample machinery that had arrived. He was so busy he all but forgot that barrel of flour. And Silas John said never a word about it. During the afternoon of the second day, he stepped outside and looked at Cooter wrassling shed timbers and shook his head mournful and went back inside. Twice on the third day he did the same. Late in the fourth day he stood in the doorway and called. When they were settled on the rear counter, he tapped his nose with the pencil in his hand.

'Cooter boy,' he said, 'I have kept my mouth from yapping so as not to disturb your muscular enthusiasm with that shed. And I wanted to give your little lost-barrel scheme plenty of play. But already it's had too much.'

'What now?' said Cooter. 'Not working?'

'It's working,' said Silas John. 'It's working too well. Thirty-seven people have paid their bills. Twenty have complained about a barrel of flour.'

'Told you they would,' said Cooter. 'Supposed to work that way.'

'Cooter boy,' said Silas John, 'you never were much good at figures. Twenty from thirty-seven leave seventeen. Up to and as of now seventeen people have paid for that one barrel of flour.'

Cooter's moustache sagged and he blew air through it. He sucked in the drooping ends and chewed them slow. His jawline stiffened and a serious squint formed at the corners of his muddy-blue eyes.

'Need the names and the money,' he said. 'Reckon to be riding around evenings paying it back.'

Three weeks went by, and Cooter James was nine games behind on the chequer chart. The flour-barrel score stood at seventy with forty-two complaints and twenty-eight payments. These last had all been returned, and he was tired of criss-crossing the countryside in the evenings. But that worry was ended. He had sent out new bills to cancel the old and no more payments were coming in. He wasn't even bothered by the fact that his evening trips had let the town and most of the territory around know about the missing barrel and easy-tongued folk were beginning to rib him about it. He strolled along the plank sidewalks after store-closing and took the joshing and enjoyed the feel of being part of a community. He built a fire in his stove and had a lazy meal and sat warm and unworrying with his old newspapers waiting for the night freight to go past and tell him to go to bed. Then one morning about sun-up a cat scrambled across his tin roof and he woke shivering and sat up in the bunk and stared at the coffee pot across the shed and began talking to it.

'Clean licked on this,' he said. 'Can't even locate that itch. Might be I need to settle this barrel business to settle my mind.'

He was early at the store and busy with a can of paint, a small brush, and the cardboard bottom of an overall carton. He needed two cardboards before he was finished with his sign. He tacked them one under the other on the inside wall by the front door.

On or about the first week of December last one barrel of flour departed these premises leaving no record in S. J. Unger's account books. Person or persons giving information of aforesaid barrel's whereabouts will receive five dollars ($5) reward and the undying gratitude of –

C. James

Cooter James's sign provided plenty of amusement for Silas John and folks coming in, and it gave the ribbing a fresh boost. But it brought no news about the barrel. Cooter worried over that and was low in his mind. He began to think he would wear out the winter without tracing that barrel. Then one afternoon, when the sun was warming towards spring, a scrawny red-haired boy came in for a piece of patching cloth and stopped by the sign and kept staring at it.

Cooter eased alongside. 'Like it, son?' he said.

'We got a barrel of flour this winter,' said the boy.

'Know anything about that particular barrel?' said Cooter. The boy shied away and started edging towards the door. 'G'wan,' he said. 'Suppose I did, I wouldn't tell you.'

'Easy, now,' said Cooter. 'No way to talk to your elders.'

'Go fry an egg,' said the boy, and skipped out the door.

It was maybe an hour later that the boy came back and with him a little waist-high girl with the same red hair in pigtails, and both of them tagging a woman in a faded gingham dress with a man's coat on over it. This woman was plump and solid inside the coat and she had a lot of red hair pulled up with old celluloid hairpins haphazard on top of her head. Her plain round face would have been pleasant with the permanent smile crinkles around the eyes except that her mouth was pursed tight right now, so tight that it pulled her plump chin into little bumps. She swung around by the door and read the sign and she turned about and started towards Silas John in the rear of the store.

'Mr Unger,' she said, trying to hold her voice firm, 'just what is the meaning of that thing on the wall?'

'Afternoon, Mrs Moser,' said Silas John. 'Any questions pertaining to that peculiar piece of writing should be addressed to Mr Cooter James here.'

She turned to look at Cooter, and for some reason he began to feel fidgety and troubled in his mind.

'So that's C. James,' she said. 'I remember him. I did business with him last time I was in here.' She glared at Cooter and the bumps on her chin started quivering. 'Well, Mr C. James,' she said, 'you open your mouth and explain that sign to me.'

'Easy, now,' said Cooter. 'Ain't much. Was missing a barrel of flour and trying to find what happened to it.'

'Well, it makes me do some wondering,' she said. 'I got a barrel of flour that week and I didn't pay for it or charge it either. You gave it to me.'

Cooter's moustache sagged, and his voice came through it feeble and fumbling. 'Did I now?' he said.

'That's right,' said the boy. 'We ain't ever eat so good.'

The woman was talking straight along so fast the words were pushing each other out of the way.

'I came in here for my winter goods and I knew exactly what I had money for and you made out the list and I paid you and I asked for a bag of flour and when you brought it out to the wagon it was a barrel and ever since my man died last fall everybody's been so kind and I've been a good customer here because I can't afford much but what I buy I get here and I thought you were being kind and I thanked you for it and you said that was all right you were pleased to do it.'

'Did I now?' said Cooter again. 'Reckon I did. But I thought – ' He shut off his talk and chewed the ends of his moustache slow and thoughtful.

'And what did you think?' said the woman. 'It surprises me you can think at all. Making a woman feel maybe she's got something she wasn't supposed to have.'

'Mrs Moser, ma'am,' said Cooter, 'all my mistake. You were supposed to have it. So busy back then slipped my mind.'

'Humph,' said the woman. 'Things like that don't slip minds easy. You stop squirming and tell me what you thought.'

'No,' said Cooter. 'Won't.'

The woman waggled her head at Cooter so hard the celluloid pins started loosening and he was afraid they might fall.

'It's not my fault I'm not a man,' she said. 'You treat me like one. You speak honest to me. You tell me what you thought.'

Cooter was caught when she talked like that and he knew it. 'Thought you were thanking me for stowing things in the wagon,' he said. He saw her chin quivering again, and he pushed his mind scurrying for words. 'Easy, now, ma'am. So maybe I didn't mean to give it you then. Do now. Didn't know about your man passing on. Glad about it now. About the mistake, I mean. Wish it had been two. Two barrels. Give you the other one now.' He started past her towards the rear of the store.

The woman's chin was quivering, but quivering mad.

'Mr C. for Cooter James,' she said, and stopped him in stride. She stared at him accusing, and the boy and the girl lined beside her and looked the same, and her words pushed each other out of the way in their hurry. 'Mr Mind-slipping James,' she said, 'I wouldn't take the tiniest speck of flour there ever was from you if me and mine were starving and you the last man on the whole earth. Doing a thing like that to a woman that's always paid her bills hard as it might be and making her find out the food she's been putting in the mouths of her babes ought to've been paid for and wasn't.'

'Don't look like babies to me,' said Cooter, beginning to be a bit peeved himself. 'Got some size on them. Want to be treated like a man you do, so I will. Stop yammering at me and wobbling your chin. Barrel's been paid for. Know what I wanted to know and there's nothing more to it.'

'Nothing more you think,' said the woman. 'I want to know who paid for it.'

'I did,' said Cooter. 'In a way I did.'

'Humph,' said the woman. 'So it's you I owe the price and just when I haven't got any cash money and don't know when I'll ever see any again with thinking the pig and the garden that isn't ploughed yet will take us through summer till I get some kind of a crop in and sold and money's always been scarce with us anyways and no extras for barrels that oughtn't to have to be paid for but do because a fool man doesn't know a person and lets his mind slip.'

'Mrs Moser, ma'am,' said Cooter, getting a firm hold on himself, 'you don't owe me the least little bit of nothing. Try to pay me a solitary single cent and I head howling for the next county.'

'Be good riddance,' said the woman. 'Howsomever, I don't have a single cent. But I'm going to pay you. I won't have a thing like that hanging on my mind, letting a man do for me what he didn't mean to. A barrel of flour costs fourteen dollars. Well, you owe me five dollars reward money as that sign there says and I make it nine dollars still owing and I'm going to pay it not knowing how right now but that I'm going to.' She waggled her head emphatic at Cooter and two of the celluloid pins fell bouncing to the floor. She stooped and grabbed them and stuck them into the pile of red hair and glared at Cooter and marched out the door. The boy and the girl took turns according to size doing the same, the glaring and the marching, and a silence settled in the store.

Then the voice of Silas John came purring from the rear. 'Cooter boy,' he said, 'that woman's got a rope on you.'

'No rope,' said Cooter. 'How's she going to pay me when I won't take it?'

'I wouldn't know,' said Silas John. 'But there's one item I do know. I know the colour of her hair.'

Cooter James went home to his shed feeling sorry for himself. 'Town life's mighty strenuous,' he said. He burned his beans chewing his moustache and forgetting them on the stove. And he couldn't stay put in his chair with his newspapers. He pulled on his jacket and took a long hike along the tracks and return to weary his muscles and worried away some hours before he fell asleep. In the morning a metal-bumping sound woke him shivering, and he lay still listening to strange noises in his shed. The tasty smell of bacon grease tickled his nose and he raised his head to peer over the blanket. The woman was there by his stove, her back to him, bustling about in a knowing manner.

Cooter lay quiet for two minutes, maybe three. He held the blanket up under his chin and raised himself to a sitting position. He had trouble finding his voice.

'Mrs Moser, ma'am,' he said, 'what in tarnation you doing here?'

'Fixing your breakfast,' said the woman. 'I figured I'd charge you a quarter each time till I was paid up. I've changed my mind and made it fifty. I'm a good cook and you keep your things dirty just like a man.'

Cooter lay back down and tried to untangle his mind and was still trying when she snapped at him.

'It's ready,' she said.

'It,' said Cooter. 'Not me. Can't get out of my bunk with you standing there.' ⁓

'Humph,' said the woman. 'Wouldn't be the first time I saw a man in his drawers. If you're so delicate about yourself, I'll look the other way.'

She did, and Cooter slipped out of the bunk and whipped on his old blue jeans and flannel shirt. With them on he felt better and able to work up the beginnings of a good mad.

'Blamed if I'm hungry,' he said.

'Eat it or don't eat it,' said the woman. 'Anyways, I've fixed it, and a man that was a man 'stead of a mind-slipper that'd take the taste out of the food a woman that pays her bills puts in the mouth of her babes would eat it hungry or not hungry and I never knew a man that wasn't hungry in the mornings anyways.'

Cooter was caught again and he knew it. He sat down and started to eat and the woman watching bothered him.

'Fixed it,' he said. 'Time to get out, and let me be.'

'Where I come from,' said the woman, 'fixing a meal means cleaning up after.'

Cooter sighed, and then his mad was boiling strong. He looked at the food, bacon and biscuits and coffee.

'Woman,' he said, 'where's my eggs?'

She jumped, and one of the hairpins fell and she stooped to pick it up and put it in place. 'Didn't know you had any,' she said.

'In that tobacco can,' said Cooter. 'Four I want. Fried and flipped.'

He ate right through every snitch of bacon, every biscuit in the pan, the four eggs, and finished with a third cup of coffee. He pulled on his boots and jacket and jammed on his hat and slammed the door behind him.

Cooter James was upset and touchy all day. He kept busy by himself in the machinery shed and hurried home before closing time. He was worrying about what he might find and his worrying was justified. The place had a different feel the moment he entered. Everything was scrubbed and polished and so neat and orderly that he shuddered when he looked around.

A flour bag had been ripped apart at the seams and the halves trimmed and put up at the side window for curtains. A bunch of winter-ivy leaves from out by the tracks was in water in a coffee cup on the table. Beside it was a note written on the edge of a piece of newspaper.

Mr C. James – 50 cents for fixing breakfast. 1 dollar for scrubbing out dirt. 50 cents for fixing curtains and such. 7 dollars owing. – Mrs A. (Agnes) Moser.

Cooter stared at the note a long time. 'Agnes,' he said. 'Was sweet on a girl named Agnes once. Didn't have red hair.' He smiled into his moustache, remembering, and started to get his supper, and each thing he wanted was in a new place. 'Women,' he said. 'Interfering things. Can't leave a man be.' By time he was ready to eat, he had a good grip on his mad again. 'Find a way to fix her,' he said, and went to bunk early, determined to be up before she arrived, and slept only in cat naps, worrying over the time. He was dressed and fed and had the place slicked, and he was by the window watching when she came in sight. He waited till she was near the door, then opened it, and came out and shut it behind him.

'Morning, Mrs Moser, ma'am,' he said. 'Had breakfast. Everything's clean.'

He went off towards the store, leaving her staring at him, and felt fine for almost the whole morning.

Along about noon worry began creeping back into his mind. Silas John beat him two more games and the afternoon seemed unusual long. He hurried home early with the worry big inside him and the woman was there in his shed by the stove preparing his supper. He pulled off his hat and leaned against the wall and sighed into his moustache.

'Stop making that silly noise,' said the woman. 'Thought you were cute didn't you sneaking up early to get breakfast ahead of me leaving a woman that's determined to pay her bills feeling that she's owing to you and why don't you act like a man that's got more sense than a fieldmouse and take off that jacket where it's warm in here so you won't catch cold if you go out again.'

Cooter James was licked and he knew it. He took off his jacket and hung it on a nail and the hat over it.

'Determined to pay the whole price?' he said.

'I am,' said the woman.

'Do it friendly, then,' said Cooter. 'Sit down and eat with me each time. Can't chew right with you just watching.'

'Maybe I might,' said the woman. 'But you mind to think straight and not go notioning that I don't get enough to eat at home because maybe we do only have bread and hominy grits most of the time with the other winter things about gone but that's filling and we'll have a garden soon – and oh, I just thought you being the kind of mind-slipping man you are you'll likely expect me to pay for what I eat.'

'Woman,' said Cooter, blowing his moustache out straight, 'man can provide food for a woman in his own house without her having to pay for it. Stop yammering and get supper ready.' He sat on the bunk and watched her bustling by the stove. He forgot the worry and began remembering yesterday's breakfast. 'Woman,' he said, 'might be we could have some of those biscuits you make?'

Two days more, and it was the end of the week and the woman didn't come on Sunday. Three days into the next week and by her figuring, two meals a day at fifty cents each, she owed Cooter only one dollar and fifty cents more.

The following morning Cooter looked across the table at her.

'Time's getting short,' he said. 'Want to know how you make those biscuits.'

'The way anyone does,' she said. 'Flour and water and shortening and a pinch of this and a pinch of that till it feels right.'

'Been making biscuits many a year,' said Cooter. 'Never taste like yours.'

'A man can't make decent biscuits,' she said. 'But about any woman could on that stove of yours.'

'That stove?' said Cooter. 'Just a fall-apart that was lying around at the blacksmith shop.'

'It's a better stove than I've had for years and years,' she said. 'And I don't mean to tell you it's not hard cooking on a stove that's got to be patched all the time and puts smoke in your face and gets you all sooty so you have to scrub all the time to be fitten for seeing.'

Cooter saw the little bumps forming on her chin and the whole chin starting to quiver. He was embarrassed and looked out the window.

'Might be,' he said, 'you'd let me get you a stove.'

She pushed up from the table and waggled her head at him so hard some of the red hair fell down by her face.

'I will not,' she said. 'I wouldn't let you give me anything. Not you. Not ever.' She sat down again sudden, and several of the hairpins bounced on the floor and she stooped to get them. When her head came up again, her eyes were snapping hard. 'Get on off to that store,' she said. 'And right away quick so I can clean this mess and get away from this place that minds me of you every time I see it.'

Cooter took his hat and jacket off the wall and slipped out the door. He walked slow to the store. He was sharp-tongued to customers all morning, and during the afternoon he managed to work up a quarrel with Silas John. When he realized what he was doing, he clamped down on his tongue and stomped out. He wandered over by the town saloon and looked in. 'Snapped me out of meanness when I was younger,' he said. 'Not now.' He wandered on and far out of town along some road, and about suppertime he wandered back towards his shed. He waited and worried a moment about opening the door, and when he did the place was empty. It was scrubbed and polished again and empty except for another note on the table.

50 cents for fixing breakfast. 1 dollar for scrubbing out a week's dirt. Makes 9 dollars now. Not a cent owing.

Cooter stared at the note. 'Fooled with that scrubbing,' he said. 'Thought a couple more meals coming.' He had been afraid at the door that maybe her chin would be quivering inside to meet him, but now he was disappointed. 'That's done, anyways,' he said. 'Done. Finished. Over with. No more of it.' He started to prepare his own supper and burned the beans, and his biscuits, even with a pinch of this and of that, were lumpy in his mouth and heavy in his stomach. He fussed around the shed and out and in a half-dozen times and started to hike along the tracks and came back as many times more till he began to think that he could call it spring and the winter over and be heading for the range again. 'Where I belong,' he said. 'In the open where figures ain't so important.'

He pulled off his outer clothes feeling better and planning an early start in the morning. He lay on the bunk and closed his eyes counting steers and checking the bigjaws and swaybacks and drifted off, counting, into sleep. A light rain began to fall tapping on his tin roof and thunder talked in the distance, and the night freight went by and he didn't hear it. Then along about sun-up a mouse skittled across a shelf and a cup made a small jangle, and he sat up in the bunk shivering and stared across the shed at the coffee pot. He stared a long time and the light grew stronger. He shook his head and sighed into his moustache. 'No sense fighting it,' he said. 'Know about that itch. Time comes to every man. Mine's now.' He sat still, thinking, and after a while a chuckle waggled the ends of his moustache. 'Not so bad at figures after all,' he said, and slipped out of the bunk and dressed himself in his town clothes. He looked down at himself and snorted and pulled the town clothes off and made himself neat as he could in his old jeans and flannel shirt.

He stopped by the door to pick up his axe, changed his mind and took the hand whetstone instead. He started towards the centre of the town and then swung along the road the woman had walked each way morning and evening coming to his place, and after a while he saw it, the unpainted two-room shack with rips showing in the tar-papered roof. A sagging small barn was at one side and two gaunt draught horses were in a makeshift corral behind it.

Cooter studied the place in the early morning light. He sniffed the air. 'Spring all right,' he said. 'Ploughing time for them's got a mind for farming.' He went to the sagging barn and around it to a pile of old wood. There was a rusty axe on the ground still wet from the night rain. He picked it up and felt the blade. 'Just like a woman,' he said, and went to work with his whetstone till he had an edge that could slice a hair of his moustache. He pulled wood off the pile and began cutting it into stove lengths. He was swinging the axe steady when he noticed the woman standing by the corner of the barn and staring at him. He stopped chopping and leaned on the axe.

'Morning, Mrs Moser, ma'am,' he said. 'Nice morning.'

'Maybe it's a nice morning,' she said, 'and maybe it isn't and I don't care what it is because I don't mean to tell you I'll not have you snooping around here and trying to make me owing to you.'

'Me that's owing,' said Cooter, taking a deep breath. 'Forgot back there you paid for a bag of flour when you got the barrel. Two dollars you paid. Means two dollars you're overpaid now. Figure to pay that back cutting wood. Twenty-five cents each morning for cutting a day's supply. Stubborn as you on things like that.'

The woman stared at him, and then the bumps were forming on her chin. 'Just like the man you are,' she said, 'to be finding ways to make fun of a woman that pays her bills and tries to get along best she can, and even so if maybe it's you that's owing it's silly with charging things back and forth all the time we might never be out straight and somebody'd always be owing somebody.'

Cooter's head came up straight and his moustache sat out stiff. 'That be so bad?' he said. 'Always doing things for each other, I mean.'

She stared at him and her chin began to quiver, and she tried to speak, but the words would not come, and Cooter swung the axe solid into a chunk of wood and left it there and faced her square on.

'Agnes,' he said, 'through talking about barrels and owing and getting things paid. Talking now like a man that's found his woman and aims to know will she have him.'

He looked at her, and she looked at him, and her voice when it came was so low he could scarce hear it. 'Babes,' she said. 'I've got two babes.'

'What's wrong with babes?' said Cooter. 'Grow up to be people, don't they?'

She looked at him a long moment and her chin stopped quivering and the pleasant wrinkles by her eyes showed plain. 'Cooter,' she said, 'that's no christened name. What's it really?'

Cooter James sighed into his moustache. 'Courtney,' he said.

The woman looked at him, and she smiled just a little, and her voice was as soft and tender as one of her biscuits. 'I think I'll call you Cooter,' she said. 'I like Cooter best.'

The Coup of Long Lance

This was a large camp, a late-spring hunting camp, more than forty lodges, set in a broad bottom by a river. The lodges stood in a wide circle with a gap, an entranceway into the central open area, at the east to face the rising sun. They were arranged, clockwise around the circle from the entranceway, in the customary order of the ten divisions or clans of the tribe. Always a Cheyenne camp of any size was made thus, even the great bustling camp of the midsummer Medicine Lodge ceremony when all the people of all the villages and camps within travelling distance gathered for eight days of feasting and dancing and careful ritual in honour of the annual rebirth of the spring now accomplished again, the re-creation of the earth and of life upon it.

This was a large camp. It slept, close to the earth in its hollow, under the moonless star-touched night of the high plains of the heartland of North America. And out across the rolling plains, scattered in small herds across the endless plains, the buffalo too were bedded down for the night in their own vast slow migration north-westward into the late-spring winds bringing their subtle sensed message of the renewing grasses.

The first faint glow of dawn crept up the eastern sky. Across from it, in the western arc of the camp circle where stood the lodges of the *Hev-a-tan-iu*, the Rope Men who used ropes of twisted hair instead of the usual rawhide, the ageing warrior Strong Left Hand stirred on his couch. He turned his head. The door flap of the lodge had been swung wide, letting in the rising light. In the centre of the lodge by the hollowed-out fireplace his wife, Straight Willow, knelt by a small pile of twigs with her fire sticks in her hands. There was a woman. A true Cheyenne woman. The mother of tall grown sons, with work-gnarled hands and deepening lines in her face, yet still strong and supple and independent, firm mistress of the lodge and its place in the camp. Always he woke with the first light of dawn and always she was awake before him, tending to her woman's duty, her woman's privilege, of lighting the lodge fire. It was no longer crowded in the lodge now that the three sons, the two real sons and the foster son, were married and living with their wives' clans as was proper, because descent and clan always passed to children through the mothers. But it was never lonely, would never be lonely, in a lodge shared with Straight Willow.

He spoke to her, using one of the silly names out of their long-ago early years together, and without looking up she called him a lazy lie-abed as she always did. He chuckled, filling the lodge with good feeling, and rose with the couch robe held about him and stepped past her and out into the morning air. Ah, it was good, fresh and clean the air, and rich colour was climbing the eastern sky. Already smoke was coming from other lodges too. Men and boys were emerging from them and heading for the river for the morning plunge that all male Cheyennes took when near water, the hardiest all though the year, even when thick ice had to be broken.

Behind him Straight Willow put larger twigs on the fire and picked up her two buckets of bullhide. She brushed past him and joined other women on their way upstream, above the swimmers, where they would dip fresh water. No Cheyenne woman, when she could avoid it, used dead water, water that had stood all night.

That was Bull Hump beckoning to him, a wide grin on his face. Bull Hump's middle daughter had been married yesterday. He was coming from her new husband's new lodge and she was in front of it, waving him on. Bull Hump spoke quickly. The young men who had visited his new son-in-law last night and feasted late and stayed in the lodge all night, according to custom, to be there to eat the new bride's first breakfast as a wife, were still asleep. They were true lazy lie-abeds. Here was a chance for some sport in the old way. But it must be a man who had counted many coups. A man like Strong Left Hand.

Strong Left Hand stepped into his lodge and dropped the robe on his couch. He came out, clad only in his manhood string around his waist with the breechclout suspended from it. He hurried towards the new lodge of Bull Hump's new son-in-law, picking up a long stout stick. He stood just outside the entrance and his voice rolled out, deep and strong, telling a coup, short and quick so the young men would not have time to get past him.

'It is Strong Left Hand who speaks. Travelling by the yellow river I met a man of the Crows on a good horse. He fled. I came up by him and pushed aside his lance and knocked him to the ground and took his horse.'

The young men were awake now. They knew what to expect. Like rabbits out of a burrow they ran headlong through the entrance and Strong Left Hand thwacked each a stinging blow with the stick. They ran, scattering, towards the river and he ran after them, thwacking those he could reach until they plunged into the water, shouting and pretending to be hurt mightily. Strong Left Hand stood on the bank laughing. It was not all pretending on their part. He was not so old after all. He had given them some good thwacks and kept up with them in the running. He tossed the stick aside and waded into the water and dived under and came up spouting. The young men splashed water at him and called out cheerful morning greetings to him and moved out of the way in the instinctive Cheyenne custom, invincible through life, of deference to one older.

When he returned to his lodge to put on his leggings and shirt and get fresh pine gum to hold his hair in a dozen bunches hanging down his back, Straight Willow had food cooking over the fire. There was no need to tell her of the thwacking. He knew by the way she looked up at him sideways, her eyes bright, that she knew. It was amazing how every woman in the camp always seemed to know almost everything as soon as it happened. And he knew she liked him to be doing things like that. She was strong on the old customs, stronger on them, as women usually were, than he was. She was of the *Suhtai* clan and even now she wore her dress longer than most women and dipping on the right side and still wore her hair in braids with little deerskin and sweet sage ornaments bunched on the back of her head, not in the new fashion of doubling them up in two humps, one on each side.

He left her with her cooking and went out beyond the camp

circle where the other men were gathering, waiting for the boys who had gone to round up the horses. Only a few horses, the most valuable, were kept in the camp at night, tied by their owners' lodges. The rest were out over the rolling ridges where the grass was good.

The horses came trotting over the last rise before the camp, the boys behind them. Strong Left Hand's eyes swept over them with the keen almost unthinking glance of the Plains Indian who, once having seen a horse clearly, could know it unerringly any time, any place. There were his six horses. Yesterday morning he had had eight horses. But Bull Hump was his cousin and yesterday Bull Hump's daughter had been married and it had simply been right that Strong Left Hand should add two horses to the presents Bull Hump was giving to the bridegroom's family. There too were his wife's twelve horses. She was very proud of them, perhaps too proud. She was the richest woman in horses in the camp. She was also the best robe-maker. But that was different. She made them to give as presents. She liked to think that newly married couples slept under her robes. She was not like that with her horses.

Strong Left Hand caught the horses with the one glance but he did not say so to the boy coming towards him, his nephew, the son of his brother, Owl Friend. This was the boy who herded for him now that his own sons were grown. It was good for the boy to feel important.

'Are they all here, little one?'

'Every one, my uncle.'

'Is any one of them lame?'

'The black one with the two white spots limped a little. It was only a stone in the hoof. I took it out.'

'You took it out? He stood for you?'

'Yes, my uncle.'

'You will be a brave man with horses, little stone picker.'

A meadow lark, startled by the many hoofs disturbing the grasses, rose out of them to the left and swooped, trilling, up into the glowing colour of the rising sun, and the heart of Strong Left Hand leaped within him. So it had been long ago, in his youth, in the time of his starving on a hill for his dreaming, and in the dawn of the third day a meadow lark had risen trilling into the rising sun and he had a vision, a vision of himself with hair thin and grey, and he had known that he would live to be an old man and count many coups. And always, after that, when a meadow lark had risen thus from near his feet, trilling for him and the morning, the day had been a good day for him. The clean sweet air of this morning was like a strong drink.

'Little lifter of horses' feet, listen to your uncle. You will tie the grey horse that is quick and fast and the spotted one that is thick and strong by my lodge. We hunt today. The others go back with the herd. You will take good care of the black one because from this moment forward he is yours. Remember what I say. You will do with him as your father tells you. Now run.'

The boy ran, leaping like a grasshopper, frantic in his hurry to tell the other boys, and Strong Left Hand turned back towards his lodge remembering when his uncle, who had given him his name, had also given him his first horse and he, too, had run leaping like a grasshopper. And now he was a man and a warrior with tall grown sons and he was a giver of horses to eager young nephews and the life cycle, endlessly repeating, moved on and it was all good, all of it, the youngness and the manhood and the drawing on towards old age, for still the meadow lark rose trilling into the sun of the morning to tell him it was good.

Back at the lodge the food was ready. Straight Willow took a small piece from the kettle of boiled Indian turnips and a small piece from the other kettle of stewed meat and each in turn she held high towards the sky, an offering to *Heamma-wihio*, the Wise One Above, then laid it on the ground by the fire. There the pieces would remain until she swept out the lodge. Once offered, they were as consumed, no longer really there. She scooped more of the food into two wooden bowls. She and Strong Left Hand sat cross-legged by the fire, eating with the ornamented spoons he had made of the horns of the first buffalo he had killed after their marriage. They talked quietly and between talkings they listened. The old crier was making his round, riding along the inside of the camp circle, calling out the news.

The chiefs (one of the tribe's four head chiefs and three of the forty council chiefs, four from each of the ten clans, were with this hunting camp) had said the camp would not be moved for many days ... The Kit Fox Soldiers would have a social dance that night ... All men should remember what had been told yesterday, that there would be a hunt today ... Word had come from Yellow Moon's camp, two days eastward, that Big Knee, chief of the Red Shields, the Bull Soldiers, had pledged to be this year's Medicine Lodge maker and the celebration would be in the first days of the *Hivi-uts-i-i-shi* moon (July, the buffalo bull rutting month) when the grasses would be long and the leaves of the cottonwoods in full growth ...

Big Knee? Ah, there was a man. He and Strong Left Hand had been boys together. They were both Bull Soldiers now, Red Shield carriers. Not many men could say that. A man could not just join the Bull Soldier band; he had to be mature and seasoned and be chosen for it. Strong Left Hand had helped persuade Big Knee to take the present term of leadership. Did Straight Willow recall the time that he and Big Knee ...

What was the old crier saying? The Dog Soldiers in the camp had challenged the Bull Soldiers to a coup-telling competition that night. They were foolish; good young men but foolish. Perhaps they thought they could win because there were more of them in the camp. They would find out. The Bull Soldiers were fewer but they were real warriors, with age and experience on them. Anyone could know that from the many red coup stripes on their wives' arms at the ceremonial dances.

Ah, this competition would be a fine thing. Strong Left Hand was full of talk. Their youngest son, Long Lance, would have a chance to tell his first coup. He was a Dog Soldier. Four days ago he had returned with the others who had gone with Many Feathers, chief of the Dog Soldiers, raiding the Crows to the north. They had gone on foot, as they had pledged to do, and they returned on horses, herding others, and they carried two scalps – but there had been no scalp dance and telling of coups, because one of them had been killed by the Crows. Long Lance could claim a coup, but he had not spoken of it, because a true Cheyenne did not go about speaking big words about his deeds; only in telling a coup did he speak of them and then he simply stated the facts. It was for others to tell what he had done in many fine words. And the others had told what Long Lance had done.

They had found a Crow camp. In the first light of morning they had crept close and started the herd of Crow horses moving away and each caught a horse and mounted and they were slipping away fast when someone, perhaps a guard hidden where they had not seen, gave an alarm and many Crow warriors, on horses kept in the camp, came after them. The chase was long and the Crows were gaining and the young Cheyennes turned, few against many and proud it was so, and charged in the swift sweeping charge their enemies knew so well, and the Crows, close now, slowed and wavered, and the Cheyennes were among them, striking and scattering them. Many Feathers was in the lead, as was right, and an arrow struck him in the shoulder and he fell from his horse, and a Crow, a brave one that Crow, swung down from his own horse and ran towards Many Feathers swinging his war club. And Long Lance, rushing up from behind Many Feathers in the charge, almost past, too far past to turn his horse in time, leaped from its back and struck bodily against the Crow and sent him sprawling. The Crow scrambled to his feet and ran and another Crow swung back and took him up behind on his horse and all the Crows were scattering and riding off except two who would ride no more. Many Feathers, not minding his wound, was on his feet and shouting to his men to come back from the chasing because the horses were stampeding. It was when the horses, most of them, were gathered and quieted and moving along together again that they saw that one of their own men was missing. Many Feathers chose Long Lance to ride back with him and they found the body. They laid it in a low hidden place with head towards the east so that the spirit, hovering near, would find the spirit trail where all footprints point the same way. They left it there because it was right that the body of a man killed in battle far from his home village should become food for the birds and the animals of the plains who would scatter his bones across the earth from which all that he now was, with the spirit gone, had originally come. Then they saw the Crows, gathered together again, coming again, and they hurried to join the others and all chose fresh horses from the herd and pushed on fast. The Crows, with no fresh horses, not eager for another Cheyenne charge, followed until late afternoon, dropping back more all the time, and then were seen no more.

Strong Left Hand was full of words, talking about their son. Straight Willow said little and then she stopped him, raising her hand. 'We are happy for him. Why is he not happy too? Look.'

Strong Left Hand looked out through the lodge doorway. Over in the eastern arc of the camp circle where were the lodges of the O-missis, the Eaters, so known because they were always good hunters and well supplied with food, his youngest son sat on the ground before his still new lodge. His hunting weapons were beside him and his hunting horses were close by and he sat with his arms resting on his knees and his head sunk low. A sadness was on him.

Strong Left Hand set aside his bowl and rose. At sight of his son in sadness a shadow seemed to be over him fighting with the clean light of the morning. He spoke to Straight Willow. 'Perhaps there is trouble with him and his wife. They are still new together. Perhaps you can be close to her today and she will speak to you.' He drove the shadowing away from his mind. It was time for the hunting. He took his stout bow made of the horns of the mountain sheep, the bow that few other men could bend, and his quiver with twenty good arrows, arrows he had made from well-grained red willow shoots tipped with edged bone heads and firmly feathered. He took his hair-rope hackamore and the single pad he used for a hunting saddle and went out to his horses.

The whole camp was abustle now. The hunters were gathering. Women and older girls were starting off with digging sticks to find the white potato roots that grew on some of the slopesides. Other women were following the path downstream where a stand of cottonwoods beckoned them to gather wood. Already small children were assembling around two of the old men who would teach them stories of the old days and of the old ways of the tribe. Older boys were splashing across the river at the ford, holding their small bows above the water, bound for the marshy land beyond where they would practise shooting wild fowl and perhaps bring in food.

Straight Willow came out of the lodge, her sewing things in

her hand, the bone awl for punching holes in tanned hides and a handful of threads, separate strands plucked from the big sinew that follows along the spine of the buffalo. Her sewing guild was meeting to help one of the women to make a new lodge. She saw Strong Left Hand swinging up on the spotted horse in the Indian way, from the off side. 'Perhaps you will bring me an untorn bull's hide. It is in my mind to make a heavy robe.' He looked at her and he knew that she meant that his arrows should sing true and that he should come back to her unharmed, and in his mind he pledged to her the biggest bull of the day's hunting. He rode off, leading the grey horse, and was one with the hunters, all the able-bodied men of the camp, moving out across the plains.

They talked and laughed as they rode, for they were Cheyennes, a gay, and talkative people, but not too much now because this was not sport, like fighting, this was the most important work of men, the obtaining of food and of materials for clothes and lodges and the necessary articles of daily life. On the success of the hunting during these good days would depend the welfare of the tribe during the long snowbound months of winter.

Strong Left Hand rode up close by his youngest son, should he wish to speak. He would not press him, for a grown Cheyenne did not interfere with the thoughts and visions of another. He spoke of such things only when that other wished to speak of them and seek counsel. But now his son rode straight ahead, silent and stern.

The hunters rode on, far out across the plains, and then Many Feathers, in charge for this day, stopped and gave his orders. Scouts had reported a herd of buffalo over the next rolling rise. Quietly they changed to their hunting horses and left the heavier burden bearers in the keeping of a young man. In small groups, as Many Feathers directed, they slipped away to come on the herd from all sides.

Silence held over the plain under the climbing sun and the endlessly moving wind, broken only by the rustling of the buffalo in the grasses and their occasional small snorts and belchings. Suddenly from the far side a shouting rose and Many Feathers and his group rushed over the last rise between them and the buffalo, and the buffalo snorted loud, facing towards this disturbance, heads up, and then they turned and ran, slow at first, then galloping in their seemingly awkward gait that could outdistance all but the best horses. Ahead of them, shouting and waving, rose another group of mounted men, pounding towards them, and they swerved to the side, and ahead was another group. The buffalo snorted and galloped, tails stiffening upright in terror, and always a group of shouting men on horses was in front of them. And now they were running in a big circle, milling around it in the frantic feeling that because they were running they were escaping.

Many Feathers raised his bow high and waved it and the hunters began swooping in close to the milling buffalo, superb horsemen the equal of any the world had known, and their arrows sang death and mortal-wound songs in the dust-driven air. Buffalo staggered and fell and others stumbled over them and now and again a stricken animal would dash outward from the milling circle at the pounding horses, and the horses, quick and fast, would dodge and twist until an arrow struck true and the buffalo went down.

Strong Left Hand swept in close, wasting no arrows, searching always for the biggest bull. He would like to kill that one himself. Two cows and a young bull had gone down under his arrows, stopped almost in their tracks by the power of the big horn bow that few men could bend. Ah, there was strength still in his left arm, his bow-string arm, that had given him his name.

Ahead of him, hazy through the dust, he saw a horse step into an animal ground hole and its rider thrown towards the milling buffalo, and a huge old bull, bloody-frothed at the nostrils, come charging out towards the man. Another horse swooped in, its rider leaning down to pick up the fallen man, and the bull swerved and its great head drove under this horse's belly and its short thick horns ripped upward and its great neck strained and horse and rider rose into the air, the horse screaming, its legs flailing, and now two men were scrambling on the ground. Other men came swooping in, Strong Left Hand foremost among them. There was no time for full bow-draw and certain aim. His arrow struck too far forward, close by the shaggy neck, and drove in only a short way, slowed by the matted hair and thicker hide there. Yet it stopped the bull, made it pause, pawing the ground, shaking its great head. But the circle of hunters was now broken. The bull rushed through the opening, bellowing, and other buffalo followed, streaming across the plain.

Now it was the chase, the hard riding, the pounding after the fleeing buffalo, the riding alongside them and in among them. But the chase did not go far because the hunters had killed enough for one day's hunting and their arrows were nearly all gone. And back along the trail of the chase lay the huge old bull with another of Strong Left Hand's arrows driven deep into its side.

Now there was no more wild excitement, only hard drudgery, bloody work that would take much of the next day too, skinning and butchering and loading the meat on the slower, stronger horses, and the patient searching for arrows to use again. Only once was there an interruption when a warrior gave warning that he had seen a man peering over a nearby rise and Many Feathers sent two men to circle around while the rest stood ready by their horses, weapons in hand. Then the two men came back, straight over the rise, and a boy was with them leading a black horse with two white spots.

Strong Left Hand smiled to himself when he saw his nephew approaching. But Owl Friend, his brother, father of the boy, stepped forward, stern of face. 'What are you doing here?'

'To see the hunt, my father.'

'And to ride your new horse. I did not say you could come.'

The boy looked down at the ground and suddenly Owl Friend smiled at him. 'You are not much bigger than a badger, but you will be a brave hunter one day.' He took the boy by the hand and led him to Many Feathers. 'Here is a small man who thinks he is a hunter.'

Many Feathers, too, was stern. 'Is this the first hunt you have seen?'

'Yes, my chief.'

'Do you know what must happen the first time?'

The boy stared at him and then Many Feathers smiled. He bent down by the carcass of a buffalo and dipped his right hand in a pool of blood there and lifted it, dripping, and smeared the blood over the boy's face. 'Now you know how it feels, still warm from the life that was in it, how it smells, how it tastes.

You must not wipe it from your face until you are home. Now the time is for work. Take this knife that is yours from this day forward and do as I show you, freeing the hide from the good meat.'

The sun was low in the west, sending long shadows into the hollows, when the hunters returned to the camp, leading the loaded horses. As they neared it they passed many boys out on the plain playing games with sliding sticks and hoops and the boys, seeing them, ran up to race about and follow them. As they came nearer a group of older girls too was approaching the camp. They had been out digging bear roots and turnips and they carried tied bunches of them. They shouted at the hunters and raised the war cry, daring the young men to try to take their roots. Some of the young men called to boys to hold their horses and they ran towards the girls and the girls quickly dropped their roots and began gathering sticks and buffalo chips and clumps of sod and one of them took her root digger and drew a line in the ground all around them. Such a line was their fort and it could be passed only by a man who had counted a coup within enemy breastworks. The young men dashed around the line-circle, leaping and laughing and teasing and dodging the missiles thrown at them. One stepped inside and told his coup and the girls had to stand aside and let him take what roots he wanted. He scooped up several bunches and tossed them to the other young men and they all went towards their horses munching on the roots and throwing back teasing remarks at the girls. They were good young men, not too tired after the day's work for leaping and laughing. But Long Lance was not with them. He sat on his horse, stern and silent, and his head drooped.

Inside the camp circle the hunters separated to their lodges. Strong Left Hand stood his tired horses in front of his lodge and went down to the river for a thorough washing. Straight Willow came hurrying from woman-talk with a neighbour and un-loaded the spotted horse. Most of the meat she put away under covering. She would be busy now, beginning tomorrow, for many weeks, cutting this meat and that from other huntings into strips and flaking it into chips to be sun-dried and smoke-cured for winter saving and the other women would be doing the same and all of them gossiping endlessly around the drying racks. Three hides were there too, Strong Left Hand's share of the day's taking, and she put these where she would peg them on the ground for scraping. Then she led the spotted horse to the river to wash away the buffalo blood and fat clinging to its short hair. She rolled up her skirt and waded into the water with the horse and then, only then, her work well in hand, she looked over the horse's back at Strong Left Hand, who was sitting for a few moments' quiet and rest in the late sun.

'It's a good, big, very big bull's hide,' she said, and he knew she was saying more than that. The meadow lark had trilled true, for it was a good day. And then the shadow was over him again, for he saw his youngest son, Long Lance, walking on down by the lower river, slow and with a sadness on him.

Straight Willow saw too. 'His wife does not know. He has been like that since they came back with the horses. But she does not know.'

Strong Left Hand went back to the lodge and took a bunch of his stored willow shoots and sat on the edge of his couch and began smoothing and shaping them for arrows while Straight Willow rebuilt the fire and began her cooking. This was one of the times he liked, the two of them together in the quiet companionship built through the long years, the good years and the bad years and all part of living. This would be one of the best of days but for that shadow in his mind.

It was a fine meal as the evening meal of a successful hunting day should be. There was much meat, and there was feasting all around the camp. Soon darkness dropped over the land and the mystic living light of the many fires lit the camp. A huge fire began to glow out in the circle where the Kit Fox Soldiers would soon be having their social dance.

Strong Left Hand took out his pipe and filled it with tobacco mixed with dried bark of the red willow. He held it by the bowl and pointed with the stem to the sky and to the earth, making his offering to the father spirit above and to the mother earth below. He pointed the stem to the four cardinal points of the compass around, making his offering to the spirits that dwell in those quarters. He took a burning stick from the fire and lit the pipe and drew in the smoke with slow satisfaction. Straight Willow sat by the fire and watched him in quiet content, for no one should move about in a lodge when the pipe was being smoked.

Music began to sound through the camp. Drumming and songs were beginning by the dance-fire. The quick lively beat of a gambling song came from a nearby lodge where some were playing the hand-hiding game. Strong Left Hand put aside his pipe and took his big red shield, his Bull Soldier shield with the buffalo head painted on it, made of the thickest bullhide with deerskin stretched over it and raven feathers around the edge. He went out and as he moved away he saw several women coming towards his lodge. He smiled to himself. Straight Willow would be having company. He went on to the big temporary lodge that had been put up during the day well out into the camp circle by the wives of the Dog Soldiers. Most of the other men were already there.

To the left inside, in a line, were the Dog Soldiers, his son, Long Lance, among them. They would give a brave account of themselves this night. There were staunch old veterans among them and two of them were men who wore black-dog ropes into battle, leather loops that passed over their shoulders and under their other arms and had ropes fastened to them with picket pins at the ends. Such a man, dismounting to fight the enemy hand to hand, must stick his pin into the ground and in the doing pledge himself not to retreat from that spot. He himself, no matter how hard-pressed, must not pull the pin loose or be dishonoured forever after. Only another of his band could free him by pulling up the pin and striking him to drive him back. Such a man counted coups or died on the spot.

To the right were the Bull Soldiers, fewer in number but the same as many in experience and honours. And at the back of the lodge, behind the central fire, sat the man who would preside, as always an old man belonging to neither of the two competing bands. He was well chosen. He was Standing Elk, twice chief of the Elk Soldiers in his younger years, now one of the most honoured men of the tribe. He was wise and just and he knew well how to keep a competition close and exciting in his calling for coups. And he wore the scalp shirt.

Only three men in the entire tribe wore scalp shirts. Such a shirt could be made only by a man who had worn one. It could be worn only by a very brave man, a man who dedicated himself to his people. When he wore it, he must be the first to advance in battle, the last to retreat. If a comrade were dismounted or fell, he must dare all dangers to pick him up. He must act always as a chief should act, be above personal angers and quarrellings, not become angry even if his wife should run away or be carried away or his horse be stolen, never seek a personal vengeance. He must take care of widows and orphans, feed the hungry, help the helpless. Some men had worn the scalp shirt and given it up. Standing Elk had worn it many years and always with honour.

Strong Left Hand waited according to custom until Standing Elk pointed to the place kept for him. He went to it, passing behind the others, careful not to be so discourteous as to pass between anyone and the fire. He placed his big shield against the lodge wall behind his place and sat down before it. Two more men arrived and they were ready to begin. Standing Elk asked one of the young men to close off the entrance. He had beside him a pile of small sharpened sticks. His pipe lay on the ground before him with the bowl towards the south, the symbol of truth-telling. No true Cheyenne would speak false in its presence.

Standing Elk passed one of the pointed sticks to the first of the Dog Soldiers. 'Which one of you has counted a coup on foot against an enemy on horseback?' The Dog Soldier passed the stick to the next man and it went down the line until it reached a man who could claim it. He told his coup. The stick went back to Standing Elk and he stuck it in the ground on the Dog Soldiers' side. He started another stick down the Dog Soldier line and it came back unclaimed. He passed it to the Bull Soldiers and he passed yet another before they were through with that question and they had two sticks in the ground on their side.

Standing Elk asked his questions. He was a wise old man. He knew the history of every man there and he framed his questions to give everyone a chance to speak and to keep the score close. Good feelings and memories of brave deeds done, always good in the retelling, filled the big lodge. And yet young Long Lance, in his place in the Dog Soldier line, sat silent, his head sinking lower and lower. Now everyone else had spoken at least once and much time had passed and the sticks were even on the two sides. Standing Elk looked at young Long Lance and then he looked at Strong Left Hand and his old eyes twinkled in the firelight. He looked straight ahead. 'This is the last. Which one of you has leaped from a horse to count a coup against a Crow warrior by striking him with your whole body to save the life of your soldier chief?'

There was a stirring among the Dog Soldiers and a chuckling and they passed the stick quickly and the one beside Long Lance thrust it into his hand. Long Lance held it, but he could not speak. And suddenly he raised his head high and spoke with the strongest truth-telling pledge a Cheyenne could give. 'I say this to the Medicine Arrows. I did not do it. I did not know Many Feathers was down. I did not see the Crow warrior. The thong in my horse's mouth had broken and I was leaning forward to grasp his nose and guide him. He stumbled and threw me and I struck against the Crow. It was not my doing.' And Long Lance tossed the stick into the fire and his head dropped again.

The heart of Strong Left Hand was big within him. There was no shadow over him even in the dim darkness of the big lodge above him. His son was a brave man, brave enough not to grasp a false bravery. But it was not for him to speak. That was for Standing Elk. The silence in the lodge held, waiting.

And Standing Elk, his old eyes twinkling even more than before, picked up another stick. 'Which one of you has counted a coup because he had a horse that knew when to stumble and throw him against an enemy?' And the laughter in the lodge, the good feeling sweeping through it, seemed enough to lift it into the air. The stick passed down the line and young Long Lance held it and he raised his head, his face shining in the firelight, and spoke: 'I claim it as a coup only for this night so that the Red Shields must provide a feast for my brother soldiers. From this time forward I give it to Many Feathers as a laughing story to tell.'

The camp was quieting, most of the lodges were dark, only embers remained of the dance-fire, when Strong Left Hand entered his own lodge again. In the dark he heard the soft regular breathing of Straight Willow on her couch. He put away his shield and squatted on his heels by her couch to tell her of their son, and because he wanted to and she wanted him to, he told it to her again.

He rose and stood tall. There was no sleeping in him yet a while. Quietly he left the lodge and walked through the outer star-touched darkness, out of the camp circle, up to the top of the first rolling rise. Behind him, in the camp, the only firelight remaining shone faintly through the entrance of the lodge where the gambling game was still being played. Always there were a few men who would keep at that until they had nothing left to stake on the next chance. They played with whispers now that would not disturb other lodges. The only sound drifting to him from the camp except the occasional muffled shifting of horses' hoofs or stirring of a dog in its sleep was the faint trembling flute song of a lover serenading his sweetheart somewhere on the far side of the circle. And even this was not a real sound but a sweet pulsing of the silence.

He stood on the rise and stretched his arms upward and from him flowed a wordless prayer of thanking to the meadow lark of the morning of a good day and through this to the Great Mystery of which it was for him his personal symbol. He sat on the ground and the small night breeze moved through the grasses and the clean sweet dark was around him and in him and he was a part of the earth beneath and the sky above and the web of life they nurtured and it was good.

Why should the thought of old Standing Elk come into his mind at this moment? Ah, there was a man. A tribe needed men like that. They were an example to the young men, even to older men who had grown sons. Strong Left Hand rose and walked quietly back to his lodge. He took off his shirt and leggings and moccasins and lay on his couch. He spoke softly: 'O my wife.'

He heard her shift a little on her couch. 'What is it, my husband?'

'In the morning I will carry the pipe to Standing Elk. I will keep my grey horse and my spotted horse for the hunting and take my other three horses and a quiver of arrows to him as an offering. I will ask him to make me a scalp shirt.'

There was silence in the lodge. Strong Left Hand sighed gently to himself. It would be hard on her, it would mean more

work and a harder time for her, too, when he wore the shirt.
He heard her shifting on her couch again. 'O my husband.
Standing Elk is a great one of the tribe. There should be more.
You will take half of my horses too. We will have need of the
others when you wear the shirt.'

Strong Left Hand breathed in so deeply that he felt as if his
lungs would burst. A meadow lark sang in his heart.

That Mark Horse

Not that horse, mister. Not that big slab-sided brute. Take any or all of the rest, I'm selling the whole string. But not that one. By rights I should. He's no damn good to me. The best horse either one of us'll likely ever see and he's no damn good to me. Or me to him. But I'll not sell him. . . .

Try something, mister. Speak to him. The name's Mark. . . . There. See how his ears came up? See how he swung to check you and what you were doing? The way any horse would. Any horse that likes living and knows his name. But did you notice how he wouldn't look at me? Used to perk those ears and swing that head whenever he heard my voice. Not any more. Knows I'm talking about him right now and won't look at me. Almost ten months it is and he still won't look at me. . . .

That horse and I were five-six years younger when this all began. I was working at one of the early dude ranches and filling in at the rodeos roundabout. A little riding, a little roping. Not too good, just enough to place once in a while. I was in town one day for the mail and the postmaster poked his head out to chuckle some and say there was something for me at the station a mite too big for the box. I went down and the agent wasn't there. I scouted around and he was out by the stock corral and a bunch of other men too all leaning on the fence and looking over. I pushed up by the agent and there was that horse inside. He was alone in there and he was the damnedest horse I'd ever seen. Like the rest around I'd been raised on cow ponies and this thing looked big as the side of a barn to me and awkward as all hell. He'd just been let down the chute from a box car on the siding. There were bits of straw clinging to him and he stood still with head up testing the air.

For that first moment he looked like a kid's crazy drawing of a horse, oversize and exaggerated with legs too long and big stretched-out barrel and high-humped withers and long-reaching neck. The men were joshing and wondering was it an elephant or a giraffe and I was agreeing and then I saw that horse move. He took a few steps walking and flowed forward into a trot. That's the only way to put it. He flowed forward the way water rolls down a hill. His muscles didn't bunch and jump under his hide. They slid easy and smooth and those long legs reached for distance without seeming to try. He made a double circuit of the corral without slowing, checking everything as he went by. He wasn't trying to find a way out. He just wanted to move some and see where he was and what was doing roundabout. He saw us along the fence and we could have been posts for all the particular attention he paid us. He stopped by the far fence and stood looking over it and now I'd seen him move there wasn't anything awkward about him. He was big and he was rough-built but he wasn't awkward any more even standing there still. Nobody was saying a word. Everyone there knew horses and they'd seen what I saw. 'Damn it to eternal hell,' I said. 'That's a horse.' The agent turned and saw who it was. 'Glad you think so,' he said. 'It's your horse. This came along too.' And he stuck a note in my hand.

It had my name on it all right. It was from a New York State man who ran some sort of factory there, made shoes I think he told me once. He'd been a regular at the ranch, not for any dude doings but once a summer for a camping trip and I'd been assigned to him several years running. It wasn't long. It said the doctors had been carving him some and told him he couldn't ride again so he was closing his stable. He'd sold his other stock but thought this horse Mark ought to be out where there was more room than there was back east. Wanted me to take him and treat him right.

I shoved that note in a pocket and eased through the fence. 'Mark,' I called and across the corral those ears perked stiff and that big head swung my way. 'Mark,' I called again and that horse turned and came about half-way and stood with head high, looking me over. I picked a coil of rope off a post and shook out a loop and he watched me with ears forward and head a bit to one side. I eased close and suddenly I snaked up the loop and it was open right for his head and he just wasn't there. He was thirty feet to the left and I'd have sworn he made it in one leap. Maybe a dozen times I tried and I didn't have a chance. The comments coming from the fence line weren't improving my temper any. Then I noticed he wasn't watching me, he was watching the rope, and I had an attack of common sense. He was wearing a halter. This wasn't any western range horse. This was one of those big eastern crossbreds with a lot of thoroughbred in them I'd heard about. Likely he'd never had a rope thrown at him before. I tossed the rope over by the fence and walked towards him and he stood blowing his nostrils a bit and looking at me. I stopped a few feet away and didn't even try to reach for the halter. He looked at me and he was really seeing me the way a horse can and I was somebody who knew his name out here where he'd been dumped out of the darkness of a boxcar. He stretched that long neck and sniffed at my shirt and I took hold of the halter and that was all there was to it....

That was the beginning of my education. Yes, mister, it was me had to be taught, not that horse. The next lesson came the first time I tried to ride him. I was thinking what a big brute he was and what a lot of power was penned in him and I'd have to control all that so I used a Spanish spade bit that would be wicked if used rough. He didn't want to take it and I had to force it on him. The same with the saddle. I used a double-rig with a high-roll cantle and he snorted at it and kept sidling away and grunted all the time I was tightening the cinches. He stood steady enough when I swung aboard but when we started off nothing felt right. The saddle was too small for him and sat too high-arched over the backbone and those sloping withers. He kept wanting to drop his head and rub his mouth on his legs over that bit. At last he sort of sighed and eased out and went along without much fuss. He'd decided I was plain stupid on some things and he'd endure and play along for a while. At the time I thought he was accepting me as boss so I started him really stepping and the instant he understood I wanted him to move that was what he did. He moved. He went from a walk into a gallop in a single flowing rush and it was only that high cantle kept me from staying behind. I'm telling you,

mister, that was something, the feel of those big muscles sliding smooth under me and distance dropping away under those
hoofs.

Then I realized he wasn't even working. I was travelling faster than I ever had on horseback and he was just loafing along
without a sign of straining for speed. That horse just liked moving. I never knew another liked it as much. It could get to him
the way liquor can a man and he'd keep reaching for more.
That's what he was doing then. I could feel him notching it up
the way an engine does when the engineer pushes forward on
the throttle and I began to wonder how he'd be on stopping.
I had an idea twelve hundred pounds of power moving like that
would be a lot different from eight hundred pounds of bunchy
little cow pony. I was right. I pulled in some and he slowed
some but not much and I pulled harder and he tossed his head at
the bit, biting, and I yanked in sharp and he stopped. Yes,
mister, he stopped all right. But he didn't slap down on his
haunches and slide to a stop on his rump the way a cow pony
does. He took a series of jumps stiff-legged to brake and stopped short and sudden with his legs planted like trees and I went
forward, bumping my belly on the horn and over his head and
hanging there doubled down over his ears with my legs
clamped around his neck. That Mark horse was surprised as I
was but he took care of me. He kept his head up and stood
steady as a rock while I climbed down his neck to the saddle. I
was feeling foolish and mad at myself and him and I yanked
mean on the reins and swung him hard to head for home and
that did it. He'd had enough. He shucked me off his back the
way someone might toss a bean-bag. Don't ask me how. I'd ridden plenty horses and could make a fair showing even on the
tough ones. But that Mark horse wanted me off so he put me
off. And then he didn't bolt for the horizon. He stopped about
twenty feet away and stood there watching me.

I sat on the ground and looked at him. I'd been stupid but I
was beginning to learn. I remembered the feel of him under me,
taking me with him not trying to get away from me. I remembered how he'd behaved all along and I studied on all that.
There wasn't a trace of meanness in that horse. He didn't mind
being handled and ridden. He'd been ready and willing for me
to come up and take him in the station corral. But he wasn't

going to have a rope slapped at him and be yanked around. He was ready and willing to let me ride him and to show me how a real horse could travel. But he wasn't going to do much of it with a punishing bit and a rig he didn't like. He was a big batch of damned good horseflesh and he knew that and was proud of it and he had a hell of a lot of self-respect. He just plain wouldn't be pushed around and that was that and I had to understand it. I claim it proud for myself that I did. I went to him and he waited for me as I knew now he would. I swung easy as I could up into the saddle and he stood steady with his head turned a little so he could watch me. I let the lines stay loose and guided him just by neck-reining and I walked him back to the ranch. I slid down there and took off the western saddle and the bridle with that spade bit. I hunted through the barn till I found a light snaffle bit and cleaned it and put it in the bridle. I held it up for him to see and he took it with no fuss at all. I routed out the biggest of the three English saddles we had for eastern dudes who wouldn't use anything else and that I'd always thought were damned silly things. I showed it to him and he stood quiet while I slapped it on and buckled the single leather cinch. 'Mark,' I said, 'I don't know how to sit one of these crazy postage stamps and I'm bunged up some from that beating. Let's take it easy.' Mister, that horse knew what I'd said. He gave me the finest ride I ever had. . . .

See what I mean, the best damn horse either of us'll ever see? No, I guess you can't. Not complete. You'd have to live with him day after day and have the endless little things happening tally up in your mind. After a while you'd understand as I did what a combination he was of a serious dependable gent and a mischievous little kid. With a neat sense of timing on those things too. Take him out for serious riding and he'd tend strict to his business, which was covering any kind of ground for you at any kind of speed you wanted. The roughest going made no difference to him. He was built to go at any clip just about anywhere short of straight up a cliff, and you'd get the feeling he'd try that if you really wanted him to. But let him loaf around with nothing to do and he'd be curious as a cat on the prowl, poking into every corner he could find and seeing what devilment he could do. Nothing mean, just playful. Maybe a nuisance if you were doing a job where he could get at you and push his big carcass in the way whiffling at everything or come up quiet behind and blow sudden down your shirt collar. Let him get hold of a bucket and you'd be buying a new one. There'd not be much left of the old one after he'd had his fun. He'd stick his nose in and flip the thing and do that over and over like he was trying for a distance record then start whamming it around with his hoofs, tickled silly at the racket. And when there'd be no one else around to see how crazy you were acting he'd get you to playing games too. He liked to have you sneak off and hide and whistle low for him and he'd pad around stretching that long neck into the damnedest places looking for you and blow triumphant when he found you. Yes, mister, that horse liked living and being around him'd help you do the same.

And work? That horse was a working fool. No. There was nothing foolish about it. The ranch was still in the beef business too in those days and he'd never had any experience with cattle before. He was way behind our knowing little cow ponies when it came to handling them and he knew it. So he tried to balance that by using those brains of his overtime and working harder than any of the others. He'd watch them and try to figure what they were doing and how they did it and then do it himself. He'd try so hard sometimes I'd ache inside, feeling that eagerness quivering under me. Of course he never could catch up to them on some things. Too big. Too eager. Needed too much room moving around. He couldn't slide into a tight bunch of cattle and cut out the right one, easing it out without disturbing the rest much. And he wasn't much good for roping even though he did let me use a western saddle for that soon as he saw the sense to it. Lunged too hard when I'd looped an animal and was ready to throw it. Maybe he'd have learned the right touch in time but he didn't get the chance. The foreman saw us damn near break a steer's neck and told us to quit. But on straight herding he couldn't be beat. He could head a runaway steer before it even stretched it legs. He could scour the bush for strays like a hound dog on a scent. He could step out and cover territory all day at a pace that'd kill off most horses and come in seeming damn near as fresh as when he started. I used to think I was tough and could take long hours but that horse could ride me right out of the saddle and act like he thought I was soft for calling a halt.

But I still haven't hit the real thing. That horse was just plain honest all through. No, that's not the exact word. Plenty of horses are that. He was something a bit more. Square. That's it. He was just plain square in everything he did and the way he looked at living. He liked to have things fair and even. He was my horse and he knew it. I claim it proud that for a time anyway he really was my horse and let me know it. But that meant too I was his man and I had my responsibilities. I wasn't a boss giving orders. I was his partner. He wasn't something I owned doing what I made him do. He was my partner doing his job because he wanted to and because he knew that was the way it ought to be with a man and a horse. A horse like him. Long as I treated him right he'd treat me right. If I'd get mean or stupid with him I'd be having trouble. I'd be taking another lesson. Like the time along about the second or third week when I was feeling safer on that English saddle and forgot he wasn't a hard-broke cow pony. I wanted a sudden burst of speed for one reason or another and I hit him with my spurs. I was so used to doing that with the other horses that I couldn't figure at first what had happened. I sat on the ground rubbing the side I'd lit on and stared at him watching me about twenty feet away. Then I had it. I unfastened those spurs and threw them away. I've never used the things again ever, any time on any horse. . . .

Well, mister, there I was mighty proud to have a horse like that but still some stupid because I hadn't tumbled to what you might call his speciality. He had to show me. It was during fall round-up. We had a bunch of steers in the home corral being culled for market and something spooked them and they started milling wild and pocketed me and Mark in a corner. They were slamming into the fence rails close on each side. I knew we'd have to do some fancy stepping to break through and get around them. I must have felt nervous on the reins because that Mark horse took charge himself. He swung away from those steers and leaped straight at the near fence and sailed over it. He swung in a short circle and stopped looking back at those steers jamming into the corner where we'd been and I sat the saddle catching the breath he'd jolted out of me.

I should have known. He was a jumper. He was what people back east called a hunter. Maybe he'd been a timber horse, a steeplechaser. He'd cleared that four-foot fence with just about no take-off space like a kid skipping at hopscotch. I'm telling you, mister, I had me a time the next days jumping him over everything in sight. When I was sure of my seat I made him show me what he really could do and he played along with me for anything within reason, even stretching that reason considerable. The day I had nerve enough and he took me smack over an empty wagon I really began to strut. But there was one thing he wouldn't do. He wouldn't keep jumping the same thing over and over the same time out. Didn't see any sense in that. He'd clear whatever it was maybe twice, maybe three times, and if I tried to put him at it again he'd stop cold and swing his head to look at me and I'd shrivel down to size and feel ashamed. . . .

So I had something new in these parts then, a jumping horse bred to it and built for it with the big frame to take the jolts and the power to do it right. I had me a horse could bring me some real money at the rodeos. I wouldn't have to try for prize money. I could put on exhibition stunts. I got together with some of the old show hands and we worked up an act that pleased the crowd. They'd lead Mark out so the people could see the size of him and he'd plunge around at the end of the shank, rolling his eyes and tossing his head. He'd paw at the sky and lash out behind like he was the worst mean-tempered mankiller ever caught. It was all a joke because he was the safest horse any man ever handled and anyone who watched close could see those hoofs never came near connecting with anything except air. But he knew what it was all about and he made it look good. The wranglers would get him over and into the outlaw chute with him pretending to fight all the way. They'd move around careful outside and reach through the bars to bridle and saddle him like they were scared green of him. I'd climb to the top rails and ease down on the saddle like I was scared too but determined to break my neck trying to ride one hell of a bucking brute. We'd burst out of the chute like a cannon going off and streak for the high fence on the opposite side of the arena. All the people who'd not seen it before would come up gasping on their seats expecting a collision that would shake the whole place. And at the last second that horse Mark would rise up and over the fence in a clean, sweet jump, and I'd be standing in the stirrups waving my hat and yelling and the crowd'd go wild.

After a time most people knew what to expect and the surprise part of that act was gone so we had to drop it. But we worked up another that got the crowds no matter how many times they saw it. I never liked it much but I blew too hard once how that horse would jump anything and someone suggested this and I was hot and said sure he'd do it and I was stuck with it. He never liked it much either but he did it for me. Maybe he knew I was getting expensive habits and needed the money coming in. Well, anyway, we did it and it took a lot of careful practice with a slow old steer before we tried the real thing. I'd be loafing around on Mark in the arena while the bull riding was on. I'd watch and pick a time when one of the bulls had thrown his rider and was hopping around in the clear or making a dash across the open. I'd nudge Mark with my heels and he'd be off in that forward flowing with full power in it. We'd streak for the bull angling in at the side and the last sliced second before a head-on smash we'd lift and go over in a clean sweep and swing to come up by the grandstand and take the applause.

Thinking of that since I've been plenty shamed. I've a notion the reason people kept wanting to see it wasn't just to watch a damned good horse do a damned difficult job. They were always hoping something would happen. Always a chance the bull might swerve and throw us off stride and make it a real smash. Always a chance the horns might toss too high and we'd tangle with them and come down in a messy scramble. But I didn't think about that then or how I was asking more than a man should expect in a tight spot that can't be avoided from a horse that's always played square with him. I was thinking of the money and the cheers and the pats on the back. And then it happened. . . .

Not what maybe you're thinking, mister. Not that at all. That horse never failed in a jump and never would. We'd done our stint on the day, done it neat and clean, gone over a big head-tossing bull with space to spare and were just about ready to take the exit gate without bothering to open it. Another bull was in the arena, a mean, tricky one that'd just thrown his rider after a tussle and was scattering dust real mad. The two tenders on their cagey little cow ponies had cut in to let the rider scramble to safety and were trying to hustle the bull into the closing out pen. They thought they had him going in and were starting to relax in their saddles when that brute broke away and tore out into the open again looking for someone on foot to take apart. While the tenders were still wheeling to go after him he saw something over by the side fence and head towards it fast. I saw too and sudden I was cold all over. Some damn fool woman had let a little boy get away from her, maybe three-four years old, too young to have sense, and that kid had crawled through the rails and was twenty-some feet out in the arena. I heard people screaming at him and saw him standing there confused and the bull moving and the tenders too far away. I slammed my heels into Mark and we were moving too the way only that horse could move. I had to lunge forward along his neck or he'd have been right out from under me. There wasn't time to head the bull or try to pick up the kid. There wasn't time for anything fancy at all. There was only one thing could be done. We swept in angling straight to the big moving target of that bull and I slammed down on the reins with all my strength so Mark couldn't get his head up to jump and go over, and in the last split second all I could think of was my leg maybe getting caught between when they hit and I dived off Mark sidewise into the dust and he drove on alone and smashed into that bull just back of the big sweeping horns.

They picked me up half dazed with an aching head and assorted bruises and put me on some straw bales in the stable till a doctor could look me over. They led Mark into one of the stalls with a big gash from one of the horns along his side and a swelling shoulder so painful he dragged the leg without trying to step on it. They put ropes on the bull where he lay quiet with the fight knocked out of him and prodded him up and led him off. I never did know just what happened to the kid except that he was safe enough. I didn't care because when I pushed up off those bales without waiting for the doctor and went into the stall that Mark horse wouldn't look at me. . . .

So that's it, mister. That's what happened. But I won't have

you getting any wrong notions about it. I won't have you telling me the way some people do that horse is through with me
because I made him smash into that bull. Nothing like that at
all. He doesn't blame me for the pulled tendon in his shoulder
that'll bother him long as he lives when the weather's bad. Not
that horse. I've thought the whole business over again and
again. I can remember every last detail of those hurrying seconds in the arena, things I wasn't even aware of at the time itself. That horse was flowing forward before I slammed my
heels into him. There wasn't any attempt at lifting that big
head or any gathering of those big muscles under me for a
jump when I was slamming down on the reins. He'd seen. He
knew. He knew what had to be done. That horse is through
with me because at the last second I went yellow and I let him
do it alone. He thinks I didn't measure up in the partnership. I
pulled out and let him do it alone.

He'll let me ride him even now but I've quit that because it
isn't the same. Even when he's really moving and the weather's
warm and the shoulder feels good and he's reaching for distance and notching it up in the straight joy of eating the wind
he's doing that alone too. I'm just something he carries on his
back and he won't look at me. . . .

Jacob

Those moccasins? Mine. Though I never wore them. Had them on just once to see if they fitted. They did. A bit tight but I could get them on.

Don't touch them. The leather's old and dry and the stitching rotted. Ought to be. They've been hanging there a long time. Look close and you can see the craftsmanship. The best. They're Nez Percé moccasins. Notice the design worked into the leather. It's faint now but you can make it out. Don't know how they did that but the Nez Percé could really work leather. A professor who studied such things told me once that design means they're for a chief. For his ceremonial appearances, sort of his dress-up footwear. Said only a chief could use that design. But it's there. Right there on those moccasins.

Yes. They're small. Boy size. That's because I was a boy then. But they're a chief's moccasins all the same. Kept them down the years because I'm proud of them. And because they mind me of a man. He had a red skin. Copper would be closer the colour. A muddy copper. And I only saw him once. But he was a man.

That was a long way from here. A long way. In years and in miles. I was ten then, maybe eleven, maybe twelve, in that neighbourhood, I disremember exactly. Best I can do is place it in the late seventies. Funny how definite things like dates and places slip away and other stray things, like the way you felt at certain times and how your first wild strawberries tasted, can remain clear and sharp in your mind. We were living, my folks and my older brother and myself, in a little town in eastern Montana. Not much of a place. Just a small settlement on the railroad that wouldn't have amounted to anything except that it had a stretch of double track where a train going one direction could pull off to let one going the other get past. My father was a switchman. Looked after track and handled the west-end switch. That was why we were there.

The Indian smell was still in the air in those days. People around here and nowadays wouldn't know what that means. It was a knowing and a remembering that not so far away were still real live free-footed fighting Indians that might take to raiding again. They were pegged on treaty lands and supposed to stay there. But they were always hot over one thing or another, settlers gnawing into their hunting grounds or agents pinching their rations or maybe the government forgetting to keep up treaty payments. You never knew when they might get to figuring they'd been pushed far enough and would start council fires up in the hills and come sudden and silent out of the back trails, making trouble. It was only a year or two since the Custer affair on the Little Big Horn south-west of where we were. No one with any experience in those things expected the treaty that ended that business to hold long.

Don't take me wrong. We didn't look for Indians behind bushes and sit around shivering at night worrying about attacks. The nearest reservation was a fair jump away and if trouble started we'd know about it long before it reached us, if it ever did. Matter of fact it never did. I grew up in that territory and never once was mixed in any Indian trouble past an argument over the price of a blanket. Never even saw any fighting Indians except this once I'm telling about and then they weren't fighting any more. It was just a smell in the air, the notion there might be trouble any time. Indians were quite a topic when I was a boy and the talk of an evening chewed it plenty.

Expect I heard as much of it as any of the boys around our settlement. Maybe more. My father had been in the midst of the Sioux outbreak in Minnesota in the early sixties. He'd seen things that could harden a man. They settled his mind on the subject. 'Only good Indian,' he'd say, 'is a dead one.' Yes. That's not just a saying out of the storybooks. There were men who really said it. And believed it. My father was one. Said it and believed it and said it so often I'd not be stretching the truth past shape to figure he averaged it couple times a week and so naturally we boys believed it too, hearing it all the time. I'll not argue with anyone wants to believe it even today. I'm only telling you what happened to me.

Hearing that kind of talk we boys around the settlement had our idea what Indians were like. I can speak for myself anyway. The Indians I saw sometimes passing through on a train or loafing around a town the few times I was in one with the folks didn't count. They were tame ones. They were scrawny mostly and they hung around where white people were and traded some and begged liquor when they couldn't buy it. They weren't dangerous or even interesting. They didn't matter more'n mules or dogs or anything like that cluttering the landscape. It was the wild ones filled my mind, the fighting kind that lived the way they always had and went on the warpath, and made the government send out troops and sign treaties with them. Can't recall exactly what I thought they looked like, but they were big and fierce and dangerous and they liked to burn out homesteaders' cabins and tie people to wagon wheels and roast them alive over slow fires, and it took a brave man to go hunting them and look at them down the sights of his gun. Days I felt full of ginger I'd plan to grow up quick and be an Indian fighter. Late afternoon, before evening chores, I'd scout the countryside with the stick I used for a gun and when I'd spot a spray of red sumac poking out of a brush clump, I'd belly-it in the grass and creep to good cover and poke my gun through and draw my bead. I'd pull on the twig knob that was my trigger and watch careful, and sometimes I'd have to fire again and then I'd sit up and cut another notch on the stick. I had my private name for that. Making good Indians, I called it.

What's that got to do with those moccasins? Not much I guess. But I'm telling this my way. It's all part of what I remember when I sit back and study those moccasins a spell.

The year I'm talking about was a quiet one with the Sioux but there was some Indian trouble all right, along in the fall and a ways away, over in the Nez Percé country in Idaho. It started simple enough like those things often did. There was this band lived in a valley, maybe seven hundred of them all told, counting the squaws and young ones. Biggest safe estimate I heard was three hundred braves, fighting men I mean. Can't remember the name of the valley, though I should. My brother settled there. But I can recall the name of the chief. That sticks. Always will. Not the Indian of it because that was a fancy mouthful. What it meant. Mountain Elk. Not that exactly. Big-Deer-That-Walks-the-High-Places. Mountain Elk is close enough. But people didn't call him that. Most Indians had a short name got tagged to them somehow and were called by it. His was Jacob. Sounded funny first time I heard it but not after I'd been hearing it a while.

As I say, this trouble started simple enough. We heard about it from the telegraph operator at the settlement who took his meals at our place. He picked up information relaying stuff through his key. News of all kinds and even military reports. Seems settlers began closing in around Jacob's valley and right soon began looking at the land there. Had water which was important in that country. Some of them pushed in and Jacob and his boys pushed them back out. So complaints were being made and more people wanted to move in, and talk went around that land like that was too good for Indians anyway because they didn't use it right, the way white men would, and when there was enough steam up a government man went in to see Jacob. Suggested the band would be better off living on some outside reservation. Get regular rations and have an agent to look after them. No, Jacob said, he and his were doing all right. Had been for quite a spell and expected to keep on doing the same. Sent his thanks to the Great White Chief for thinking about him but he wasn't needing any help. So after a while the pressure was stronger and another government man went in. Offered to buy the land and move the band in style to a reservation. No, said Jacob, he and his children – he called them all his children though he wasn't much past thirty himself – he and his children liked their land and weren't interested in selling. Their fathers had given up land too much in the past and been forced to keep wandering and had found this place when no one wanted it, and it was good and they had stayed there. Most of them then living had been born there and they wanted to die there too and that was that.

Well, the pressure went on building and there were ruckuses here and yonder around the valley when some more settlers tried moving in and a bunch of young braves got out of hand and killed a few. So another government man went in, this time with a soldier escort. He didn't bother with arguing or bargaining. He told Jacob the Great White Chief had issued a decree and this was that the whole tribe was to be moved by such and such a date. If they went peaceable, transportation would be provided and good rations. If they kept on being subborn, soldiers would come and make them move and that would be a bad business all around. Yes, said Jacob, that would be a bad business but it wouldn't be his doing. He and his children wouldn't have made the storm but they would stand up to it if it came. He had spoken and that was that.

So the days went along towards the date set which was in the fall I'm telling about. Jacob and his band hadn't made any preparations for leaving and the officer in charge of this whole operation thought Jacob was bluffing and he'd just call that bluff. He sent about four hundred soldiers under some colonel into the valley the week before the moving was supposed to happen, and Jacob and the others, the whole lot of them, just faded away from their village and off into the mountains behind the valley. The colonel sent scouting parties after them but couldn't make contact. He didn't know what to do in that situation so he set up camp there in the valley to wait and got real peeved when some of Jacob's Nez Percés slipped down out of the mountains one night and stampeded his stock. Finally he had his new orders and on the supposed moving day he carried them out. He put his men to destroying the village and they wiped it level to the ground, and the next morning early there was sharp fighting along his upper picket lines and he lost quite a few men before he could jump his troops into the field in decent force.

That was the beginning. The government wanted to open the valley for homesteading but couldn't without taking care of Jacob first. This colonel tried. He chased Jacob and his band into the mountains and thought overtaking them would be easy with the squaws and young ones slowing Jacob down, but Jacob had hidden them off somewhere and was travelling light with his braves. He led this colonel a fast run through rough country and caught him off watch a few times and whittled away at his troops every odd chance till this colonel had to turn back, not being outfitted for a real campaign. When he, that'd be this colonel, got back he found Jacob had beat him there and made things mighty unpleasant for those left holding the camp before slipping away again. About this time the government realized what it was up against and recalled the colonel and maybe whoever was his boss, and assigned a general – a brigadier – to the job and began mounting a real expedition.

We heard plenty about what happened after that, not just from the telegraph operator but from my brother who was busting the seams of his breeches those days and wanting to strike out for himself, and signed with the freighting company that got the contract carting supplies for the troops. He didn't see any of the fighting but he was close to it several times and he wrote home what was happening. Once a week he'd promised to write and did pretty well at it. He'd send his letters along to be posted whenever any of the wagons were heading back, and my mother would read them out to my father and me when they arrived. Remember best the fat one came after he reached the first camp and saw Jacob's valley. Took him two chunks of paper both sides to tell about it. Couldn't say enough about the thick green grass and the stream tumbling into a small lake and running quiet out again, and the good trees stepping up the far slopes and the mountains climbing on to the end of time all around. Made a man want to put his feet down firm on the ground and look out steady like the standing trees and stretch tall. Expect that's why my brother quit his job soon as the trouble was over and drove his own stakes there.

Yes. I know. I'm still a long way from those moccasins. I'm over in Idaho in Jacob's valley. But I get to remembering and then I get to forgetting maybe you're not interested in all the sidelines of what I started to tell you. I'll try to move it faster.

As I was saying, the government outfitted a real expedition to go after Jacob. A brigadier-general and something like a thousand men. There's no point telling all that happened except that this expedition didn't accomplish much more than that first colonel and his men did. They chased Jacob farther and almost penned him a few times and killed a lot of braves and got wind of where his women and their kids were hidden, and forced him to move them farther into the mountains with them getting out just in time, not being able to carry much with them. But that wasn't catching Jacob and stopping him and his braves from carrying on their hop-skip-and-jump war against all whites in general and these troops in particular. Then a second general went in and about a thousand more soldiers with them and they had hard fighting off and on over a couple hundred miles and more, and the days drove on into a deep winter and Jacob was licked. Not by the government and its soldiers and their guns. By the winter. He and his braves, what was left of them, had kept two generals and up to two thousand troops busy for four months fighting through parts of three states and then the winter licked him. He came to the second general under truce in what remained of his Chief's rig and took off his headdress and laid it on the ground and spoke. His children were scattered in the mountains, he said, and the cold bit sharp and they had few blankets and no food. Several of the small ones had been found frozen to death. From the moment the sun passed overhead that day he would fight no more. If he was given time to search for his children and bring them together he would lead them wherever the Great White Chief wished.

There. I'm closer to those moccasins now even though I'm still way over in Idaho. No. Think it was in western Montana where Jacob surrendered to that second general. Well, the government decided to ship these Nez Percés to the Dump, which was what people called the Indian Territory where they chucked all the tribes whose lands weren't just cut down but were taken away altogether. That meant Jacob and his children, all that was left of them, about three hundred counting the squaws and kids, would be loaded on a special train and sent along the railroad that ran through our settlement. These Nez Percé Indians would be passing within a stone's throw of our house and we would have a chance to see them at least through the windows and maybe, if there was need for switching, the train would stop and we would have a good look.

Wonder if you can scratch up any real notion what that meant to us boys around the settlement. To me maybe most of all. These weren't tame Indians. These were wild ones. Fighting Indians. About the fightingest Indians on record. Sure, the Sioux wiped out Custer. But there was a lot more Sioux than soldiers in that scuffle. These Nez Percés had held their own mighty well against a big chunk of the whole United States Army of those days. They were so outnumbered it had got past being even a joke. Any way you figured, it had been about one brave

167

to six or seven soldiers and those braves hadn't been well armed at the start and had to pick up guns and ammunition as they went along from soldiers they killed. Some of them were still using arrows at the finish. I'm not being funny when I tell you they kept getting bigger and fiercer in my mind all the time I was hearing about that long running fight in the mountains. It was notches for Nez Percés I was cutting on my stick now and the way I felt about them, even doing that took nerve.

The day came the train was to pass through, some time late afternoon was the first report, and all of us settlement boys stayed near the telegraph shack waiting. It was cold, though there wasn't much snow around. We'd sneaked into the shack where there was a stove, till the operator was peeved at our chattering and shooed us out, and I expect I did more than my share of the chattering because in a way these were my Indians because my brother was connected with the expedition that caught them. Don't think the other boys liked how I strutted about that. Well, anyway, the sun went down and we all had to scatter home for supper and the train hadn't come. Afterwards some of us slipped back to the shack and waited some more while the operator cussed at having to stick around waiting for word, and one by one we were yanked away when our fathers came looking for us, and still the train hadn't come.

It was some time past midnight and I'd finally got to sleep when I popped up in bed at a hammering on the door. I looked into the kitchen. Father was there in his nightshirt opening the outside door and the operator was on the step cussing some more that he'd had word the train was coming, would get there in half an hour, and they'd have to switch it and hold it till the westbound night freight went past. Father added his own cussing and pulled on his pants and boots and heavy jacket and lit his lantern. By time he'd done that I had my things on too. My mother was up then and objecting, but my father thought some and shushed her. 'Fool kid,' he said, 'excited about Indians all the time. Do him good to see what thieving smelly things they are.' So I went with him. The late moon was up and we could see our way easy and I stayed in the shack with the operator and my father went off to set his signal and tend his switch. Certain enough, in about twenty minutes the train came along and swung on to the second line of track and stopped.

The telegraph operator stepped out and started talking to a brakeman. I was scared stiff. I stood in the shack doorway and looked at the train and I was shaking inside like I had some kind of fever. It wasn't much of a train. Just an engine and little fuel car and four old coaches. No caboose. Most trains had cabooses in those days because they carried a lot of brakemen. Had to have them to wrangle the hand brakes. Expect the brakeman the operator was talking to was the only one this train had. Expect that was why it was so late. I mean the railroad wasn't wasting any good equipment and any extra men on this train, and it was being shoved along slow when and as how between other trains.

I stood there shaking inside and the engine was wheezing some and the engineer and fireman were moving slow and tired around it, fussing with an oilcan and a tin of grease. That was the only sign of life I could see along the whole train. What light there was in the coaches, only one lantern lit in each, wasn't any stronger than the moonlight outside and that made the windows blank-like and I couldn't see through them. Except for the wheezing engine, that train was a tired and sleeping or dead thing on the track. Then I saw someone step down from the first coach and stretch and move into the moonlight. He was a soldier, a captain, and he looked tired and sleepy and disgusted with himself and the whole world. He pulled a cigar from a pocket and leaned against the side of the coach, lighting the cigar and blowing out smoke in a slow puff. Seeing him so lazy and casual, I stopped shaking and moved into the open and closer to the coach and shifted around trying to find an angle that would stop the light reflection on the windows and let me see in. Then I stopped still. The captain was looking at me. 'Jee-sus,' he said. 'Why does everybody want to gawk at them? Even kids.' He took a long drag on his cigar and blew a pair of fat smoke rings. 'You must want to bad,' he said. 'Up so late. Go on in take a look.' I stared at him, scared now two ways. I was scared to go in where those Indians were and scared not to, after he'd said I could and just about ordered I should. 'Go ahead,' he said. 'They don't eat boys. Only girls.

Only at lunchtime.' And suddenly I knew he was making a joke, and it would be all right, and I went up the steps to the front platform and peered in.

Indians. Fighting Indians. The fighting Nez Percés who had led United States soldiers a bloody chase through the mountains of three states. The big and fierce redmen who had fought many times their own number of better armed soldiers to a frequent standstill in the high passes. And they weren't big and they weren't fierce at all. They were huddled figures on the coach seats, two to a seat down the twin rows, braves and squaws and young ones alike, all dusty and tired and hunched together at the shoulders in drowsy silence or sprawled apart over the window sills and seat arms in sleep. In the dim light they looked exactly like the tame Indians I'd seen, and they seemed to shrink and shrivel even more as I looked at them and there was no room in me for any emotion but disappointment, and when I noticed the soldiers sleeping in the first seats close to me I sniffed to myself at the silly notion any guards might be needed on that train. There wasn't the slightest hint of danger anywhere around. Being on that train was no different from being off it except that it was being on a stopped train and not being outside on the ground. It didn't even take any particular nerve to do what I did when I started walking down the aisle.

The only way I know to describe it is that I was in a sort of trance of disappointment and I wanted to see everything and I went straight down the aisle looking all around me. And those Indians acted like I wasn't there at all. Those that were awake. Each of them had his eyes fixed somewhere, maybe out a window or at the floor or just at some point ahead, and didn't move them. They knew I was there. I could tell that. A feeling. A little crawling on my skin. But they wouldn't look at me. They were somehow off away in a place all their own and they weren't going to let me come near getting in there with them or let me know they even saw me outside of it. Except one. He was a young one, a boy like me only a couple years younger, and he was scrooged down against a sleeping brave – maybe his father – and his small eyes, solid black in the dim light, looked at me, and his head turned slow to keep them on me as I went past and I could sense them on me as I went on till the back of the seat shut them off.

Still in that funny trance I went into the next coach and through it and to the third coach and on to the last. Each was the same. Soldiers slumped in sleep, and the huddled figures of the Indians in different pairings and sprawled positions but the effect the same and then at the end of the last car I saw him. He had a seat to himself and the headdress with its red-tipped feathers hung from the rack above the seat. He was asleep with an arm along the window sill, his head resting on it. I stopped and stared at him and the low light from the lantern near the end of the coach shone on the coppery texture of his face and the bare skin of his chest where it showed through the fallen-apart folds of the blanket wrapped around him. I stared at him and I felt cheated and empty inside. Even Jacob wasn't big or fierce. He wasn't as big as my father. He was short. Maybe broad and rather thick in the body but not much, even that way. And his face was quiet and – well, the only word I can ever think of is peaceful. I stared at him and then I started a little because he wasn't sleeping. One eyelid had twitched a bit. All at once I knew he was just pretending. He was pretending to be asleep so he wouldn't have to be so aware of the stares of anyone coming aboard to gawk at him. And sudden I felt ashamed and I hurried to the back platform to leave the train, and in the shadow there I stumbled over a sleeping soldier and heard him rousing himself as I scrambled down the steps.

That started what happened afterwards. Expect I'm really to blame for it all. Mean to say it probably wouldn't have happened if I hadn't been hurrying and wakened that soldier. He didn't know I was there. He was too full of sleep at first and didn't know what had awakened him. While I stayed in the dark shadow by the coach, afraid to go out into the moonlight, he stood up and stretched and came down the steps without noticing me and went around the end of the train towards the wider shadow on the other side, and as he went I saw him pulling a bottle out of a pocket. I felt safe again and started away and turned to look back, and the light was just right for me to see movement inside through the window by the last seat. Jacob was standing up. All kinds of wild notions poured through my mind and I couldn't move and then he was emerging through the rear door on to the platform and I wasn't exactly scared because I wasn't conscious of feeling anything at all except that I couldn't move. Time seemed to hang there motionless around me. Then I realized he wasn't doing anything and wasn't going to do anything. He wasn't even aware of me or if he was I was without meaning for him and he had seen me and dismissed me. He was standing quiet by the rear railing and his blanket was left inside and the cold night air was blowing against his bare chest above his leather breeches but he didn't appear to notice that. He was looking back along the double iron line of the track towards the tiny point of light that was my father's lantern by the west switch. He stood there, still and quiet, and I stayed where I was and watched him and he did not move and stood there looking far along the westward track and that was what we were doing, Jacob and I, when the soldier came back around the end of the train.

Thinking about it later I couldn't blame that soldier too much. Maybe had orders to keep the Indians in their seats or not let them on the rear platform or something like that. Probably was worried about drinking on duty and not wanting to be caught letting anything slip with the tang plain on his breath. Could be too he'd taken on more than he could handle right. Anyway he was surprised and mad when he saw Jacob standing there. He reached first and pulled some object off the platform floor and when he had it I could see it was his rifle. Then he jumped up the steps and started prodding Jacob with the rifle barrel towards the door. Jacob looked at him once and away and turned slow and started to move and the soldier must have thought Jacob moved too slow because he swung the gun around to use the stock end like a club and smack Jacob on the back. I couldn't see exactly what happened then because the scuffle was too sudden and quick but there was a blur of movement and the soldier came tumbling off the platform to the ground near me and the gun landed beside him. He was so mad he tripped all over himself getting to his feet and scrabbling for the gun and he whipped it up and hip-aimed it at Jacob and tried to fire it and the breech mechanism jammed some way and he clawed at it to make it work.

And Jacob stood there on the platform, still and quiet again, looking down at the soldier with bare breast broadside to the gun. I could see his eyes bright and black in the moonlight and the shining on the coppery firmness of his face and he did not move and of a sudden I realized he was waiting. He was waiting for the bullet. He was expecting it and waiting for it and he would not move. And I jumped forward and grabbed the rifle barrel and pulled hard on it. 'No,' I shouted. 'Not like that.' And the soldier stumbled and fell against me and both of us went down and someone was yelling at us and when I managed to get to my feet I saw it was the captain and the soldier was up too, standing stiff and awkward at attention. 'Damned Indian,' the soldier said. 'Trying to get away.' The captain looked up and saw Jacob standing there and jerked a bit with recognizing who it was. 'He was not,' I said. 'He was just standing there.' The captain looked at the soldier and shook his head slow. 'Jee-sus,' he said. 'You'd have shot that one.' The captain shook his head again like he was disgusted and tired of everything and maybe even of living. 'What's the use,' he said. He flipped a thumb at the soldier. 'Pick up your gun and get on forward.' The soldier hurried off and the captain looked at Jacob, and Jacob looked down at him, still and quiet and not moving a muscle. 'There's fools of every colour,' the captain said and Jacob's eyes brightened a little as if he understood and I expect he did because I'd heard he could speak English when he wanted to. The captain wiped a hand across his face. 'Stand on that damned platform as long as you want,' he said. He remembered he had a cigar in his other hand and looked at it and it was out and he threw it on the ground and swung around and went towards the front of the train again, and I wanted to follow him but I couldn't because now Jacob was looking at me.

He looked down at me what seemed a long time and then he motioned at me and I could tell he wanted me to step out further into the moonlight. I did and he leaned forward to peer at me. He reached a hand out towards me, palm flat and down, and said something in his own language and for a moment I was there with him in the world that was different and beyond my own everyday world and then he swung away and stepped to stand by the rear railing again and I knew I was outside again, outside of his mind and put away and no more to him than any other object around. He was alone there looking far down the track and it sank slow and deep in me that he was looking far past the tiny light point of my father's lantern, far on where the lone track ran straight along the slow-rising reaches of distance into the horizon that led past the longest vision at last to the great climbing mountains. He was looking back along the iron trail that was taking him and his children away from a valley that would make a man want to put his feet firm on the earth and stretch tall and was taking them to an unknown place where they would not be themselves any longer but only some among many of many tribes and tongues and all dependent on the bounty of a forgetful government. It wasn't an Indian I was seeing there any more. It was a man. It wasn't Jacob, the tamed chief that even foolish kids could gawk at. It was Mountain Elk, the Big-Deer-That-Walks-the-High-Places and he was big, really big, and he was one meant to walk the high places.

He stood there looking down the track and the westbound night freight came rumbling out of the east and strained past, and he stood there watching it go westward along the track and his train began to move, creeping eastward slow and feeling forward, and I watched it go and long as I could see him he was standing there, still and quiet, looking straight out along the back trail.

Well. I've taken you to where I was headed. It's only a hop now to those moccasins. I tried to tell the other boys about it the next day and likely boasted and strutted in the telling and they wouldn't believe me. Oh, they believe I saw the Indians all right. Had to. The telegraph operator backed my saying I was there. Even that I went aboard. But they wouldn't believe the rest. And because they wouldn't believe me I had to keep pounding it at them, telling it over and over. Expect I was getting to be mighty unpopular. But Jacob saved me even though I never saw him again. There was a day a bunch of us boys were playing some game or other back of the telegraph shack and sudden we realized someone had come up from somewhere and was watching us. An Indian. Seemed to be just an ordinary everyday sort of tame Indian. But he was looking us over intent and careful and he picked me and came straight to me. He put out a hand, palm flat and down, and said something to me in his Indian talk and pointed far off to the east and south and back again to me and reached inside the old blanket he had fastened around him with a belt and took out a dirty cloth-wrapped package and laid it at my feet, and went away and faded out of sight around the shack. When I unrolled that package there were those moccasins.

Funny thing. I never wanted to go around telling my story to the other boys again. Didn't need to. Whether they believed or not wasn't important any more. I had those moccasins. In a way they made me one of Jacob's children. Remembering that has helped me sometimes in tough spots.

Harvey Kendall

My father had two pair of boots. He had a pair of shoes too but he wore those only when my mother made him, to church on Sundays and to funerals and the like. The boots were what you'd call his regular footwear. One pair was plain, just rough and ready old-style cowboy boots, nearly knee high, made of stiff cowhide with canvas pulling-straps we used to call mule ears that dangled and flapped on the outside when he walked along. He wore those at work on weekdays. He was cattle in-spector at the local stockyards, where the ranchers for quite a stretch around brought their stuff to be checked and weighed before being shipped out. He'd pull out of bed in the morning and pad around the house in his socks, or when Mother got after him, in the slippers she'd bought for him, until after breakfast and then he'd squat on the edge of a chair and heave and yank at those boots till they were on and tuck his work pants down inside the tops and stand up and stretch and say, 'Another day, another dollar,' which was sort of silly because he earned more than a dollar a day, and out the door he'd go with those mule ears flapping.

We lived a short ways out of town and sometimes he'd walk in those boots down to where the stockyards spread out beside and behind the station about a half-mile away, and sometimes he'd saddle his old cow pony and ride down and maybe during the day circulate some through the pens helping the handlers move the stuff around, which he didn't need to do because he wasn't paid for that. 'Can't let this Mark horse get too lazy and fat,' he used to say but that was only an excuse. The truth was he plain liked the feel of that horse under him now and again and the tickle of dust rising up in a man's nose saddle high and the fun of shooing a few steers through some tricky gates.

It reminded him of the old days when he was a free-roaming cowhand with a saddle-roll for a home before my mother herded him into the same corral with a preacher and tied him down to family responsibilities.

Those cowhide boots were just everyday knockabout working boots. The others were something else again. They didn't reach quite as far up the legs but they had high narrow heels that curved under in back with a real swoop and they were made of soft calfskin that fitted like a glove over the feet and ankles and then opened out some to take care of the pants if those were folded over neat and tucked in careful. The tops were curved up on the sides with little leather pulling-straps that stayed out of sight inside and those tops were made of separate pieces of the calfskin darker brown in colour than the bottoms and they had a clever design of a rope loop stitched into them. He wore those boots on Sundays after he came home from church and on special occasions like meetings of the stockmen's association and when he was riding old Mark near the front in the annual Fourth of July parade. They reminded him of the best part of the old days, the times he was representing whatever range outfit he was with that season in the early rodeos and showing the other cowhands from the whole country roundabout what a man could do with a good horse and a good rope.

When he wore those calfskin boots my father always wore the belt that went with them. It was made of calfskin too and it was so wide my mother had to fix new belt straps on every pair of new pants she bought for him. It had a big solid slide-through silver buckle that had three lines of printing engraved in the metal. The first line said 'First Honours' and the second line said the one word 'Roping' and the third line said 'Cheyenne 1893'. That belt and that buckle, tight around his waist above those calfskin boots, reminded him of the best thing of all about the old days, the time he set a record busting and hog-tying a steer, a record that stood seven years before anyone beat it and then it was beat only because they shortened the run some and changed the rules a bit and fast work was really easier to do.

Anyone knows anything about kids knows which pair of those boots I liked. Cleaning and polishing both pairs with good saddle soap to keep the leather in right condition was one of my regular chores every Sunday morning before church. I'd get out the soap and a moist rag and if my father wasn't around watching I'd give those old cowskin boots a lick and a promise and then I'd really go to work on those calfskins even though they didn't need much, not being worn often. Sometimes I wouldn't do more than just run the rag quick over the old cowskins and figure my father wouldn't notice I'd let them go because that old leather was rough and stiff all the time anyway and then like as not I'd be enjoying myself on the calfskins and suddenly I'd look up and there my father would be watching me with his eyebrows pulled down till they about met over his nose. 'Gee-rusalem, boy,' he'd say. 'One of these days you'll rub those boots clean through. It's the others need the limbering so my feet don't ache in them. Get busy on them now afore I sideswipe you one.'

Mention of sideswiping points to maybe one reason I didn't like working on those old cowskins. Whenever I'd done something wrong, broke one of the rules my folks made for me or messed up some chore when I should've known better, my father would come after me from behind and hop on his left foot and turn his right foot toe outward and swing his right leg so that the side of his foot swiped me hard and hurting on my rump. He'd sideswipe me a good one or two or three according to how bad it was that I'd done and until I began to get some size there were times he raised me smack off the ground. Just about every time he did that he had those old cowskins on. But likely that didn't have too much to do with my feeling about them. I never was mad after a thumping or went around being sulky. My father sideswiped me only when I had it coming and he'd do it quick and thorough and tell me why, and then to show it was over and done and he was ready to forget about it he'd tell me to stick close around after supper and we'd saddle old Mark and he'd let me sit in the saddle and get in some practice-throws roping a fence post before dark.

The truth was I didn't like working on those old cowskins because they were tough and hard to do anything with and old-fashioned and pretty well battered and they didn't mean a thing to me. Working on those others, those fine-looking calfskins, meant plenty. I'd rub away on that soft dark-shining leather and talk proud to myself inside. Not many boys had a father who had been a roping champion and in country where roping was real business and a man had to be good at it just to hold an ordinary ranch job. Not another boy anywhere had a father who had made a roping record that stood seven years and might still be standing if changes hadn't been made. I could work on that leather and see in my mind what I never saw with my eyes because all that was over and finished before I was born, my father on old Mark, young then, firm and straight in the saddle with the rope a living thing in his hands, my father and young Mark, working together, busting the meanest toughest trickiest steer with the hard-and-fast method he always said was the best. I could see every move, as he had told them to me over and over, young Mark reaching eager for speed to overtake the steer and knowing what to do every second without a word or a touch on the reins and my father riding easy and relaxed with the loop forming under his right hand and the loop going forward and opening and dropping over the wide horns and Mark slowing as my father took up the slack and pulled the loop tight and Mark speeding again to give him slack again enough so he could flip the rope over to the right side of the steer and then Mark swinging left in a burst of power and speed and the rope tightening along and down the steer's right side and pulling its head around in an outside arc and at the same time yanking its hind legs out from under it and making it flip in a complete side-winding somersault to lie with the wind knocked clean out of it and then all in the same motion Mark pivoting to face the steer and bracing to keep the rope taut and my father using that pivot-swing to lift and carry him right out of the saddle and land on his feet and run down the taut rope with his pigging string in his hand and wrap it quick around three of the steer's legs and draw it close and tie it and Mark watching and keeping the rope taut ready to yank and make that steer behave if it started causing trouble and then easing some slack at the right instant so my father could cast the loop loose and stand up to show the job was done and walk casual back to Mark without even looking at the steer again like he was saying in the very set of his head on his shoulders that's that and there's a steer hog-tied for branding or earmarking or anything anybody's a mind to do with it.

Well, what I'm telling about this time had a lot to do with those boots and that belt and my father and old Mark too but mostly my father. It began the night before the sort of combination fair and rodeo at our town that year. The committee running things had some extra money available and they'd telegraphed and persuaded Cal Bennett to agree to come for the price and they'd plastered the town with bills saying the topnotch champion roper of the big-town circuit would be on hand to give some fancy exhibitions and everybody'd been talking about that for days. We were finishing supper, my father and my mother and me, and I notched up nerve enough and finally I said it. 'Father,' I said, 'can I wear your belt tomorrow? Just a little while anyway?'

My father settled back in his chair and looked at me. 'What's on your mind, boy? Must be something special.'

'I'm sick of it,' I said. 'I'm sick of all the other kids talking about that Cal Bennett all the time. There's a new kid too and I was trying to tell him about you setting a record once and he won't believe me.'

My father kept on looking at me and his eyebrows pulled down together. 'Won't believe you, eh?'

'That's it,' I said. 'If I was to be wearing that belt and let him see it then he'd know all right.'

'Expect he would,' my father said and he leaned back farther in his chair, feeling good the way he usually did with a good meal inside him, and he said in a sort of half-joking voice, 'Expect he would even more if I was to get out there tomorrow and swing a rope in the free-style steer busting and show everyone around here a thing or two.'

That was when my mother started laughing. She laughed so she near choked on the last bite she was chewing and my father and I stared at her. 'Gee-rusalem,' my father said. 'What's so blamed funny?'

My mother swallowed down the bite. 'You are,' she said. 'Why it's eleven years since you did anything like that. You sitting there and getting to be middle-aged and getting thick around the middle and talking about going up against young fellows that are doing it all the time and could run circles around you nowadays.'

'Oh, they could, could they?' my father said and his eyebrows were really together over his nose.

'That horse of yours too,' my mother said and to her it was still just something to chuckle at. 'He's the same. Getting old and fat and lazy. He couldn't even do it any more.'

'He couldn't, eh?' my father said. 'I'll have you know being young and full of sass ain't so all-fired important as you seem to think. It's brains and know-how that count too and that's what that horse's got and that's what I've got and like riding a bicycle it's something you don't ever forget.'

He was mighty serious and my mother realized that and was serious too. 'Well, anyway,' she said, 'you're not going to try it and that's final.'

'Gee-rusalem,' my father said and he thumped a fist on the table so hard the dishes jumped. 'Just like a woman. Giving orders. Tie a man down so he has to keep his nose to a grindstone getting the things they want and start giving orders the moment he even thinks a bit about maybe showing he still can do something.'

'Harvey Kendall,' my mother said, 'you listen to me. I saw you near break your neck too many times in those shows before we were married. That's why I made you stop. I don't intend to have anything happen to you.'

They were glaring at each other across the table and after a while my father sighed and looked down and began pushing at his coffee cup with one finger the way he always did when they've been having an argument. 'Expect you're right,' he said and he sighed again and his voice was soft. 'It was just an idea. No sense us flaring at each other over a little idea.' He turned to me. 'Wear the belt,' he said. 'All day if you've a mind to. If your feet were big enough you could wear the boots too.'

In the morning my father didn't go to work because that day was a local holiday so we had a late breakfast and he sat around quiet like he was thinking things over in his mind the way he'd been all the evening before after supper. Then he pulled on the calfskin boots, looking a bit different in them without the belt on up above, and he went out and saddled old Mark and rode into town to help with the preparations there. I couldn't go along because just before he left he told me to stick close to my mother and watch out for her, which was a backhand style of putting it because she would really be watching out for me and that was just his usual little scheme to tie me to her so I wouldn't be roaming around and getting into any devilment. Soon as he was gone I got out the belt and put it on and it went around me almost twice but I could fix it so the buckle was in the middle in front as it should be and I stood on a chair to admire that part of myself in the little mirror my father used for shaving. I waited while my mother fussed with her good dress and the trimmings, doing the things women do to make themselves look what they call stylish, and then the two of us, my mother and me, walked the half-mile into town and the day's activities.

We stopped at all the exhibits and saw who had won the prizes for jams and jellies and raising vegetables and the like and we spent some time looking over the small pens where the prizewinning stock animals were. I stood on one foot and then the other and chewed molasses candy till my jaws were tired while my mother talked to women and then more women and I didn't get a chance to roam around much and show off that belt because she was watching out for me just about every minute. Three or four times we bumped into my father busy circulating all over the place as the cattle judge and one of the local greeters of out-of-town folks and he'd stop and talk to us some and hurry away. He was enjoying himself the way he always did at these affairs, joshing with all the men and tipping his hat to the women, and he was developing a sort of glow from a drink or two with the other greeters.

He joined us for a quick lunch at the hotel. He was feeling good again and he joked me over being about half hidden inside that belt and as soon as we were through eating he hustled us out and to the temporary grandstand along one side of the main stockyard pen so we all could have good seats for the rodeo doings. He picked a place in the third row where he always said you could see best and he sat in the middle with my mother on one side of him and me on the other and it wasn't till we had been there a little while and the two of them were talking hearty with other folks around that I had my chance to slip away by sliding through and under the grandstand and go find some of the other kids so I could strut and show off that belt. I went hunting them proud and happy as I'd ever been and I found them and in maybe five minutes I was running back under the grandstand as mad and near crying as I'd ever been too. I knew where to crawl up through by my father's boots and I did and he felt me squirming through against his legs because the stand was filled now and he took hold of me and pulled me up on the seat beside him. 'Quiet now, boy,' he said. 'We wouldn't want your mother to know you've been slipping away like that.' He swung his head to look at her on the other side and saw she was busy talking to a woman beyond and he swung back to me and saw my face. 'Gee-rusalem, boy,' he said. 'What's eating at you?'

'Father,' I said, 'he doesn't believe it about you.'

'Who doesn't believe it?' he said.

'That new kid,' I said.

'Did you show him that belt?' my father said.

'Yes,' I said. 'But he just laughed. He said it's a fake. He said if it isn't you just found it somewhere or got it from some old pawnshop.'

'Found it?' my father said. His eyebrows were starting to draw down together but the people all around were starting to buzz louder and things were beginning out in the big pen that was the arena for the day. 'All right, boy,' my father said. 'We'll do something about that when this shindig's over. Maybe a good sideswipe'd do that kid some good. Be quiet now, the bronc riding's coming up.' He didn't pay any more attention to me because he was busy paying attention to what was happening in the arena but not all his attention was out there because he kept fidgeting on the plank seat and every now and then he was muttering to himself and once he did it loud enough so I could hear. 'Pawnshop,' he said and kept on fidgeting around and didn't seem even to know he was doing that.

Plenty was happening out in the arena, the kind of things I always enjoyed and got excited about, but I wasn't in any mind to enjoy much that day and then suddenly there was an extra flurry of activity and the main gates swung open and the people began to shout and cheer. A man came riding through the gateway on a beautiful big buckskin that was jouncing with each step like it had springs in its feet and you could tell right away the man was Cal Bennett. He was slim and tall and straight in the saddle and he was mighty young-looking and mighty capable-looking all at the same time. He had on boots just like my father's calfskins, maybe not exactly the same but so close to it there wasn't much difference, and a wide belt like the one I was wearing, and sitting there so easy on that jouncing saddle like he was glued to it he was about the best-looking figure of a man I ever saw. He had a coiled rope in his hand and shook out a loop as he came forward and began spinning it and it grew bigger and bigger and suddenly he flipped it up and over and it was spinning right around him and that buckskin and suddenly he flipped it again and it was spinning big and wide in front of the horse and he gave a quick little wriggle with his heels and the horse jumped forward and he and that horse went right through the loop and it was spinning behind them and then the people really went wild. They shouted and clapped and stomped their feet. Cal Bennett let the loop fall slack on the ground and bowed all around and took off his big hat to the women and put it back on and coiled in his rope and rode over to the side of the arena where he'd wait for time to do his real roping stunts and still the people shouted and stomped. And my father sat there beside me and pulled up straight with his head high, looking around at the shouting people, and his face got tight and red and he shrank down till he was hunched low on the seat and he sat very still. He didn't fidget any more or mutter to himself. He just sat still, staring out at the arena and things happened out there, and then the announcer was shouting through his megaphone that the free-style steer busting for the local championship was next and suddenly my father turned and grabbed me by the arm. 'Hey, boy,' he said, 'take off that belt.'

I fumbled with it and got it off and handed it to him and he stood up right there on the grandstand and yanked off the ordinary belt he was wearing and began slipping that big belt through the special pants straps my mother had sewed for him. She saw him looming up there beside her and what he was doing and she was startled. 'Harvey Kendall,' she said, 'just what do you think you're going to do?'

'You keep out of this,' my father said and the way he said it would have made anybody shy away. He pulled the belt tight through the buckle and started down towards the arena, pushing through the people in the two rows ahead. He stepped to the ground and turned to look back at my mother. 'Just keep your eyes on that arena,' he said, 'and you'll see something.'

He squeezed through the fence rails into the arena and went straight to the little bunch of men who were acting as judges for the rodeo events. He was reaching in his money pocket as he went and he took out two dollar bills. 'I'm in this one,' he said to the men. 'Here's my entry fee.'

They all turned and stared at him. 'Lookahere, Harve,' one of them said. 'You want to show us how you used to do it, that's fine. That's wonderful. We'll be proud to have you. But don't you go trying to do it racing against a stop watch.'

'Shut up, Sam,' my father said. 'I know what I'm doing. You just take this money.' He pushed the bills into the man's hand and swung away hurrying and by the time the other entries were lined up he was back leading old Mark and with a good rope he'd borrowed somewhere in his hands. He took a place in the line and the judges put all the names on slips of paper in a hat and pulled them out one by one to get a running order and my father's name was one of the last. He stood there among those younger men and their horses, quiet and waiting by old Mark, just running the rope through his hands to see it had no kinks and coiling it careful and exact, and all the while the excitement was building up in me, and my mother sat still and silent on the plank seat with her hands tight together in her lap.

One after another the others made their runs, flipping their steers and dashing in to hog-tie them, and they used a lot of different methods, some forefooting the steers and some going straight for the heads and quick pull-arounds, some risking long throws to save time and some playing it safer and chasing till they were close in, and some of them were good and some maybe better than just good but you could tell easy enough none of them was in the real champion class, and then it was my father's turn. He led old Mark out and walked around by old Mark's head and reached up a hand to scratch around the ears and he whispered something to that old horse nobody could hear and he came back around and swung up to the saddle.

Seeing him there, straight and sturdy in the saddle, I couldn't hold it in any longer. I jumped standing right up on the seat. 'Father!' I shouted. 'Father! You show them! The whole bunch of them!' My mother pulled me down quick but she was just as excited because her hands trembled and out there in the arena my father didn't pay any attention to anything around him. He sat quiet on old Mark checking the rope again and a hush spread over the whole place and off to the side Cal Bennett reined his big buckskin around so he could watch close and sudden my father let out a whoop. 'Turn that critter loose!' he yelled and the bars on the chute were yanked away and a big rangy steer rushed out into the arena and as it crossed the starting line the timer slammed down with his hat and old Mark was leaping forward. Not three jumps and there wasn't a person watching didn't know that old horse knew what he was doing and maybe he was a mite slower than the young cow ponies that'd been performing but he was right up there in the champion class with the know-how. The steer was tricky and started twisting right away and old Mark was after it like a hound on a hot scent, keeping just the right distance to the left of it and closing in steady. My father was riding high in the stirrups and a loop was forming under his right hand and while he was still a ways back the loop whipped forward fast like a snake striking and opened out over the steer's head and the steer twisted and the loop struck on one horn tip and fell over the other horn and pulled off.

'Gee-rusalem!' My father's voice roared out over that whole arena. 'Stick with him, Mark!' And old Mark was hard on that steer's tail with every twist and turn and my father yanked in the rope and whipped out another loop and it settled smack over the horns and head and he pulled it tight and flipped the rope over to the steer's right side and old Mark swung left, head low and ploughing into the sudden strain coming, and that steer spun like a cartwheel somersaulting as it spun and was down flat and old Mark pivoted to face the steer and keep the rope taut and my father tried to use that pivot swing to lift him out of the saddle and his foot caught on the cantle going over and he went sprawling on his face in the dust. He scrambled up and scrabbled in the dust for the pigging string and started down the taut rope trying to run too fast and stumbled and went down again. He came up this time puffing with his face dark red and ran on and just about threw himself on that steer. He grabbed at the legs and got the string around three of them and tied it quick and jumped to the steer's head and old Mark eased some on the rope and he loosened the loop and threw it off and straightened up. He didn't even turn to look at the timekeeper. He didn't look around at all. He just looked down at the ground and walked slow towards old Mark. And while he was walking there, slow and heavy-footed, the one thing that could rule him out even if he'd made good time and was the worst thing that could happen happened. The steer had some breath back now and was struggling and the knot had been tied in such a hurry that it slipped and the steer got its feet free and pushed up hot and mad and started after my father. Maybe it was the shouts that warned him or maybe it was old Mark shying back and snorting but anyway he turned and saw and dodged quick and began to run and the steer was right after him and suddenly a rope came fast and low to the ground and the loop in it whipped up and around that steer's hind legs and tightened and the steer hit the ground again with a thump and at the other end of that rope were Cal Bennett and his big buckskin.

The people went wild again and they had a right to because that was about as fast and tricky a job of roping as they'd ever seen anytime and it wasn't just a show-off stunt, it was serious business, but my father didn't pay any attention to the shouting or even to Cal Bennett. He just stopped running and looked around once and started walking again towards old Mark, slow and heavy-footed with those calfskin boots all dusty. He reached and took hold of the reins and went right on walking and old Mark followed him and he remembered the rope dragging from the saddle horn and stopped and unfastened it and coiled it in and went on walking and old Mark followed and together they went to the outside gate and someone opened it enough for them to go through and he left the rope hanging on a gatepost and they went outside and along around the fence towards the road, the two of them alone together, my father walking like an old man and sweaty old Mark tagging with his head low. I felt plain ashamed of being me, of being a boy with a father who'd made a fool of himself like he had, and I wanted to crawl away somewhere and hide but I couldn't do that because my mother was standing up and telling me to come along and starting down out of the grandstand right in front of all those people. She had her head high and she looked like she was just daring anyone to say anything to her. She marched along in front of the grandstand and around the side towards the road and I had to follow, trying not to look at anybody. She hurried a little and came alongside my father and he kept staring at the ground ahead of him and didn't seem to notice but all the same he knew she was there because he put out a hand and she took hold of it and they walked on along the road towards our house like that, neither one of them saying a word.

It was sad-feeling and mournful around our place the rest of that afternoon. My father was as silent as if he'd forgotten how to speak. After he took care of Mark he came in the house and pulled off those calfskin boots and tossed them in the hall closet with the other pair and put on his slippers and went out and sat on the back steps. My mother was just as silent. She hustled around in the kitchen and it looked like she was baking things but for once I wasn't interested in that. I didn't want to be anywhere close to my father so I took the front steps and I sat there whittling some and chewing on my knuckles and being miserable. I was mad at what he'd done to me, made me feel ashamed and fixed it so the other kids would have something to torment me about and so that new kid never would believe it about him. 'He ain't so much,' I said to myself. 'He's just an old has-been, that's all he is.'

Then we had supper and we were all just as silent as before and Mother had fixed the things my father liked best, which was kind of a waste because he only picked some and at last he looked up at her and grinned a sick little grin and looked down and began pushing at his coffee cup. 'I told you you'd see something in that arena,' he said. 'Well, you did.'

'Yes,' my mother said. 'I did.' She hesitated a moment and then she found something to say. 'And I've been to a lot of those shows and I never saw a steer slapped down as hard and thorough as that one.'

'That wasn't me,' my father said. 'That was Mark.' He pushed up and turned away quick and went out again to the back steps.

It was only a while later and I was on the front steps again when I saw something that made me jump up and my heart start to pound and what I saw was a big buckskin coming along the road and turning in at our place and sitting easy in the saddle was Cal Bennett.

'Howdy, bub,' he said. 'Is your father handy?'

'He's around back,' I said. He nudged the buckskin and started around the house and all at once it came rushing up in me and I had to shout it at him. 'Don't you dare make fun of him! He was better'n you once! He made a record nobody's ever really beat!'

Cal Bennett reined in his horse and leaned over towards me and his eyes were clear and bright looking down at me. 'I know that,' he said. 'I wasn't much bigger'n you are now when I saw him make it. That's what started me practising.' He straightened in the saddle and went on around the house. I stood still in the surprise of his words and then I had to follow him and when I went around the rear corner of the house there was my father sitting on the steps looking up and there was Cal Bennett on that big buckskin looking down and they were holding a silence there between them for what seemed a long while.

My father shifted a little on the steps. 'Nice of you to come around,' he said. His voice was taut and careful. 'I forgot to thank you for pulling that steer off me this afternoon.'

'Shucks,' Cal Bennett said. 'That wasn't much. You've done it yourself many a time. There ain't a man ever worked cows ain't done it often for another man out on the range.'

They kept looking at each other and the tightness that had been in my father's face all those last hours began to easy away and when he spoke again his voice was steady and friendly the way it usually was. 'I sort of messed it up out there today, didn't I?'

'Yes,' Cal Bennett said. 'You did kind of hooraw it some.' He chuckled and suddenly my father chuckled too and then they both grinned like a pair of kids.

'From what I hear,' my father said, 'you're good. You're damn good.'

'Yes,' Cal Bennett said and his voice was easy and natural and he wasn't boasting at all. 'Yes, I am. I'm as good as a man named Harvey Kendall was some years back. Maybe even a mite better.'

'Expect you are,' my father said. 'Yes, I expect you are.' He leaned backward on his elbows on the steps. 'But you didn't come here just to chew that kind of fat, pleasant as that can be as I used to know.'

'No,' Cal Bennett said. 'I didn't. I've been figuring. This rodeo business is all right for a young fellow long as he's young but there ain't any future in it. It's getting to be more fancy show for the crowds and less real roping all the time anyway. I've been saving my money. With what I collected in town a while ago I've got the tally I was aiming at. Now I'm figuring to get me a nice little spread somewhere in this territory and put some good stock on it and try raising me some good beef.'

'Keep talking,' my father said. 'There's a lot of sense in what you're saying.'

'Well, now,' Cal Bennett said. 'I figured to ask you to help me some getting started.'

My father straightened on the steps and he cocked his head to one side, looking up. 'Tell me something, Bennett,' he said. 'There's a woman mixed up in this somewhere.'

'Yes,' Cal Bennett said. 'There is.'

'And she wants you to quit risking your fool young neck showing off with a rope in front of a lot of shouting people.'

'Yes,' Cal Bennett said. 'She does.'

'And she's right,' my father said. 'And now you tell me something else. Why did you come to me?'

'Simple,' Cal Bennett said. 'I been asking questions round about for some months. Found out a few things. Found out there's one name signed to a checklist on a cattle shipment that'll be accepted without question anywhere the rails run and that name's Harvey Kendall. Heard people say and for quite a ways around these parts that when you want good stock picked out and straight advice on how to handle them right you go find that same man. Heard them say that man never did another man dirt and never will. Heard them say – '

My father put up a hand to stop him. 'Whoa, now,' my father said. 'No need to pile it on too thick. Of course I'll help you best I can. You knew that before you started all that palaver. Hop down and squat on these boards and tell me just what you have in mind.'

And there the two of them were side by side on the steps talking quiet and friendly and the buckskin wandered off far enough to find a few grass tufts by our little pasture fence and whiffle some over the rails at old Mark and I was standing by the house corner with the strangest feeling in me. Somehow I didn't want to disturb them or even let them notice I was there and I stepped back soft and around the house again, wondering what was happening to me, and then I knew what I wanted to do. I went in through the front door and past my mother sitting quiet in the front room with our old photograph album in her lap and I went straight to the hall closet. I hardly even looked at those calfskin boots even though they were mighty dusty and could stand a cleaning. I took out the rough old cowskins and I got the saddle soap and a moist rag and I went over by the back door, where I could sit on a stool and hear them talking, and I really went to work on those old boots. I wanted to make that hard old leather comfortable as I could for his feet. I wanted to make those old boots shine.